Cactus
Flowers

Anne,

I hope you enjoy

Frederick

Frederick Patten

Published by Pomegranate Press,
Dolphin House, 51 St Nicholas Lane,
Lewes, Sussex BN7 2JZ
pomegranatepress@aol.com
www.pomegranate-press.co.uk

British Library Cataloguing-in-Publication Data.
A catalogue record for this book is available from the British
Library.

ISBN 0-9548975-6-0

Printed by CPI Antony Rowe, Highfield Industrial
Estate, Eastbourne, East Sussex BN23 6QT

*A*mong the many harrowing experiences of children evacuated to the countryside during the Second World War, the suffering of Dennis O'Neill was the worst. An orphan placed with foster parents on a farm, he was starved for months and was reduced to sucking the udders of cows for sustenance. The 13-year old boy weighed a mere four stone when the farmer battered him to death. His body was discovered in a shallow grave on the farm.

The case produced a campaigning fervour that swept away the dreadful climate of the Poor Law, which had not differentiated between young offenders destined for correction in approved schools and those children under eighteen years of age who, abandoned or abused, had been deprived of a normal home life.

The resulting Children Act of 1948 created a new breed of staff in local government, dedicated to preventive work with the deprived and those delinquents whom the juvenile courts felt were capable of rescue from a life of crime. Initially given considerable autonomy to overcome the image of the undeserving poor, they were innovative in creating a comprehensive support service for young people at risk.

Frederick Patten was one of the first of these children's officers, and Cactus Flowers draws on his experiences with deprived youngsters and their families during the early 1950s.

ACKNOWLEDGEMENTS

Although this is my second published book, this one is a novel, intended to fulfil an ambition to pay tribute to many disadvantaged children – unloved, abandoned, abused – who still made good. Most of these young people, like those in *Cactus Flowers*, blossomed because there were special people out there who cared for them and loved them when it was most needed.

My thanks are due to Catherine, Jennifer and the many friends who offered continuous support, enabling me to write about this extraordinary period in the social history of this country when the pressure of public opinion caused the abandonment of the blind cruelty of Poor Law legislation.

It was important to have accuracy and authenticity in respect of the period, so it is impossible to measure the research and attention to detail provided by Janet in her role as proof-reader. I am indebted to her for her assistance and encouragement.

It would not be fair to omit reference to my publisher David Arscott, whose ready wit hid a real understanding of my need to aim for a good read on a subject dear to my heart.

Frederick Patten
mail@fcpatten.plus.com

1

Bright sunshine temporarily blinded Peter Kemp as he glanced up at the remains of a sign that hung askew. The damaged board had once read LONDON COUNTY COUNCIL'S CHILDREN'S DEPARTMENT, AREA 4. The square, featureless building he was about to enter, a target for vandals, was dwarfed by the huge blocks of flats of Hackney's new Montgomery Estate. His life was centred here and he hoped this would continue for some time.

He dusted down his grey suit, adjusted his collar and tie, stuck his hat at an angle on his head and reached for his attache case. He locked the door of his four-year-old Rover for the second time that morning. His blue eyes gave the hint of a sense of humour but not a glimmer of the sadness that had marred his childhood.

He looked at his watch. It was almost nine o'clock. He had spent the last thirty minutes sitting at the bottom of the concrete steps of the adjacent block, talking to an old woman whom he had never met before. Her young grandson had been sleeping beside her and Kemp wondered if his intrusion was justified.

Glancing back at the flats, he thought that not even a sunny day could make these blocks look appealing. Yet the gritty old lady had a different perspective. 'Me house was bombed,' she had said, 'but we carried on living in it. Then we had to wait six years to come here. I live like royalty now, with hot and cold running water all the time.'

He passed the double doors of Reception and headed for the back door of the two-storey building. Unlocking it, he ducked as he went into the small hall – the ceiling was a hazard for anyone slightly taller than average –

and quickly climbed the stairs. He needed some privacy to plan his day, making up for the kind of emergency he had inflicted on himself this morning.

In his office, shafts of sunlight were doing their best with the bare white walls and dark brown linoleum, contriving to produce a brighter shade of cheerlessness. Hanging up his hat he went to make his regular check of the flowering cactus on the windowsill, his sole attempt at personalising his room. In a sanguine moment he had bought it as a symbol of both the prickly behaviour of his charges and their potential for changing dramatically for the better.

As he crossed the room to his desk he took a fountain pen from his jacket pocket and reaching for a memo pad wrote:

Mrs Boulton,
I have met a Mrs Stevens from the adjacent block. I hope she will come in to see you about her grandson Jamie, Flat 204. It would be helpful if you could make a few discreet enquiries – there is a possibility that the child may be at risk.
P.K.

He blotted the note before placing it in his 'Out' tray then went to the grey metal filing cabinet. Unlocking it he extracted two files from his caseload of twenty-four and placed them on the ink-stained desk.

The telephone rang. He picked it up and heard the voice of Andrew McGovern, his new Scottish boss. The man hadn't been free to take up his position until six months ago, but it was clear why the London County Council had been prepared to wait for him to join the new Department. His experience as an enlightened prison governor made him an important ally in the fight to place the emphasis on prevention and rehabilitation for the deprived and delinquent. His role was to coordinate the work of the field officers and his energy and enthusiasm rivalled that of many a younger man.

'Morning, Kemp. I was looking out for you from my office window – your car was there a long time before you came in.'

'I was distracted by an old lady and her grandson, sir,' Kemp explained. 'We may need to help them.'

'I shouldn't have thought we had to go looking for work! What are you proposing?'

'I've just written about it to T.O.B,' said Kemp.

'Our formidable Theresa Olive Boulton.'

'Terrible old battle-axe,' Kemp amended.

'Yes, I do know how you all refer to our senior clerk, but you won't find many like her, believe me.'

'I've enormous respect for Mrs B,' Kemp replied, 'but I do wish she'd stop trying to marry me off!'

'Come, you're her pet project!' McGovern laughed. 'It's the price you pay for being the youngest field officer in the service. Twenty-six, unmarried and, rumour has it, no girl friend. Mrs Boulton won't let up until you've found yourself a good woman to take care of you.'

Kemp wanted to object, but McGovern's voice faded. He faintly heard him say, 'Come in, Mrs Boulton. I'm speaking to Kemp about you.' Kemp wondered if the senior clerk would detect the amusement in her boss's voice. 'He's written a memo for you. Could you collect it from his office?'

His voice came loud again.

'Mrs Boulton's brought me some papers to sign, Kemp. She's going to collect the memo you've spoken of and you can give her the background. After she's gone I need to speak with you. I'll come to you, if that's all right?'

'Fine, thank you.'

Replacing the receiver in its cradle, Kemp opened one of the files on his desk. Within minutes there was a knock on the door and Mrs Boulton walked briskly into the room. Her greying hair was the only indication that she was in her mid-fifties, for her skin was remarkably unlined and she was attractive. Her businesslike manner did not hide the warmth of the smile she gave Kemp. He noted the cup of tea she was carrying and instantly forgave her for meddling in his life.

'Good morning, Peter. Mr McGovern tells me you've a message for me?' She placed the tea on his desk.

Kemp drew up a chair for her. They had joined the Department at its inception and had high regard for each other's ability and commitment.

'Thanks, Mrs B.'

She took the memo from him, holding it at a distance to read, and squinted. 'I hurried here and forgot my spectacles. What's the background?'

'When I drove up this morning I noticed a hunched figure, a bundle beside it, at the bottom of the steps of the block next door. The shape of the bundle disturbed me so I went back and saw Mrs Stevens and the child – his head cradled in her lap. It troubled me because although it's a sunny morning, it's not warm enough to be sitting around on concrete.'

'Do you suspect abuse?'

'I believe the child's at risk.'

'So you went across and spoke to them?'

'Yes. Mrs Stevens thought this place was still the estate office. I explained that we now use the building, told her what we did and that we're a relatively new Department. It gave me an excuse to sit down beside her. I managed to check that the child's breathing was regular and he seemed unmarked.

'Apparently he'd run out of his parents' flat and up three flights to her, because they were fighting. She said he's done it several times. Jamie's only four so naturally she worries about him going up and down all those stairs.'

'I should think so too.'

'They all used to live together before being re-housed. Her son can't get a job and her daughter-in-law goes off every now and again – he doesn't know where. That's what this morning's row was about. Mrs Stevens tried to take Jamie back to his parents but, as she put it, "they were still going at it hammer and tongs", so she carried on down until it was over.'

'I'm amazed she told you all this – they're usually so reticent.'

'The situation looks potentially fraught to me so I suggested she pop in to see you. I told her you'd give her good advice.'

Mrs Boulton smiled at the compliment.

'I'll make some enquiries. If Mrs Stevens comes to see me, I'll give what advice I can. If it sounds serious, I'll pass it on to Margaret Beckwith. Her caseload of girls isn't so large at the moment.' She stood up. 'I'll let Mr McGovern know that you're free.' She stopped by the door. 'I don't suppose you've had any breakfast?'

She didn't wait for an answer.

Soon after her departure there was a knock on the door and Kemp rose. A tall, grey-haired man walked across the room and, choosing one of the chairs provided for visitors, draped his thin frame uncomfortably on it.

'Sit down, Kemp.'

Typically, McGovern waited to be sure he had the young man's full attention. Abandoning the discomfort of the chair, he perched on the corner of the desk.

'I'm sorry to add to your workload but I've an important visit I need you to make.'

'Is it a priority? You gave me two new cases on Wednesday.'

'Yes, I'm afraid it is. And it's different. This one hasn't come to us via the juvenile courts. It's about a lad named Michael Grant, under supervision in a private hostel in Streatham. His elder brother, who's known as Bobby G, attacked a member of the staff when he visited Michael. Not surprisingly, the management want the lad out of there. The family live in Hackney Wick so he's our responsibility.'

'Will the management prosecute?'

'Possibly – subject to your report, and how quickly he's moved. Interestingly, the parents have registered a counter-complaint saying Michael should've been allowed home earlier.'

'So, a few complications?'

'The legal team want us to check on the suitability of the parents to have their son back. They've promised the Grants that someone will call this morning around ten-thirty, and suggest it should be a male officer because of the possibility of further aggression. If there's a likelihood of violence, it might be desirable to take someone with you as a backup.'

'No thanks,' Kemp said. 'I'll be all right. Two of us visiting might inflame the situation.'

McGovern drummed his fingers on the desk.

'Do be careful, Kemp. This Bobby G is an unpleasant character by all accounts. I recall that you've done a bit of amateur boxing but bear in mind that this young bully has done time and won't observe the Queensbury rules.'

McGovern stood up, placing the Grant file on the desk. 'On the other hand, I suppose bachelors are relatively expendable.' He gave a friendly nod and left the room.

Grimacing, Kemp opened Michael Grant's file and scanned it, then rang the hostel to speak to the deputy warden. He held on while the man was found.

'Mr Kemp? John Cartwright. Sorry to have kept you waiting but I was dealing with a security issue. Since Bobby Grant's visit we've considered it necessary to increase our safeguards.'

'I'm so sorry to hear about the attack on you.'

'Michael's brother is a thug, and that incident brought out the worst in the boys. Afterwards I spotted a small group, including Michael, having a laugh at my expense.'

'That's very disappointing for you.'

'It is. I listened to them for two or three minutes before they saw me and heard one of them crowing about "the mess Mikey's brother made of old Cartwright's face". It's upsetting because he's a boy I've a lot of time for. Another boy said that he wished he'd been there to see me "get done over". We do our best for the boys but it's not going to be easy with Michael here as a reminder of his brother's behaviour.'

'I do understand. What was Michael's contribution?'

'Not unnaturally, he was revelling in the limelight. The group wanted to know if his brother had been to prison, and whether it's true that he's the leader of a gang in Hackney.'

Kemp was absorbed. He might gain useful information that would be helpful in deciding whether to allow the Grants to have their young son back.

'What did Michael say?'

'He said, "Oh yeah, me brother's done time and he's got a gang." He went on to say, "Me and me brother got nabbed stealing lead off a church roof. He's going to get me out of here".'

'I can see why you want him to leave as soon as possible.'

'I'm sorry for the trouble that gives you,' Cartwright said. 'I've told Michael that he isn't staying here, but I haven't said there's a likelihood of him going home. That would really give the wrong impression to the other boys.' He began to chuckle, then hissed.

'I've just discovered that it really does hurt to laugh,' he said ruefully.

'I'm afraid we're bound to look at the prospect of him going home,' Kemp said. 'If he does, he'll come under my supervision.'

'I don't envy you. I heard Michael boast, "Me Dad's been done two times over by the police for being drunk and disorderly. Nobody messes with my family". You'll need to be careful of the father as well as Bobby.'

'If I decide he should go home I'll tell you, but you can keep it from Michael until he's left the other boys.'

'That's helpful. Thank you.'

Cartwright sounded relieved as he replaced the phone.

Kemp locked the three files in his safe. Passing Mrs Boulton on the way out he called, 'I'm out on a new case Mrs B. I'll tell you about it when I get back.'

'Well, make sure you take care of yourself.'

He hurried out of the office, aware that her efforts to take him under her wing were increasing. She had been widowed in the Great War and was childless. With that history he found it difficult to be cross with her for long.

Once he was on his way to Hackney Wick he forgot about office politics. Apprehensive only because another attempt at violence would destroy Michael's chances, Kemp turned into the street where the Grants lived. It curved as it followed the direction of the railway. There were many gaps in the line of tiny terraced houses, the result of a protracted attack with fifty-pound cluster bombs in 1940. According to popular belief the objective had not been to destroy the railway, but to break the morale of the residents of the thickly populated East End.

Ahead, Kemp saw three houses with open space on either side of them. The gap nearest to him revealed a substantial fence built along the rear of the properties, preventing access to the railway lines. On the far side was a large billboard, sporting the remains of a battered ROWNTREES KIT KAT poster. It uncomfortably reminded him that Mrs Boulton was right: he had missed breakfast.

Now closer, he could see that a sheet of corrugated iron boarded up the bottom front window of the middle house, and patrolling in front was a heavily built young man. Kemp assumed he was the notorious Bobby G, apparently intent on intimidation from the outset. The thrust of his hands deep into his trouser pockets emphasised the exaggerated swing of his shoulders. The peak of his cap, pulled low over his brow, partially concealed his dark hair.

Parking his Rover behind a van, Kemp slid across to the passenger seat. The objective of this visit was simply to see if it was possible for Michael to return home. Bobby's influence was a real concern. He mustn't be allowed to claim that his violence had been the prime reason for his young brother's release.

Bobby Grant hove into view again and turned away as he reached the parked van, giving Kemp the opportunity to leave his car.

He walked up to Bobby, who turned theatrically when he heard footsteps. Kemp noted the scowl. The cigarette hanging from the corner of his mouth no doubt explained the number of small holes in his Fair Isle pullover.

He met Bobby's stare and gave a slight smile.

'Good morning. Would you know where the Grants live please?'

Bobby seemed taken off his guard and Kemp wondered whether he had expected an older, desk-bound variety of council officer. Quickly recovering his poise he looked at Kemp with narrowed eyes, and then without a word swaggered to the middle house. Pushing the front door open with his foot he entered without a backward glance and yelled, 'Ma, that geezer's here.'

Kemp reacted quickly. He followed and stood behind Bobby, but left enough space to avoid any wide swing he might attempt.

'I'm from the Children's Department and my name is . . . '

The bully turned.

'I know where you're from but that don't give you no right to come into a private house without permission.'

'Oh, I'm sorry! I thought you meant me to follow you when you walked in without speaking.'

'What we got here?' demanded a loud female voice.

As Bobby turned to the speaker, Kemp moved swiftly past him. He faced a well-built, middle-aged woman whom he assumed was Michael's mother. A cigarette dangled loosely from her fingers. A few strands of red hair had slipped under the scarf wound around her head and were lying limply on her forehead.

'Good morning. Mrs Grant? I'm Kemp, from the Children's Department. I've come to discuss Michael's situation.'

'Oh, lordy! If it ain't a young hoity-toity type. Are you sure you know who you're dealing with? Listen sonny, we don't want no discussion. You'd do yourself a favour just to bring our Mikey back.'

She contemptuously blew cigarette smoke in his direction. 'Ernie!' she called, stepping back through a doorway.

A big man with a large beer belly squeezed past her. He was wearing a distinctly off-white vest that stretched tightly across his stomach. He rubbed his eyes, yawned then growled, 'You heard her!'

This had to be Michael's father and it seemed the confrontation might be early in the day for him. Kemp hoped this meant that without the stimulus of alcohol Grant would be of a milder disposition than his wife and elder son. Mrs Grant stood behind her husband and nudged him.

'Go on! Ask him! Ask him if he's going to let our Mikey come home.'

Bobby moved closer.

'That's what I've come to discuss, Mr Grant.'

Bobby interrupted, placing his thumbs in the armholes of his pullover.

'Look, mate, if you don't do what you're asked you'll be sorry.'

Kemp didn't intend to be caught unawares like Cartwright. Aware that with this posture Bobby could quickly strike out at him, he placed his own hands higher, ostensibly holding his jacket lapels. Putting his back against a door he adjusted his weight evenly and watched the Grants. He became conscious of a sour smell but couldn't make out its source.

Mrs Grant's patience was running out.

'What you waiting for, Ernie? If he won't let us have our Mikey home, do him!'

Grant didn't move. Bobby hesitated, seeming to have taken account of the way Kemp had repositioned himself. He dropped his hands by his side.

'Round one to me,' Kemp thought.

Addressing Grant he said, 'You must realise that this won't bring Michael home.'

The two men studied him, seemingly disconcerted by his confidence. He stood between them, knowing that every second of inactivity was to his advantage. It allowed them time to reconsider an action that might prove counter-productive.

He breathed deeply, reminding himself of the ice-breaker at office meetings when each field officer was asked to create an amusing headline for one of their dramatic moments during the previous month. Having placed himself in a narrow passage between two men bent on making his mind up for him, and urged on by a woman seeking to see his blood spilt, he thought INEPT COUNCIL OFFICIAL GETS DONE seemed an appropriate title to bring to the next meeting – if he survived. He smiled.

Both men appeared disconcerted by this.

Bobby G re-designed his threat.

'Me and me mates can do you anytime we like. We know where your office is. We'll have you.'

Kemp ignored him and turned to the older man.

'Let's talk about it, Mr Grant. I'm sure we can find an answer.'

Shunting his wife before him Grant said, 'Come on, Doll.'

Kemp let breath escape before following them into the small kitchen. The roll of flypaper, covered in dead flies, immediately caught his attention. It hung down from the light shade, directly over the centre of the table. The frayed, well-worn carpet felt glutinous beneath his feet. Grant made a half-hearted attempt to clear the kitchen table of dirty crockery and cutlery.

'Dump them in the sink,' his wife ordered.

Scowling, she sat down on one of the chairs around the table and jerked her thumb at another chair, indicating where Kemp was to sit. Cigarette ash fell on the table; she brushed it off with an angry jerk of her wrist. Grant deposited the dishes in the stone sink with a clatter, then joined his wife.

Bobby G slumped disconsolately into an armchair by the window. Through the dirty glass Kemp could see the corrugated iron curve of an Anderson air-raid shelter at the back of the house, almost covered by dandelions.

Mrs Grant took charge.

'So what've we got to do then? My Bobby said the warden bloke got no more than he asked for.'

'I haven't come to talk about that, but it would have been better if it hadn't happened.'

'What's that?'

Bobby G looked malevolent.

'The reason for allowing Michael back early is so that he returns to a balanced home life.' Kemp looked directly at Bobby. 'His case isn't helped if his brother assaults the hostel staff.'

'Shouldn't have bossed me kid brother about then, should he?'

'It's the warden's job to maintain discipline.'

Bobby clenched his fists.

'Look, mate!'

'Shut up, Bobby!' Mrs Grant turned to Kemp. 'What we got to do to get our Mikey back?'

Kemp smiled at her but her expression remained hostile.

'You need to show that you can provide satisfactory accommodation and can keep Michael from further trouble.'

If she was affronted, she managed to conceal it. She awkwardly eased herself off the chair.

'Come on then, you'd better have a nosey round.'

The men remained seated. Mrs Grant led the way in to a small room off the kitchen. It contained a hand basin, and a tin bath was propped up against the wall, scum marks clearly visible. There was a pervasive smell of damp.

'The lav's out there,' she said, pointing through the small window at a wooden shed opposite the kitchen door.

They went back through the kitchen and climbed the bare stairs. The dingy sheets on the double bed in the main bedroom were tangled and the bedspread was on the floor, together with a pile of clothes. The wardrobe leant at an angle, one of its doors open. Curtains hung unevenly at the window and dust lay thick on a chest of drawers. A small alcove on the landing housed a stained sink with a dripping tap. Opposite, Bobby's room barely had space for the sagging single bed and small wardrobe.

Mrs Grant started down the stairs.

'You've seen it all,' she said in a loud voice. 'We're turning the front room into a bedroom for Mikey. That's it. You satisfied?'

He couldn't allow her ploy to work, as much as he would have liked to. The front room had to be the one with the corrugated iron at the window. He turned the door handle then stepped back to allow Mrs Grant to go first. She didn't move.

As the sour stench assailed them, Kemp realised this was what he had smelt earlier. They were looking in to a room where water from the sink upstairs had seeped through and brought down a small patch of ceiling, exposing the latticework. A stained mattress, spilling its grey stuffing, lay beneath a huge mound of rubbish. Mildewed milk bottles, yellowing newspaper, greasy chip paper and kitchen waste covered the surrounds.

Feeling nauseous, he hastily closed the door.

2

Her face scarlet, Mrs Grant shouted, 'You'd no business going in there!'

With trembling hands she lit another cigarette and turned to her husband, demanding that he join them. Grant was furious.

'Can't believe they'd stop Mikey living at home, just because he ain't got a proper bedroom. During the war we used to have six in a bed and the government didn't say nothing then, did it?'

Where did they expect Michael to sleep, Kemp wondered? Was he going to share Bobby's single bed? Or would it be in the armchair in the kitchen, after everyone had gone to bed?

Most of the time he dealt with unwanted children, but here were parents desperately wanting their son home. Unable to reach a different conclusion, he took a deep breath.

'I'm afraid this won't do for a teenager. Under the circumstances it's impossible to approve Michael returning to you.'

Bobby was beside him before the sentence was completed. Kemp gave him a dismissive look and then concentrated on the parents.

Mrs Grant's eyes gleamed. She clearly wanted his blood but Grant was physically restraining her. Bobby flexed his hands, obviously looking for his chance to join in as Mrs Grant's fingers clawed towards Kemp.

'It won't do no good, Doll,' Grant said.

Ignoring the threatened violence, Kemp said, 'Your contact with Michael is very important. Could you see him more often, or do you have relatives nearby he could stay with?'

Grant put his face in front of his wife and said forcibly, 'What about Linda?'

She stopped struggling but he retained his hold. She stared at him. He nodded eagerly and released her.

'Me married daughter don't live far from us,' she said, straightening her pinafore. Glaring, she added, 'They've got a spare room.'

She frowned and tossed her head at Bobby G, signalling him to move away. 'We could get a bed in there, but I suppose they're too bleeding young or something?'

Apparently unable to wait for an answer she continued, 'But then again, if you can go around telling people what to do with their children, I can't see you can have any bleeding complaint. I reckon you ain't that much older yourself.'

Grant winced at his wife's abusive tone. 'She don't mean nothing by that,' he said hurriedly, looking anxious.

'How old are they, Mr Grant?'

His wife butted in.

'Linda's twenty. Her hubby's twenty-four – him with his good job and all the airs and graces.'

'Shut it, Doll. Geoff's a good bloke and he looks after our Linda.'

'As Michael won't actually be fostered by them, their age is less of a problem – assuming they want the responsibility and could cope. I'll need to visit.'

'She should be in now,' Grant said, swiftly. 'She only works part-time and this ain't one of her days on. She ain't far away. We can go now.'

They all looked at Kemp. He was being pressurised. It was usually wise to let things calm down rather than respond to pressure, but he was unhappy about adding to the separation of a child from its parents.

'It would be a bit much for us all to descend on her.'

Mrs Grant sneered. 'I thought for a moment there you really wanted to help.'

Obviously worried that his wife's sarcasm might upset a possible solution, Grant rounded on her.

'Pack it in, Doll.' To Kemp he said, 'Me daughter would love to help, Mister. There's only the four of us to call on her, and we're all family except for you.'

'How far is it?'

'Only a couple of miles. It wouldn't take long in your car.'

Kemp saw the glance exchanged between mother and son. Were they waiting for the suggestion to fail, perhaps perversely wanting it to?

'You ought to introduce me anyway,' he said. 'Let's go. But I make no promises.'

'Fair enough. Come on, Doll.'

Mrs Grant looked astonished but jerked her head at her son. 'Come on, Bobby.'

Kemp wished he had an acceptable reason to exclude him.

Grant beat his wife to the car and climbed in to the front passenger seat. He gave directions to Linda's flat.

A plump, pretty girl opened the door. Her eyes widened in surprise as she looked at her visitors. She gave Kemp, standing slightly apart from the group, a brief sidelong glance but ignored Bobby.

'What's up? Is something wrong?'

'No, Linda love,' Grant hastened to reassure her.

His wife jostled him but he pushed her back and hurriedly explained the situation.

Linda beamed. 'I'd love to have Mikey here, if that'll get him home. I know Geoff will agree.'

She turned to Kemp. 'I could cope with school times.'

Still ignoring Bobby, she stood in her mother's path.

'Now, Mum, you all wait in there. This place ain't so large to have you all trailing behind when I'm showing Mr Kemp around.'

Chattering, she took Kemp proudly around a home very different from the one he had just left.

'This is me spare room, Mr Kemp. I does me ironing and sewing on that table but I can move it out so that the room is only for Mikey to use.'

'With a single bed in here this will do very well. It's a pleasant room and you've made a comfortable home.'

Linda flushed at the praise. 'But how do you think your husband will feel about Michael living here? It can be difficult having someone else in your home, and in the case of Michael it's a big responsibility. He's got to be kept out of trouble and away from bad influence.'

Linda rubbed her forehead. 'I know who you mean. Geoff won't have Bobby in our home – he'd be mad he's here now. You can bet that Bobby won't be seeing Mikey in our place. As for me Mum, Geoff can't stand her but puts up with her because he has to. He likes Mikey. He feels sorry for him and used to take him out sometimes. We'd do our best to look after him.'

While Kemp was relieved that Bobby's access to Michael would be restricted, much depended on Geoff and Linda controlling and influencing the youngster. He wondered how difficult that would be for them.

He was reassured soon after when Linda said

pointedly, 'If he's round your place at night, you've to send him back to us on time, Mum. And it's not to be too late because Geoff's got to be up early for work. I don't want his hours messed up.'

'Of course, love.'

'I mean it, Mum. We can't be staying up all night waiting for him, only to find you and Dad have allowed him to sleep over. Geoff will get ratty.'

Mrs Grant briefly glared at her daughter before forcing a smile. 'Don't you worry, love. We'll get Mikey back to you in good time.'

Kemp looked closely at Linda.

'Are you sure your husband will accept this? We seem to be taking his agreement for granted.'

'Don't you worry about Geoff. I'll keep him happy.'

Mrs Grant pushed in between them.

'So if you're satisfied, Mr Children's Officer, when can Mikey come home then?'

Her husband and daughter remonstrated with her. Grant stepped in front of his wife.

'How soon can my boy come, Mr Kemp?'

Mindful of the hostel's impatience to be rid of Michael, Kemp quickly assessed his own time.

'If you can get hold of a bed and have it delivered by tomorrow, Mikey could come home this weekend.'

There was a murmur of excitement from the family. Grant was delighted and looked pointedly at his wife.

'No one delivers on a Saturday,' Linda said anxiously. 'Can you get hold of transport, Dad?'

'That ain't a problem, girl.' Grant smiled broadly. 'Jimmy, next door, will pick it up in his van for the price of a beer or two. Now petrol ain't rationed he's happy to help out.'

'Let's go down the second-hand shop when Mr Kemp leaves, Mum, and see what they've got.'

Bobby G was sulking, which Kemp took to be a good sign. Addressing Mrs Grant he said, 'You'll need to do something about Mikey's attendance at school. We can't leave that to chance.' Bobby snorted derisively.

'Me and Geoff will do that,' interjected Linda, flashing a knowing look at her mother. She paid no attention to her brother. 'We can go this afternoon after Geoff finishes work. He's on an early shift today.'

Kemp guessed she could see the importance of settling Michael down quickly, and didn't trust her mother to be civil to the headmaster.

'Subject to your husband's agreement, we can accept Mikey coming to you on a trial basis,' Kemp told her. 'I'll go back to the office to set things in motion.'

The sight of Bobby G looking triumphantly at his mother dented his enthusiasm. In an attempt to diffuse a conflict that might poison his relationship with Michael, he went over to him.

'See that he doesn't get into any more trouble, Bobby. He'll take notice of you.'

Bobby G's leer faded for a moment.

'Yeah!'

Blinking rapidly, his father said, 'You listen, Bobby. We don't want to lose Mikey again.'

His voice was gruff with emotion.

Shaking hands with Grant and nodding to Mrs Grant, Kemp followed Linda to the front door. Once outside she said, 'You done a good job there, mister. Me family can be trouble but we really do miss Mikey. When Mum and Dad visit he keeps asking when can he come home. They get upset, specially Pa.'

She looked up at him. 'Me ma's not easy to deal with, is she? She hates the council. You was lucky.'

Kemp nodded ruefully.

'I mean for her to even talk to you. She gets these fits. Me and Geoff will make sure she don't go near the headmaster so there won't be no trouble there.'

'Before you go to the school, I'll need confirmation from Geoff that he's willing for Michael to stay with you both. We don't want anything to go wrong.'

'We'll come to your office on the way and sign any papers you need. You'll get on like a house on fire with Geoff. Like I said, he don't have a high opinion of me Mum but he stomachs her for my sake. You can choose your wife, he says, but not your in-laws. I told you I'll keep him happy.'

That confident last phrase had firmly registered with Kemp. He had little doubt that Linda would succeed and fleetingly wondered what it was like to be so sure of someone. He handed her his card. 'Will you be able to find your way to the office this afternoon?'

She read the address. 'I know the Montgomery Estate. That's where those big blocks of flats are.'

'My office is at the bottom of the road, immediately after the flats. It's the only small building on the estate. If you ever need to come on your own, do so in daylight as it can be a bit threatening in the dark. It's noisy, with groups of youths with time on their hands and no place to go.'

'I've heard all about it.'

'If I'm not available and you need urgent help, ask for Mrs Beckwith. She looks after teenage girls but she'll assist. The person who'll most probably answer the telephone is Mrs Boulton, our senior clerk. Speak to her if I'm out. She'll give you good advice and will make sure I get any messages from you.'

'Mikey will be fine with us and we won't be afraid to ask for help.'

She tentatively added, 'It'd be good if you'd give us as long as possible to let him settle before you come to see us.'

'I appreciate that it'll take a little longer for the three of you to adjust, but if I'm to give you a bit more time before I visit, it's even more important that you let me know immediately if a problem arises.'

They shook hands. Kemp went to his car, pleased with the outcome. Back at the office, however, McGovern's compliments were qualified as he said, 'That's a satisfactory result and a very quick one. I'll let the legal department know.'

He frowned. 'But it does mean you've let work take over your private life yet again. You need to learn to look after your weekends, young man.'

Kemp merely nodded. 'I'll get the report done before I leave the office this evening.'

During the afternoon he was told that Linda's husband was waiting in reception and went down to meet him. Geoff was studying the posters on the wall and turned when he heard Kemp's footsteps. Transferring his crash helmet and goggles to his left hand, he offered his right hand to Kemp, smiling as he did so. They went out to Linda, standing beside a motor-cycle side-car.

'Hello again, Mr Kemp. I told you me hubby would have Mikey to stay with us, didn't I?'

'It's good we can help Mikey,' Geoff said. 'We should look after our own.'

'We found a bed, Mr Kemp.' Linda held her husband's arm. 'We've put a deposit on it.' Looking up proudly at her husband she added, 'Geoff has a good job. He's a bank messenger.'

'Yes, and I can't be doing with no trouble because of that.'

'You won't get any trouble, love. Mikey's only a kid.'

'I want him kept away from Bobby G, that's all I want.'

Linda's smile disappeared.

'We'd best be off,' she said hurriedly. 'We mustn't keep the headmaster waiting.'

'Before you go, I need you both to sign these forms, confirming that you're willing to be responsible for Mikey.'

Kemp waited to see them leave. Geoff adjusted his goggles while Linda opened the sidecar's door and settled on the low seat. Her husband swung the perspex canopy over her before kick-starting the engine.

Kemp was back in his office only a moment before McGovern knocked and entered.

'I've been watching from the window. They seem a decent couple.'

'Yes, I think they are. Once I have confirmation tomorrow that they've had a bed delivered, I'll take Michael to their flat.'

'You've worked fast on this.'

'The right time always seems to be now.'

'You need to slow down. We've never had time for a chat since I came. You might like to know your name came up at a meeting at County Hall yesterday. I met the Director of Education for Northumberland. He said that when you were at the teacher training college, you set up a youth centre in a difficult patch in his area and encouraged the students to get involved.'

'Bill Evans. Yes, he came on to the management committee.'

'So I understood. Why isn't that information on your CV?'

'I don't think it's particularly relevant, Mr McGovern. It was something I did voluntarily in the evenings and at weekends.'

'You might be surprised to know it was relevant enough to bring you here. Apparently, Bill Evans spoke about you to our chief executive when this Department was being formed. That's how you came to be invited to apply.'

Kemp was thoughtful. It was something he had never understood.

McGovern studied him for a moment.

'Well, you obviously aren't inclined to talk so I'll drop the subject – but suffice to say Bill Evans sent his regards.'

'Thank you.'

'Apart from taking Michael Grant home,' McGovern frowned, 'what other plans do you have for the weekend?'

Kemp's face twisted into a grin.

'Don't worry, sir, I've given up voluntary youth work. I'll settle for a long walk in Epping Forest and catching up on some reading.'

'No female companions?'

Kemp was alerted. It seemed that Mrs Boulton had been infecting McGovern with her preoccupation with his private life. As a diversion he moved across to the filing cabinet, pulling out a file he didn't need. To his chagrin his boss remained seated by his desk, waiting for an answer.

'The trouble with girlfriends, Mr McGovern,' he said at last, 'is that sooner or later they get serious. Frankly, I don't want dependency. My passion is for these children, and for the time being I feel privileged to be doing what I'm doing.'

He turned his attention to the papers on his desk. McGovern stood up.

'Our gain is some poor girl's loss,' he grinned. But at the door he paused. 'Don't overdo it, Kemp. We all need to have a life of our own.'

Mrs Boulton heard the last words as she came into the room.

'Have you been talking to Peter about easing off a little?'

'I've been talking about our young friend working at the weekend.' Then he caught the irritation on Kemp's face and abruptly changed the subject. 'How long will it take property maintenance to replace our sign?'

'I reported it first thing this morning and they complained it's the third sign that's been damaged in the short time we've been here. What do they expect when there are no amenities for young people and the estate is so isolated?'

She returned to the initial topic.

'I think Peter should find a nice young woman then he wouldn't be so lonely!'

McGovern saw Kemp bridle and hastened to say, 'It's possible to be alone without being lonely, Mrs Boulton.'

He gave her a warning glance and left the room. Mrs Boulton stayed, sorting through the papers she was carrying. Kemp sat back in his chair, watching her. On his guard but softening towards her he asked, 'Is there something for me, Mrs Boulton?'

'Yes, I think this might be of interest to you. Do you have time to look at this now?'

She held out a letter. He took it and scanned it rapidly. It gave details of a conference 'for professionals in the field of social work'.

'I think you should go,' she said.

He was furious. What was going on in her mind? He struggled to contain his anger at this continued invasion of his privacy.

There was a long silence. He knew her persistence was based upon concern and he had no wish to damage their working relationship, but she was probing an area that was extremely painful for him.

She appeared to take his silence as interest.

'If you've got nothing in your diary for that period, I'll book it for you.'

Making an effort to make light of the interference he said, 'You obviously think I'm in need of an overhaul?'

'Nothing of the sort,' she said frostily, 'but I do think you need to pay more attention to your life outside of work. I dare say you were used to your own company as a child - and that's made you the independent person you are – but if you don't socialise you'll end up a miserable and insular old man.'

Her face was crimson as she hurried to the door, obviously aware that she had said more than she intended, or had the right to say.

'Harsh words, Mrs Boulton,' Kemp called after her, but she had already left the room.

3

Kemp started after her, wondering which of them felt most damaged by the sudden altercation. Twice he reached for the door handle then drew back, pacing the office. It was extraordinary that his boss and the senior clerk should both want to talk to him about his non-existent private life.

He couldn't tell them that he still grieved for his parents and was devoid of any desire to be dependent. He had been so safe, so well loved, and then suddenly his roots had been torn from him.

Disturbed, he sat down, overcome by the recollection of the moment at boarding school when he had been told that his parents had been buried alive in the rubble of their home. Sent to stay for a short time with his paternal grandmother, he found she had been destroyed by the tragedy and was only a pale imitation of the grand old lady he had known. Several times in those two weeks he had caught her looking at him with tears in her eyes, but it was almost as if he wasn't there. Occasionally they would sit together, holding each other and gazing at nothing. Back at boarding school and destined to go to her at term end, he learned that she had a stroke and passed away.

At her funeral he had overheard someone say, 'She had nothing left to live for.' It had hurt him even more, knowing he belonged nowhere and to nobody. Bitter and angry at not being able to say goodbye to his parents, he vowed that he would never allow anyone to get that close to him again.

He half accepted that it was an immature decision

made by an adolescent. Maybe it did need reviewing, but he wasn't ready. Thankfully, his extreme distress had forged a depth of compassion for other young people deprived of a normal home life. It had confirmed his choice of subjects for university and determined his profession.

At university, a professor of psychology had early on questioned his single-mindedness. In an over-simplistic cover up he had answered, 'I just want to do good.' The man had come back witheringly and ungrammatically, 'Has it occurred to you that people don't want to be done good to?'

It was a useful lesson for although he empathised with his young clients, he knew better than to allow his understanding make him a soft target.

When the Children Act had been debated, Parliament had spoken of 'the failed trust of the eager disappointed.' It adequately described the majority of the youngsters in his charge, and was his mandate. Yet because he spent every minute using the insight so painfully gained, his colleagues viewed his dedication as unwise or unhealthy. No doubt they were taking the more detached view that if one didn't find a balance between work and private life, ultimately judgement could become impaired.

He squirmed in his seat, feeling frustrated.

Making up his mind, he went downstairs to put things right with Mrs Boulton. She was on her own in her office, putting files away. 'Mrs B,' he began, 'we mustn't be at cross purposes.'

Looking crestfallen she said hesitatingly, 'I'm sorry, Peter. I should never have intruded.'

'I know you meant well, Mrs B. Look, everybody will

be gone soon so why don't we have a chat over a cup of tea? I'll bring in some of my tea ration on Monday to replenish our stock here.'

'That isn't necessary, Peter. I've said I'm sorry.'

He went up to her and took her hand.

'I ought to tell you a little about my background. It might help you to understand how I feel.'

She nodded.

'I'd like that, but please ignore what I said. I sometimes get carried away, worrying about the children and you field officers working so hard for them.'

Kemp thought carefully about what he would tell her.

Shortly after she brought a tray into his office, and needing no encouragement to sit down, she poured their tea and looked expectantly at him. He began his carefully tailored story.

'I went to boarding school at eight because my father was an irrigation engineer overseas and my mother was with him much of the time. I missed them but never felt abandoned because Mother wrote almost every day and Father once a week. I liked my school and there was always plenty going on, especially sport. In fact, I was rarely alone so it was often difficult to find somewhere quiet to sit and read. I looked forward to the end of term because, with everybody gone, I had the library to myself. Also, I used to get boxing lessons from one of the admin staff. He was a distinguished amateur and I'd train at his club.'

'Your father worked in India, didn't he? There's so much hardship there.'

'Yes, he did. I joined them in India during the summer holidays. It's a wonderfully vibrant country but confusing, and some aspects of it were ugly. Extreme wealth and poverty existed alongside each other and there were big divisions by caste, religion and race, made infinitely worse by famine. Whenever we left the compound we were told not to give to the hungry or we'd be surrounded by scores of children chanting, "Buksheesh, No mamma, no poppa".'

Mrs Boulton sipped her tea.

'It must have been very distressing.'

'It was the sort of experience in which one was helpless – and we rarely get a chance to make amends. I'm sure you can see now how tremendously I value this opportunity.'

He paused, hoping he had said enough.

'Yes,' she said quietly, 'I do know how you feel, Peter. Many of us felt much the same after World War 1. When it was over we felt a duty to make things better, if only because of all those poor men who didn't come home, including my poor husband.' Her eyes were moist. 'I attended rallies supporting the creation of The League of Nations, even visited Geneva twice. When this last war started, I felt an enormous sense of personal failure.'

She shook her head, sighed and then almost pierced his armour.

'I believe the war left you an orphan?'

Kemp avoided answering by gathering up their cups. He hadn't realised she knew. Not looking at her, he missed the sympathy in her eyes.

'Do you have other relatives, Peter?'

'No.' He needed her off this subject, but one short word might be too revealing. He added, 'I hope you understand now how I feel about this job, Mrs B?'

'I do understand, but please realise how important it is to keep a balance – not to be so self-contained.'

Kemp shrugged.

'I've a sense of vocation and that's not unusual. We all have in this office, and we enjoy the challenges – you know that.'

'I agree wholeheartedly, but doing this sort of work is emotionally draining.' She stood up, attempted a smile, and picked up the tray. 'It's so important to be able to detach ourselves when we're away from it.'

Reasonably sure that his limited disclosure had repaired a dangerous rift he said quietly, 'I'll give you a lift home, Mrs B.'

'Thank you – and thank you for confiding in me. I'll lock up and wait for you.'

Looking pre-occupied, she left the room.

Before going downstairs Kemp rang the hostel to ask Cartwright to ensure that Michael would be ready to leave the next morning. Gathering up his hat and attache case, he pulled at the filing cabinet drawers to check they were locked and switched off the lights.

Mrs Boulton was making a final security check, so he waited for her in Reception. As they drove he told her about the arrangements he had made for Michael.

They drew up outside her house.

'Will you come in for a drink?'

He hesitated. 'It's very kind of you but I've an early start, and . . . '

'Yes, I know,' she coaxed, 'but please come in for one quick drink. I'll then feel forgiven for what I said in the office.'

'It's over and done with Mrs B, so don't worry about it. But yes, thank you, I'll come in for short time.'

He switched off the engine and assisted her out of the car. Mrs Boulton led the way into an immaculate house. As she poured their drinks Kemp wandered around the room, looking at her paintings and photographs. One, of a serious-looking young man in army uniform, caught his attention.

'That's my late husband,' she said.

She held out a small silver tray. Kemp took his glass and raised it to her. Sipping her sherry she looked at the photo.

'We went to a studio to get that taken because I so much wanted a really good photograph of him. It was very extravagant of us as we didn't have much money, but I've been thankful so many times that we did that. He'd been badly injured and was home on medical leave. Ten days after that photo was taken he went back to France – and never came home.'

Kemp touched her arm.

'I'm sorry Mrs B. I didn't mean to pry. He was a fine looking chap.'

'It's all right, Peter. It's so long ago – I can talk about it. He died in April 1917 at Arras. He'd just had his twenty-second birthday. Look,' she turned to a small table, 'here's our wedding photo.'

Kemp studied it for a few seconds then looked at her. 'Gosh Mrs B, you were a fine looking couple.'

She blushed.

'Forgive me.' He hesitated. 'Did you never think of marrying again?'

'George and I grew up together. I never wanted anyone else.'

'But – Mrs B – haven't you been lonely?'

'Of course I have, and I wished so much we'd had time together to have a child. I wanted a family but it wasn't to be. I loved George and felt I owed it to him to live as full a life as I could, otherwise what he fought for, what he died for, would have been for nothing.'

Lost in reverie, every syllable demonstrating her resolve she said, 'I won't pretend it was always easy, but I found that the more I reached out to people the easier it became.'

Kemp was fascinated: this was another side to Mrs Boulton. She ran her fingers lightly over her wedding photo before placing it back on the table.

He realised how similar their tragedies were, but she had stood up to the loss of her husband and the failed dreams of having their baby, whereas his reaction had been to run away from ever becoming dependent on anyone again.

'I must go, I've to be up early,' he said quickly.

Driving to his flat, he resolved to let his anger go. He took a deep breath, wondering if he could use the learning points he acquired while dealing with his caseload as stepping stones on a personal journey of rehabilitation. He knew that his parents wouldn't have wanted him to go on grieving and remaining fearful of entering into a meaningful relationship.

At Michael's hostel the next morning the warden clearly tried to make amends for the ultimatum that the boy should be gone in days, emphasising that the London County Council was a valued client. Kemp confirmed that he supported Cartwright's action.

Reassured, the warden gave his opinion.

'Michael's impulsive, excitable, easily led and unable to see the consequences of his actions,' he said.

Kemp thought of Bobby G and was momentarily discouraged.

He found Michael impatient to go, his face alive with anticipation. He was a lanky youth, untidily dressed, and clearly seeing Kemp merely as a means of transport to freedom.

Mrs Boulton confirmed that Geoff had phoned to say the bed had arrived.

'You do know that you can't live at home but that your sister turned up trumps for you?'

'Yeah. Mr Cartwright told me.'

'Did he also tell you that your brother very nearly mucked it up for you, and this is only a trial to see how you get on with Linda and Geoff?'

The lad nodded, only half listening.

'Do you like Geoff?'

'Oh, yeah, I used to go fishing with him sometimes. But will I still be able to see me mum and dad?'

'Of course. Your parents are happy you're coming back. They'll all be waiting for you at your new home.'

Michael's eyes shone.

The Grant family was present in force at the flat and, predictably, Michael was fussed over, but Kemp was disturbed by the boy's obvious idolatry of Bobby, laughing at everything his brother whispered to him.

'How did you get on with the headmaster?' Kemp asked Geoff.

'Very well. Mikey can start on Monday.'

This was the first Michael had heard of his new school. He grimaced and looked imploringly at his mother, who didn't react.

When Kemp left, Mikey barely responded to his farewell. Kemp understood this well enough – but Bobby's smirk disturbed him.

4

At eight-thirty on Sunday morning the phone rang in Kemp's flat.

'Peter? I'm sorry to phone you so early but I'm going off to church soon and need to tell you about a call I had from the Cambridgeshire police. I was the emergency contact last night.'

'What's the problem, Mrs B?'

'A young lad by the name of Norman Wills. He's sixteen. The police think he might have been involved in a break-in before they caught up with him. He's in a place of safety near Cambridge and has to be removed by lunchtime tomorrow.'

'Why Cambridge?'

'That's where he was making for, and that's where the nearest place of safety was with space to take him. He's our responsibility because his grandmother lives in Hackney and he's the subject of a Fit Person Order. She's reluctantly been acting in loco parentis. Norman has run away several times but this time his grandmother has refused to have him back. He's had only temporary jobs and has never appeared before the courts.'

'What else do we know about him?'

'We've a file. I seem to remember that he's described as being unusually intelligent but without ambition. Several attempts have been made to challenge him but he's never responded.'

'All right, Mrs B. Tell me where to look for his papers and I'll read them on the train to Cambridge.'

'I'll be in the office by eight. I'll have the file ready.'

'Thanks, Mrs B. That's very helpful.'
'And I'll mark all the key points for you.'
'You spoil me.'

Kemp parked his car at Liverpool Street Station. The first priority was to find Norman accommodation, a decision that would confront him once he came back to London. He read the timetable carefully: he needed a slow train on the return journey to have more time to assess the lad.

Settling back into the corner seat, he began reading. According to the social worker's notes, the boy was unhappy with his grandmother, who saw him as a burden. Allegedly, she was embittered by the behaviour of her daughter who, before running off and leaving her baby, had confessed to not knowing who his father was. This had given the grandmother cause to remind Norman repeatedly that he was a mistake, and that if it were not for her he would be on the streets.

While at elementary school an I.Q. test had shown Norman to be within the top quartile of a grammar school intake, but he had made no effort to live up to that potential.

Creating a mental picture of Norman, Kemp listed adjectives that applied to him: intelligent, homeless, uncooperative and work-shy. It was a challenging mix and it took little imagination to believe that he was destined for a life on the wrong side of the law.

There was plenty of evidence that Norman was resentful towards well-meaning adults offering advice, so Kemp wondered if appearing uninterested would evoke a response. Once in his charge Norman might become apprehensive about his future and open a dialogue. Unenthusiastic about his plan but unable to improve on it, he opened the carriage window for fresh air. The noise of the train increased, communicating a monotonous clanking rhythm. Relieved to leave the train at Cambridge, he joined a taxi queue. When he gave the cab driver the address the man snapped, 'It's only a short distance. You could walk it in fifteen minutes. You sure you want me to take you?'

'I don't have much time.'

Grunting, the driver crudely pointed to the door behind him.

Already in the role he would use for dealing with Norman, Kemp matched the taxi driver's surly behaviour and didn't tip. The driver muttered something unintelligible but Kemp ignored it.

The warden greeted him. 'I'm pleased you arrived early. We don't usually take in youngsters for such a short time as it isn't financially worth our while.'

Kemp grimaced at the unwelcoming manner. He wondered why everybody was being so miserable and concluded that it was a reflection of the sour persona he had adopted.

In a monotonous tone the warden continued, 'The boy doesn't seem very bright. He hasn't talked to any of the other residents, staff, or inmates. He went missing a short while ago and we found him in the staff quarters, having lost his way. There are plenty of notices. Can't he read?'

Kemp's eyes narrowed. Clearly, Norman had been trying to find a way out.

It was an oddly silent meeting when Norman entered the room. He failed to look up.

'So this is Wills,' Kemp said flatly.

In spite of his own taciturn manner, the warden raised his eyebrows at the curtness of the comment.

The youngster wore a khaki jacket, army surplus trousers and running shoes. He was of medium build with brown hair and, in spite of the bowed head and sluggish movements, Kemp suspected that he was alert and very fit.

Norman avoided eye contact – probably, Kemp thought, because his eyes would have shown cunning beyond his years. It wasn't going to be easy to get Norman to communicate, but it was essential to do so in order to help him.

'I'll arrange for a car to take you to the station,' the warden offered, 'but you've no need to go yet. The train's not due for some little while.'

'Thanks, but we'll go now,' Kemp said, knowing that he needed as much time as possible with Norman. 'We'll walk. I could do with the exercise.'

Having seen too many people ignoring his advice, the warden merely raised his eyebrows again. Kemp signed off and led the passive youth away. The lad appeared oblivious of the silence and irritatingly lagged half a pace behind throughout the journey.

They reached the station without a word exchanged and there was silence for forty minutes in the station waiting room. Norman maintained his indifference while Kemp, pretending to be engrossed with papers from his attache case, was increasingly concerned about the immediate future. He had learnt so much since leaving university that he rarely thought of his professional training, but with the limited time available he knew he would need all the skills he possessed if he was going to achieve a breakthrough with this young man. He could place Norman in a secure hostel but it was a certainty that the lad would find a way to abscond and get into deeper trouble.

When the train arrived Kemp chose an empty compartment and sat opposite Norman, staring at him. Although Norman never met his gaze he was sure that the youngster knew he was under scrutiny.

'I suppose you want to know where you're going,' Kemp said gruffly.

'Nope.'

'You know you're due to go to a detention centre and the police suspect you of a burglary?'

'I suppose.'

'Don't you care?'

'Nope.'

Annoyed with himself for giving the boy the chance to answer 'yes' or 'no' to his close-ended questions, Kemp tried again.

'What are you aiming to achieve?'

Norman looked out of the window at the passing fields and rushing telegraph poles, the view criss-crossed by birds wheeling freely across the sky. Kemp guessed at the emptiness in the boy's world and abandoned his strategy. Speaking in a gentler tone, and observing him carefully as he did so, he said, 'If you had your way right now, what would you choose to do with yourself?'

'Daft question, ain't it?'

'Try. What would you do right now if you had your way?'

'Disappear.'

'You'd probably have to steal to survive,' Kemp said irritably. 'You'd get picked up by the police again and be locked up for a long time.'

'It's a chance, ain't it?'

'Not much of one.'

Norman was intelligent so he ventured further, all the time watching for any signal, odd gesture, inflection in his voice or movement of his eyes, which were mostly downcast.

'Look, I'm supposed to do some kind of assessment of you but if we can't get on you'll be sent to a detention centre while a decision is made about your future. I want to give you an opportunity to plan your life. If it's a possibility, we'll examine it carefully.'

Silence.

'Come on,' Kemp urged doggedly. 'If you had your choice what would you really want to do?'

'Disappear.'

'It makes no sense. You'd last a few days on the run, a week at the most. Think again.'

'Disappear.'

'All right, if that's all you want,' said Kemp, pretending irritation at the stubbornness.

'What?'

'Disappear! Go! Why should I worry about you? I'll write an absconder's report.' Kemp's disgust was apparent as he added, 'You'll be picked up sooner or later but you'll be off my plate.'

'You're kidding?'

'Nope. I'm not kidding,' Kemp mimicked, willing Norman to look at him. 'I've responsibility for you at the moment and I'm your last chance. I'd like to help you but if you won't be helped, it's no good, is it?'

After a long silence Kemp added coldly, 'If you don't want to talk and all you want to do is run away, then so be it. It's your choice. I find that so empty headed that

I'll improve the odds for you. If you do go, I promise not to report you until I get to London.'

With unfortunate timing, the train began pulling into a station. Norman stood up. Kemp's eyes followed him, willing him to think again: making a bid for trust so early in these circumstances had been the height of folly.

'Do you mean what you said?'

'I never break my word.'

The train ground to a halt and Norman almost fell, but Kemp made no move to catch him.

At last the boy was looking at Kemp. As he moved slowly to the door his wary brown eyes watched the man intently, his jaw slack in apparent disbelief. Kemp remained motionless.

After what seemed like a moment of indecision, Norman stepped out of the compartment and sped down the corridor to the exit door.

5

The train was in the station for a long time. Through the window Kemp could see people walking along the platform, but he sat motionless. Norman might be watching and interpret any movement as breaking his word. He had gambled too much too quickly, he thought miserably.

The guard's whistle signalled for the train to leave. The carriages bumped against each other before moving off in a steady rhythm. Kemp couldn't keep still any longer. He went to the window and looked back at the disappearing platform, half-expecting to catch a glimpse of Norman, two fingers held erect in triumph.

Leaving the compartment he glanced down the corridor, and then rapidly looked again to see if he was mistaken. At the far end Norman, looking sheepish, leant against the side of the coach.

Kemp smiled. 'I'm glad you're still here. It's time to make some plans.'

The lad didn't move.

'Come on,' Kemp said, retreating into the compartment. 'Let's see what we can work out.'

Dragging his feet, Norman came in. He sat on the edge of the seat, directly opposite his new advisor but Kemp crossed over to sit next to him.

'Sorry, but we're on the same side now. Let's talk.'

Norman shifted.

'What do you want to know?'

'Why do you keep running away from your grandmother?'

'I hate living in that horrible basement. Gran

watches me like she's my jailer. She moans at me all the time. She keeps telling me I got bad blood in me veins and one day I'll find myself in big trouble.'

Raising his voice, he mimicked her: 'And you needn't think I'm sorting things out for you.'

Kemp nodded sympathetically.

'I tell myself I don't care, and I don't really, but . . . what I hate most is when people speak to me as if I'm something to be sorry for, like some kind of pet that's been badly treated.'

'Is that because they know you haven't got parents?'

'It's true I ain't got no parents, but what you've never had, you never miss. I don't suppose I'd like me mother even if I met her.'

'Do you want to talk about her?'

'Not really. Gran destroyed all the photos but I've tried to picture what she's like. I don't blame me mum for wanting to escape. As for me dad, from what me mates say it's not always a good thing to have one of them.'

'You're an intelligent boy. Why did you do so badly at school?'

'The teachers always went on at me to do better. I got bored and they complained I didn't listen.'

'Could that be true?'

'I told you, I get bored.'

'If you'd done better at school you could have become more independent.'

'I am independent.'

Kemp shrugged. 'I suggest you think about that, bearing in mind your current circumstances. What did you do when people tried to help you?'

'I'd start to take the mickey, wouldn't I?'

'Who was the loser?'

Norman didn't answer and stared stolidly into the distance. Kemp thought that boredom had set in.

'You said at the beginning you were running away. For me to help you, I need you to tell me what your next word is after running away. Is it *from* or *to*? You have to understand what an enormous difference there is between those two words.'

'What do you mean?'

'Are you running away *from* something? Or running away *to* achieve something?'

'I told you I hated where I was,' Norman said vehemently.

'You did. So your reaction to that driving thought is negative. You're running away *from* – do you understand? It's the difference between being negative or positive. If you're going to help yourself, you must learn to think positively.'

'Most of the time I don't run away, I just decide not to listen.'

He seemed to want to argue, which pleased Kemp. It was an improvement on being passive.

'Of course, and that's a form of running away, like the proverbial ostrich who sticks his head in the sand. It's negative.'

'Yes, but if you accept everything people say . . . '

'Beginning a sentence with a 'Yes, but' is another way of being negative.'

'Yes, but . . . '

Norman stopped and couldn't help but grin. He relaxed into his seat.

'If you're to be the man you have the potential to be,' Kemp said, 'you must learn to be positive. Stop telling yourself what you don't want and think of what you do want. Aiming for a desired destination, even if it seems out of reach, is surely more fun than drifting and being confronted by the unexpected.'

'I've always hated where I was living and that's got to be where I start. I can't think beyond that.'

'That's all right. The first step can often be what you don't want, but you need to take the second step.'

'What's that?'

'What you do want.'

The lad shook his head in disbelief.

'That sounds like a fairy story. That's not being real, Mr Kemp.'

'Do you know how to eat an elephant, Norman?'

'I ain't heard that one, mister.'

'In small bites.'

Norman laughed, his mood lifting, and looked at Kemp with interest.

'Don't think you won't get frustrated when you aim for things and don't achieve them, but that's the challenge you accept. You learn that way, adding to your experience until you stop being a loser and become a winner.

'The fact is, you can't always do it by yourself. Another negative you've been practising is to push people away when they offer to help. Instead, why don't you try looking around for all the help you can get.'

'I feel put down when people help me.'

'So you erect a barrier which makes certain they can't help you. How would you rate that as intelligent behaviour on a scale of one to ten?'

Norman was defensive. 'It's difficult to start.'

'Well, we haven't got all that much time, Norman, so

I'm giving you credit for having the ability to think through and accept the soundness of what I'm saying. You need to get off that slippery slope and change immediately. I need to summarise now because we'll soon be in London.

'My view is that "running away from" has become your only solution. The result is that you're starving your growing curiosity. The feeling of freedom when you run away is an illusion. Without something to aim for you're losing the opportunity to make the most of your undoubted potential.'

Kemp stood up and went to the window.

'I think you're ripe for adventure. You've intelligence and a kind of dogged courage. Use it.'

Norman was thoughtful.

'I've always felt I was being helped because people were sorry for me and I didn't want that so I'd play 'em up. I'm not a charity, Mr Kemp.'

'Then prove it.' Kemp remained at the window. 'It seems to me you ought to seek challenge and adventure in something like, say . . . the Merchant Navy. They have a junior sea training school.'

There was a gasp behind him.

'Cor! Wouldn't that be something? That'd be my dream,' Norman said, sitting upright.

'It could've been yours.' Kemp turned to face him. 'To succeed now would require real hard work and not a little good fortune.'

Norman was on his feet.

'Why not now?'

Kemp watched him closely.

'You've never had a conviction, have you?'

'No!' Norman was indignant but Kemp had noticed

the involuntary movement towards his right leg, where there was a bulge. He caught Kemp's eye and looked guiltily away.

'What have you got in that pocket?'

'Only this Swiss army knife.'

He pulled it out from his army trousers.

'That would be a useful instrument in a burglary.'

Norman swallowed hard. The discussion had taken an unpleasant turn.

'I think you'd better tell me about it. Best get it out of the way. If we're to work together we need to be able to trust each other.'

Norman looked everywhere but at Kemp. He struggled, blinking several times.

'I've never . . . '

'Tell me about the burglary, Norman.'

After a few seconds the boy began to speak.

'I got this book about a spy and copied some things he did. I had to get enough money to set myself up somewhere. I picked a house that looked like rich folk lived there, and I thought they'd leave some money about. I didn't want much.'

His voice was hoarse.

'I'd broken some glass to get in and then trod on it. I was so frightened about the noise but kept looking and found this.' His hands rummaged in the lining of his jacket, extracting a tightly rolled ten-pound note. 'The police didn't find it.' He sat down, misery on his face.

Kemp moved away from the window and sat close to him. After a silence he said, as if deep in thought, 'So you've no convictions. We could at least try to get an interview at the sea training school, but you'd have to work very hard to give yourself a reasonable chance.'

Norman went rigid. Only his eyes moved, searching Kemp's face. The switch of conversation was unbelievable.

'I really would work hard,' he whispered.

'You've no choice,' said Kemp brutally. 'You'll have to achieve a transformation to even be invited for interview. Everything you've been doing has led you away from such an opportunity as this. Being easily bored, lazy, avoiding challenge, turning away those who would help you, refusing to be part of a team, all those things have prepared you for failure – not only for this dream, but for any other.

'This is a wake-up call Norman. Maybe it gives you time – I don't know – but I think you owe yourself a chance.'

The train stopped again but it was of no interest to either of them. The solitary boy seemed to be struggling to understand the opportunity; a vision of a future very different from the one he had originally intended for himself. It was as if he realised he didn't deserve it.

As Kemp watched Norman he understood only too well how difficult it was to rid oneself of a dominating belief, even though it might be nothing more than a defence mechanism, destructive of the future. He recognised that it was a first important stepping stone for him too, but he ceased the introspection immediately and concentrated on the young man.

'You've become an expert at the power of withdrawal, Norman,' he said. 'Now you have to reverse direction. You'll need to work on English, maths and geography and you'll have to pass a medical and an aptitude test. Three months of preparation should be enough to get you in front of the selection board with a chance.'

Kemp wondered if Norman would have the willpower to sustain this new approach and dramatically change his behaviour. Commitment was needed and just at this moment he was enjoying the fact that Norman was hanging on to every word.

'Do you think I could pass?'

Kemp grinned. 'You've the brains – that is, when you think things through. Your academic record is rubbish so you'll have to score well in subjects that have bored you. I think the aptitude test will be your opportunity to shine. I'll coach you, if you want this enough. But it's not a dream, it's an aim.'

They spent the remainder of the journey in earnest conversation. Norman could finally see how, as an outsider, he had developed an independence that always set him at odds with authority. It was now imperative to consolidate the ground covered in such a short time.

'You need to have an address. Do you think you can manage a hostel where you're free to come and go as you please?'

'If you say I must.'

'You have to live somewhere! What do you suggest?'

'Could I live in lodgings? I wouldn't make no trouble.'

'Well, I could find some easily enough, and I'd visit you regularly to coach you until you have your interview,' Kemp began. 'But no, that's not going to work.'

'Why?'

'Well, I'd only be able to pay the first two weeks lodgings for you, and you haven't got any money to pay for them after that.'

Norman looked at Kemp as though he thought he was nice enough, but not very bright.

'I'd get a job, any job.' His eyes widened and he grinned. 'You knew that!'

Kemp grinned too.

'Your days of being Nomadic Norman are over, for the time being at least. You'll need to have a half decent work record to interest the Merchant Navy,' he said. 'At the very least you'll have to prove that you can hold down a job long enough to earn a good testimonial from your employers.'

'I'll have a bloody good try. Oh, sorry, sir.'

Kemp felt the beginnings of affection.

'I think you can make it. By the way, in spite of your denial. I think you're the best charity I know at the moment so you'd better keep the ten pounds you told me about. But never again, promise?'

'I promise,' answered Norman hurriedly, putting the money out of sight.

'I believe that anybody who tries playing that sort of game aboard ship gets thrown overboard.'

Norman reddened.

Collecting Kemp's car at the station, they began a search for lodgings from a list Kemp had compiled from his advertisements. He had already visited and assessed their suitability and their work concluded successfully at a small house in Stamford Hill. Alice Windsor was a pleasant middle-aged lady, alert and busy. She seemed thrilled with her potential lodger.

'My husband died in 1947. Perhaps you remember I told you that when you first called, Mr Kemp? I'm looking forward to the companionship of this young man, and the extra bit of income will help, because my husband's pension doesn't stretch very far.'

'I ought to warn you,' Kemp said, 'that Norman may

not stay very long because he's aiming to get in to the Merchant Navy.'

'It's me dream,' said Norman. He looked at Kemp. 'I mean aim.'

Kemp explained. 'We've been talking about turning wishes into reality.'

'And how do you do that?' Mrs Windsor asked.

'By eating an elephant,' Norman said swiftly.

'Perhaps you'll explain that to me later,' she said, looking puzzled. 'But business first. I'll give you breakfast and an evening meal to make sure you're eating properly.'

To Norman's delight his room had a table that would be his desk, and he learned that he would be free to come and go as he pleased. As he pranced about with obvious pride he overheard his landlady tell Kemp that she would like her new lodger to keep reasonable hours.

'What do you think are reasonable hours, Missus?' he interrupted.

Mrs Windsor smiled.

'By ten o'clock sounds reasonable to me, and if it's after that I'd expect you to be very quiet.'

'I ain't very interested in staying out late. I've got a lot of work to do. But how would I get in if you've gone to bed?'

'You would use your key of course.'

She handed it to him and he took it thoughtfully. Only a couple of evenings ago he had committed his first burglary and now this lady was handing him the key of her house.

'I ain't never had a key before. I'd take me shoes off if I was ever late, Missus.'

'Windsor,' said his landlady. 'You're welcome, Norman.'

She held out her hand and he self-consciously shook it.

Kemp telephoned to arrange for Norman to attend an interview with the personnel manager of a large laundry nearby. He would almost certainly get a job in the dreaded vat room.

'It's a very ordinary job but it pays well, and you can practise showing humility under trying circumstances.' He chuckled. 'All good experience for a life at sea.'

He went with Norman to his room and disclosed that he had given Mrs Windsor some money so that she could buy him underwear and socks. He declared he was leaving and wished him luck for tomorrow. The boy's eyes began to look suspiciously watery. Kemp guessed that it was probably the first time that Norman had permitted himself to be vulnerable in a long time so he hurried from the room.

He remembered the boy saying fervently, 'I'm not a charity'. Sympathy wasn't wanted. What the lad needed from him was empathy, and he could have that in abundance.

6

Having collected the Merchant Navy's application form, Kemp called in to the office briefly and met McGovern, who had been informed of the emergency call from the police.

'So what did you do with the runaway?'

'He's in lodgings.'

'In lodgings, man! You surely haven't? Och! Is this a joke?'

'No. He's lodging with a very pleasant lady. I'm going to see him shortly.'

'With his history, he won't be there when you go back.'

'Oh, I'm sure he will, Mr McGovern.'

'Kemp, you can't be starry-eyed about all your charges. I'm afraid you've made a mistake this time.'

'I don't think so, sir.'

McGovern opened his mouth to say more, but recognising the confident tone merely said, 'You got through to him, did you?'

He glanced out of the window a short while later and saw Kemp drive off.

Mrs Windsor was cleaning the brass on her front door when he arrived.

'We arrived home from the library about an hour ago, Mr Kemp, and I haven't seen him since. He went straight to his room with his geography books. Go through to the sitting room while I let him know you're here.'

Norman looked depressed after studying the application form.

'I ain't got nothing to offer,' he said, turning it over several times.

Kemp scrutinised the form.

'Perhaps you've a point,' he said. 'Look, why don't we write a good letter telling them of your interest, and ask for details about jobs in the Merchant Navy? It'll be a little while before that information comes through, which gives you time to get some satisfactory work experience. They don't know that the form I collected was intended for you, so there's no harm done.'

'This ain't bad,' Norman decided some time later, checking the letter for the last time. 'They might interview me, don't you think?'

As they were leaving the house Mrs Windsor wished him luck. She put her hand out to touch Norman then checked herself.

With his fingers crossed, Norman pushed the letter in to the post box. Kemp left for the office, telling Norman he would be back to see him in a few days.

Mrs Boulton waylaid him on his return.

'I've had a visit from Mrs Stevens, the old lady who lives in one of the flats next door. You met her and her grandson recently and encouraged her to come and talk to me.'

'Yes I did. About Jamie. I knew you'd give her some sound advice.'

'Well, she came in and I think there's a problem. Mrs Stevens describes her daughter-in-law as a bad lot. She quarrels with her husband and disappears for a couple of days. Be that as it may, I've asked Margaret to keep an eye on things. I thought you'd like to know.'

Kemp thanked her and ran up the stairs, his thoughts turning to priorities. Michael Grant was top of his list but he had to accept that things must be going well or he would have been contacted. He mentioned this to McGovern when he saw him.

'Linda wanted time to allow Michael Grant to adjust to the routine of their home. She's his sister, so I'm leaving it a while.'

'It's your decision, laddie.' McGovern laughed. 'As long as you're not doing it because the lassie's got a pretty face.'

Kemp had an uncomfortable feeling that there might be a flicker of truth in the comment.

Going through his files he was pleased to find that he was up to date with the statutory visits to the young people he supervised. Each must be visited at least once every six weeks. While he was checking, his phone rang.

'Peter, I've a problem I'd like to share with you.'

The deep voice was unmistakably that of Ben Sears, the superintendent of the Wellington Residential School. The manner, too – straight to the point.

'Good morning, Ben. How can I help?'

'I'll get to that in a moment. First, I've a youngster who's due to leave us in the summer. He's applied for army junior leadership training. He has an interview in the not-too-distant future at Blackheath. It's likely to be close to our Open Day, which is a busy time for us and, to make matters more difficult, I've a shortage of staff this term. I thought I'd ask if you could escort him there. Can you help out?'

'I'll do my best to fit it in.'

'Good. My main problem concerns another youngster. Are you free to come over? It's a quarter to twelve now. I could provide you with a late lunch. Bubble and squeak's on the menu today.'

'You know how to tempt a man but I'm not free until after three o'clock.'

'Then it's tea and biscuits. See you later.'

Kemp smiled as he put the phone down. His dealings with Sears were rather like encountering a whirlwind for the man was never still – a consequence of being responsible for more than a hundred youngsters, of all ages, resident in the children's home. Every year a dozen or so would have to leave when they reached their fifteenth birthdays. They would then be the responsibility of all areas in London. Forecasts showed that Area 4 were likely to receive about three boys a year to supervise.

Completing a routine visit, Kemp went on to the school. Sears was in his office, doing three jobs at once. He lived on the premises but his wife took no part in the running of the school. Once again he came straight to the point.

'Have a seat, Peter. The tea's just been made – pour yourself a cup. I've organised for you to meet Ronald Stone and his housemaster at four o'clock, so you can make arrangements about taking him to Blackheath.'

'Good.'

'Now I'd like to talk to you about Eric O'Reilly. His mother's dead, so he's been in care most of his life. She was living with an Irishman who deserted her soon after Eric's birth. She named him as the father. He's never been in contact with his son in all the time the lad's been here, but now he's suddenly turned up and wants to have Eric to live with him.

'I don't like the man and I suspect his motives, but as he is the putative father we need to have good reason to intervene. After his visit here Eric's housemaster reported that the boy was very dour about it: not excited, as one would expect him to be, having found his long lost father. Nevertheless, O'Reilly has applied to have Eric for the long weekend at half term and Eric wants to go.'

Sears took his glasses off to clean them and peered at Kemp.

'Could you take a professional look at this situation?'

'I'll see what I can do. I'll have a word with his housemaster before I leave.'

'O'Reilly has made noises about taking Eric away at term end so we need to have a good reason for refusing before then. I know the lad isn't due to come to you for a year but it would relieve my mind if you could give us an opinion.'

'The long weekend should tell us a lot. In the meantime I'll research his file.'

'You've earned yourself another cuppa,' Sears grinned.

Kemp spoke briefly to Ronald Stone, promising to collect him for his interview in a few weeks time.

Eric's housemaster, who was due to be transferred, could add nothing useful, but the boy's former teacher, an attractive tomboy, was pointed out to him. He was about to introduce himself when she said, 'You're Peter Kemp, aren't you? Someone told me who you were on a previous occasion. I'm Kathleen Ashley. Can I help?'

'It's about Eric. Do you know him well?'

'Oh yes, a terrific little all-round sportsman. Popular, but doesn't give much away. His schoolwork was average. He's playing football for the school this evening so it's not a good time to speak to him. Tension is high as it's near the end of the season and the Wellington boys are determined to keep their top position. That's the best I can do for the moment as I'm due on the netball court.'

She whirled out of the room, leaving him to wonder whether the words 'human dynamo' appeared in the job specifications at Wellington.

Kemp left: he saw no point in interviewing Eric without having knowledge of his background. To get the youngster's file he would need to show him as a temporary extra to his caseload. As a source of information, he added the young teacher to the list of people he would visit the next time he came.

Anxious to keep abreast of his admin, he reached the office earlier than usual the following day. At the top of the stairs he saw Mrs Boulton and Jennifer Bowlby in the kitchen, earnestly talking. Jennifer was primarily responsible for adoption cases. They looked up and moved apart as a signal for him to join them. He pretended to miss the gesture and with a quick, 'Good morning,' disappeared into his office.

Some time later one of the clerks came to empty his out tray, taking his request for Eric O'Reilly's file along with other papers. Not long after McGovern rang to ask him to come to his office.

'I understand you've been asking for the file on an Eric O'Reilly. Is he an extra you're thinking of taking on?'

'Yes.'

'Is there any particular reason?'

'Ben Sears is concerned about him and, in any case, seeing a youngster before he's actually due to leave eases the transition from school to work. There are enough other changes occurring then – like leaving friends and becoming part of new families.'

'Don't you think you've enough on your plate?'

'Do you object, sir?'

'As you know, I want you to be free to make your own decisions, but I'm concerned at the time you spend working. I don't want to see you overloaded. I hate to interfere, but I'll do a deal with you.'

'What is it, sir?'

'I want you to have a break. I'd like you to attend the conference that Mrs Boulton mentioned to you. It seems very sound.'

'Do you insist?'

'Of course not. That's no way to enjoy a break. I simply think that once you get there you'll enjoy meeting new people.'

Kemp considered McGovern's words. He respected him and thought him wise.

'All right, I'll apply and, unless there's some unlikely emergency, I'll attend.'

'Good man,' said McGovern, looking relieved.

Soon afterwards Mrs Boulton knocked on Kemp's door, bringing his post and an urgent message.

'Mr Drew's been on the phone, wanting to talk to you. He's gruff to the point of being rude.'

'It's probably because he hates asking for help, Mrs B.'

'I can't stand the man. His son's been missing for four days and he has something to tell you about what might've happened. I tried to get him to say more but he refused. He said it was men's talk. Men's talk indeed!'

'He's worried, Mrs B. Dennis may be nearly seventeen, but he's retarded. He lacks initiative, is over anxious to please and is very trusting. I know his father's manner alienates people, but he's done all he can for his son since his wife abandoned them.'

Mrs Boulton was not easily appeased.

'Forgive me if I can't quite believe that ungracious man could be thought of as caring – particularly as Dennis has now been missing for four days. How did he first come under our wing?'

'The police found him wandering the streets about three years ago. He told them he was looking for his mother. He was placed with Dr Barnardo's.'

Mrs Boulton shook her head slowly. 'Poor lad.'

'The mother never returned but Drew visited regularly. When the Act came in Dennis was transferred to us and Drew was allowed to have the boy home on holiday. I visited and found Dennis sleeping on two armchairs which had been pushed together.'

'What happened to the boy's bed? Had he sold it?'

Kemp grimaced.

'That's not very kind. Drew only has a one-bedroom flat. When the boy was smaller I guess it worked, but I told Drew that the living arrangements weren't good enough now to allow Dennis home permanently.'

'Quite right. He can't really love the boy.'

'Hang on, Mrs B. Your pet hate of the moment immediately turned the small dining room into a bedroom for Dennis. There's a strong bond between father and son. It's reflected in the boy's demeanour, and you have to admit we've not had any trouble since I agreed he could come home permanently just over a year ago.'

'I suppose you're right, but I dislike bad manners.'

'I wonder if Dennis's disappearance has any connection with Mrs Drew's whereabouts? They're still unknown, and I understand she's never contacted her husband or son again.'

'The boy's had a rough deal.'

'So has the father,' said Kemp.

'All right, I'll be gentler with him next time. That's if Dennis turns up and hasn't been abused.'

'You're a lady of strong convictions, Mrs B.'

As she turned to leave the room he said, 'Oh! Can you resurrect that invitation to the conference, please? I propose to go if there are any places left.'

He was unable to interpret the look on her face as she closed the door.

Telephoning Dennis's school he was told that the place was closed for the day but Dennis's form mistress was in. After speaking to her Kemp put the phone down slowly, pondering on a surprising piece of information. He went to see Mrs Boulton on his way out.

'It appears that Dennis has run away from home but is still attending school.'

'What did I tell you, Peter? His father's abused him in some way, you mark my words.'

'We'll see,' said Kemp, mystified.

Within minutes he was pulling up outside Drew's flat. The worried father was waiting, anxious as ever that his neighbours shouldn't know his business. He let Kemp in through a half open door then quickly closed it. A tall, stooping, morose man, somewhat uncouth in appearance, Drew wore a bushy moustache and beard.

'You've come,' he said, 'and about time too. Me lad's being enticed away.'

Kemp ignored the rudeness.

'Have you rung the school, Mr Drew?'

'No. I didn't want them knowing my business.'

'So you don't know that Dennis is still attending school?'

Drew said nothing, wrinkling his brow in apparent surprise although Kemp suspected that he must have been to the school gates to look for his son.

Another tenant came down the stairs. Waiting until the woman was out of earshot Kemp said, 'I think we'd better go upstairs and you can tell me what's really been happening.'

Drew looked unwilling to move but led the way up to the top floor. His reluctance to take Kemp into his flat was explained when they walked into the kitchen. Dirty cups and the remains of half-eaten meals littered the table. A big armchair, which Kemp hadn't seen in the kitchen on previous visits, was draped with a heavy overcoat, suggesting that Drew hadn't slept in his bed the previous night or, perhaps, for several nights.

'It's kept me up,' Drew said, following Kemp's glance. 'I thought he might come home late, having lost his way or something.'

'How many days has he been missing?'

'He ain't been home for three nights.'

'He could hardly lose his way three nights running and still go to school each day.'

'I didn't know he were going to school, did I?'

Drew was becoming truculent but Kemp persisted.

'I don't think you're telling me the whole story, Mr Drew.'

'There ain't no story. I thought you'd be out there looking for him by now.'

'Is that what you've been doing?'

'Course I have. There's no sign of him.'

'And yet he's been attending school. You could have met him at the school gates.'

'I didn't know that, did I? Look Mister, I've had

enough. We ought to be out there searching the neighbourhood.'

Drew stood up and paced the small room. Kemp noticed, for the first time, that when under stress his anxiety mirrored the behaviour of his son. Kemp rose too.

'Let's stop beating about the bush. Did you chastise him over something?'

'Only about staying out late. These streets ain't safe at nights.'

'Did you strike him?'

'No I didn't!' Drew glared at Kemp. 'He was coming home later and later. I told him three times about it.'

'Then what did you do?'

'I told him he was not to go out in the evening any more.'

He was close to tears.

'And the next evening he didn't come home at all. Am I right?'

Kemp spoke gently for he had confirmed his original summing up of Drew.

'Easily taken advantage of, he is,' said Drew. 'I don't know what's come over him, coming home later and later.'

'Have you no idea at all where he might be or whom he might be with?'

Drew struggled for a while then blurted out, 'He's being picked up by a woman in this fancy car. She lives somewhere over the other side of the Wick. It's got a bad reputation, that area.'

'How do you know this?'

'I saw 'em, didn't I?' Drew looked abject then confessed. 'Saw him being picked up at the school gates in this posh car.'

'What's the address? Do you know that?'

'No I don't. This bloke only said where she came from. She's a foreigner, Indian or something like that. You've got a car, that's why I thought you could help. I ain't got no car but I got the number.'

He went to the kitchen table and handed Kemp a torn cigarette packet.

'I'll see what I can find out,' Kemp said. In a kinder voice he added, 'You did right to call me but I wish you'd been honest with me from the start.'

Dejected, Drew simply grunted.

'If you've told me all you know, I expect I'll be bringing him back.' He looked about the kitchen. 'How about tidying things up? I'm sure you'll want Dennis to come back to a welcoming home. And as he loves you so much he won't want to see you looking a wreck, so why not spruce yourself up too?'

'Do you think you can find him?' Drew blew his nose on a very crumpled and dirty handkerchief. 'I've let things go a bit.'

His woebegone expression deepened and he avoided Kemp's eyes as he passed him to go down the stairs.

Stoke Newington police station was Kemp's next port of call. He had visited it on more than one occasion but unfortunately there was no one on duty at the desk that he knew. He produced his credentials.

'I need to know the address of the owner of this car, please, and anything else you may be able to tell me.'

He handed over the torn cigarette packet with his card and the constable raised his eyebrows.

'We won't keep you long, sir,' he said. 'Do you have any clue as to who the owner is? A name perhaps?'

'No. I'm sorry.'

'All right, sir. We'll be as quick as we can.'

Kemp waited for twenty minutes. He was drumming his fingers on the table in front of him when the station sergeant appeared. Drawing himself up to his full height he appraised Kemp.

'Is this something we're likely to be involved with in the near future, sir? We like to be forewarned.'

'I sincerely hope not. It would have a very unfortunate outcome if that were so. I'm simply following up enquiries concerning one of our youngsters in care.'

The sergeant grunted.

'The owner of the car is known to us. Her name is Rashida Bannerjee and we do have her address.'

He handed over a form with the details and asked Kemp to sign for it. As Kemp turned away he added, 'There's been a reaction to her and her Indian husband living there. I had to call at the house because things were thrown at the windows and there were threats, that sort of thing. That's how I know about her. She's Anglo-Indian, an interesting lady.'

As an afterthought he said, 'I don't tolerate colour prejudice. India's been a very important part of the Empire and people shouldn't forget that.'

'Why is she an interesting lady, sergeant?'

'It wouldn't be fair to encourage you to pre-judge her, sir. I think you must see for yourself.'

7

A well-preserved vintage Bentley was parked outside the house. Guessing this was the 'posh car' to which Drew had referred, Kemp parked in front of it.

This part of Stoke Newington boasted large, once superior, three-storey houses. Unfortunately there were no signs of the renovations that were going on in other parts of the borough. The buildings appeared to huddle together in mute protest at the deterioration that was gradually overtaking them. Several were derelict and there was an air of desolation.

Why was Mrs Bannerjee 'an interesting lady'? Intrigued, he considered the fact that she had described herself as Anglo-Indian to the police sergeant might provide the answer: it sounded defiant. He remembered his parents telling him how the child of Anglo-Indian parents tended to be shunned by both communities. He wondered if prejudice was operating here. If Dennis was staying in this household, the racial tension might harm him because he was ill-equipped to cope with stressful situations.

He lifted the heavy brass knocker on the front door and after some delay, through the coloured glass panes, he saw the shadow of a figure approaching. A wrinkled man, dressed from head to foot in white, opened the door to him. He looked old, but it might have been the effect of the grey goatee beard and the parchment-like skin.

'I'm looking for a Mrs Rashida Bannerjee,' Kemp announced. 'I'm from the London County Council.'

The man made no eye contact but inclined his head,

almost deferentially. He spoke carefully, his Asian accent very pronounced.

'I am Mr Bannerjee. You will follow me, please?'

He led the way up the stairs into a room thoroughly reminiscent of several Kemp had seen in India, whose influence was everywhere about him. He looked around for the source of the incense that permeated the room. There were many collectors' items, and particularly admirable were the woven silk rugs on the walls. Rather coarser rugs were underfoot. Mr Bannerjee motioned towards a chair, bowed again and left the room. In moments he was back.

'She is coming,' he said. Clearly not inclined to converse with the visitor, he solemnly assumed a meditative pose in front of the fireplace.

When Mrs Bannerjee appeared, her demeanour was very different from her husband's. The woman who came unhurriedly to meet him was tall and distinguished, with a perfect olive complexion and long, black, shiny hair. A wide headband gathered the sleek blackness of it together before her hair fell to rest on her shoulders and then cascaded to the small of her back.

She was elegantly dressed in a silk sari. The blue, green and gold of its pattern combined to produce a peacock that entwined itself around her figure. The sari was draped across the upper part of her arm; her wrists revealed gold bangles and her long slender fingers held many rings. She had attractively manicured nails. He couldn't believe that this was everyday dress and wondered where their income came from.

Kemp looked into soft, deep brown, almost luminous eyes. Her make-up, sparingly applied, emphasised her good looks. She bowed a welcome to him without offering her hand. She, too, had an air of detachment but one very different from her husband's for she was totally attentive to her visitor.

He guessed her to be in her mid-thirties. With such poise and charm he could have imagined her anywhere but in this house, married to this man. He gave her his card.

In a well-modulated voice with hardly a trace of eastern accent she said, 'You are welcome in our house, Mr Kemp. My name is Rashida Bannerjee. This is my husband.' She gestured towards the crouched, motionless figure by the fire. Quietly she added, 'How can we help you?'

'I'm making enquiries about a young man named Dennis Drew,' Kemp said, refusing to be overawed. 'Do you know of him?'

'Would you like to please sit down?'

She waved a hand towards a chair as if she hadn't heard the question. Feeling a loss of control because of her deceptive manner, Kemp was mildly irritated and responded rather gruffly.

'This is an official visit, Mrs Bannerjee. Please answer my question. Do you know the whereabouts of a Dennis Drew?'

Rashida Bannerjee smiled.

'We do. He is not in any trouble is he?'

'That's something I think I should ask you, Mrs Bannerjee.'

She inclined her head and, without further comment, led him up the stairs to the third floor of the house. They passed an open bedroom where a mattress was laid on the floor and children's possessions were scattered everywhere.

In the second bedroom Dennis was curled up alongside a youth of roughly his own age, and both boys had playing cards in their hands. Dennis scrambled to his feet. Tall and slim, he looked wide-eyed at Kemp, colour mounting in his cheeks. Dropping his gaze he noticed the untidiness of his grey shirt and crumpled trousers and rapidly proceeded to adjust his dress.

The other youth looked extraordinarily like Rashida Bannerjee. He was beautiful, dressed in white loose clothes that served to enhance his olive skin and slight figure. He was not as tall as Dennis and looked younger. He had inherited a finely chiselled face and a slightly aquiline nose from his mother, as well as the jet-black hair that crowned his good looks. Long lashes hid his eyes as his head was slightly bent and he never once looked at Kemp.

'This is my son, Deta,' said Mrs Bannerjee proudly. 'The boys are good friends. Dennis is welcome here.'

Deta placed his hands together, made the traditional bow and moved to stand beside his friend. Not wishing to ignore the courtesy, Kemp gave an awkward half bow in reply before turning to Mrs Bannerjee.

'Has Dennis been staying here for several days?'

'Yes, he's happy here.'

'But what about his father?'

He turned to Dennis.

'You must know that your father's very worried about you, and very unhappy.'

Looking crestfallen, the lad started to fidget.

'Please get your things together,' Kemp told him. 'We'll be driving home to your father shortly.' To Mrs Bannerjee he said, 'May we go downstairs to wait for Dennis?'

Back in the living room Mrs Bannerjee said, 'Dennis can stay here as long as he likes.'

'You're mistaken,' Kemp told her firmly. 'Don't you know that he's under the supervision of a court order and that he's not been home for three nights?'

'He is a poor little devil,' she replied. 'There is no woman in his life to look after him.'

The cadence in her voice as she said 'devil' was appealing.

'Dennis goes to the same school as Deta,' she went on. 'He is handicapped too. I can take them in the mornings and collect them in the afternoons. My husband is home when I am out working. Dennis is welcome here.'

She had retained her composure throughout. It was very disarming and her eyes, holding his, were appealing for him to agree.

'It's not possible,' he insisted, wondering at the same time about the nature of her work. 'Don't you realise that his father loves him? Can't you imagine how very worried he is?'

She ignored the implied criticism.

'Deta and Dennis are very happy together. I have money – I could look after him.'

'It's not possible.'

'But it must be awful for him and for his father to manage without a woman to look after them.'

Struck by her persistence, Kemp had a moment of intuition.

'Did you know Mrs Drew?' he asked

'That was clever of you!' she said, after a moment's pause. 'Yes, we knew each other quite well.'

'Is she involved in this?'

'No, but she was my friend.'

'And is she likely to come back?'

'That is also not possible.'

She smiled at him in her gentle way. He waited for her to say more but she held her silence, sending his mind racing. Rashida Bannerjee had hinted that a special relationship had existed. How had she met Mrs Drew - surely not through work? He settled for a different question.

'Are you in touch with Mrs Drew?'

'No.' She paused. 'Are you going to prevent Dennis coming here?'

He didn't answer. He was finding it difficult to conduct this interview normally. Mrs Bannerjee was totally non-combative and utterly disarming. She was setting him a problem and he took a moment to re-evaluate the situation. He couldn't leave the premises without taking Dennis with him: the boy was a ward of the court and therefore technically his responsibility.

Dennis hurried into the room, agitated. His eyes kept darting from Mrs Bannerjee to Kemp, as if he saw the two of them as protagonists. Deta followed.

Kemp hadn't seen Dennis so distraught before. It was clear he was set to be defiant. If he resisted and the Bannerjees encouraged him, it could involve the police and he might end up back in an institution– a tragedy for Dennis and a terrible disappointment for his father.

Dennis's agitation was communicating itself to Deta, who was showing alarming signs of anguish. Under stress it was apparent that Deta was indeed retarded. Those soft brown eyes he had inherited from his mother, though dull by comparison, were showing white, and he began to claw at her sari.

While appearing stern, Kemp was nonplussed. Out of the corner of his eye he saw the hitherto trance-like figure of Mr Bannerjee turning slowly and deliberately towards him. He found it surprisingly threatening. Against the backdrop of the eastern carpets on the wall and the mixture of incense and scent, the situation showed every indication of spiralling out of control. Kemp focused on Mrs Bannerjee, deciding that she held the key, but she was ahead of him.

'You must go to see your father, Dennis, and show him you are safe, then perhaps he will let you come here again.'

Her serene tones calmed the explosive situation. Her son ceased to shake. Dennis's shoulders drooped but her intervention was decisive. She took his hand.

'We have been rather naughty and thoughtless, have we not? Take your father some of my cake as a peace offering, then maybe he will let you come again.'

Deta stopped clutching at her sari. She led Dennis into the kitchen, emerging with a cake. Taking her time wrapping it, she placed it in a large paper bag and handed it carefully to Dennis while caressing his back with her free hand.

To Kemp the scene had been riveting and a privilege to watch. Her gentle voice had seemed almost hypnotic.

Dennis went meekly to Kemp.

'I do want to see me Dad and ask him if I can come again,' he said.

Rashida Bannerjee turned to Kemp.

'You will allow them a little time to say goodbye to each other?' Kemp nodded. 'Then may I be allowed to be hospitable to you and provide you with some tea?'

He couldn't refuse; he had no wish to refuse. The

tension had evaporated. She motioned to her husband, who gestured with a half bow for Kemp to follow him into the next room. The boys sped happily in the opposite direction, the ugly situation forgotten.

It was a relief to both men when Mrs Bannerjee rejoined them, for they had sat in an awkward silence. Kemp stood up as she came in, took a large, heavy tray from her and placed it on a small table. She handed him a tiny cup of tea before taking one to her husband.

As she sat down Kemp said, 'As Dennis's father didn't know where you lived, I went to the police station to see if they could help. I was surprised when the sergeant said he knew you both.'

She sighed.

'Our acquaintance with the police has come about for unfortunate reasons. My husband reported an 'assault on his person', I think you call it, and we are often abused with ugly words. Sometimes stones come at the windows. I have to garage my car each night. It seems to inflame these unkind people.'

'What has given offence to the neighbours?'

'It is the colour of our skin that offends them. In this country it is directed at my husband more than me, but it was no different in our own country. I was rejected because I had an English father. Neither the Indian community nor the British would accept me socially. Can you explain this prejudice that shames humanity?'

'Indeed I can't,' Kemp said, with feeling.

Images came flooding back of the prejudice, based on race and class distinction, that he had witnessed from the shelter of his father's compound. It was a refuge that had not prevented sleepless nights about those many inequalities.

'I do not understand why people should be so unkind but I forgive them,' she said with a gentle laugh. 'When they throw a stone it has no message wrapped around it to tell us why they are unhappy.'

Kemp had to go because he wanted too much to stay. He found her presence beguiling. He would have loved to hear her talk of the country that he and his parents had shared for a while.

'Will Dennis be able to come again, Mr Kemp?'

'I'll do my best, Mrs Bannerjee. It'll depend on what Mr Drew says.' He smiled. 'I'm sure the home-made cake will help.'

He was certain that it would be beneficial for Dennis to enjoy her hospitality. She was providing the undemanding maternal affection that Dennis had been deprived of for most of his life. He was not about to stop that, but it depended on the boy's father.

Dennis underlined this as he said goodbye to his young friend and to Rashida. The parting was emotional and punctuated by promises more in keeping with a pending trip round the world than a journey across to the other side of Stoke Newington.

'I hope it'll work out well and that he can come back,' Kemp said, offering Rashida Bannerjee his hand. Her gentle smile remained in his mind long after the house was out of sight.

Kemp and Dennis were quiet during the drive to the boy's home. It was possible, he thought, that their thoughts were similar.

They saw the front door open immediately they pulled up at the flat. Drew didn't come out but stood back to allow them both to pass, following in silence.

When they were all in the kitchen Dennis put his

arms round his father's waist and said simply, 'Sorry, Dad.'

Drew said nothing but stroked the top of the boy's head. They remained locked together until, conscious of Kemp's presence, he said, 'You had me worried, son,' and released the boy's hands.

To Kemp he said, 'He's been all right then. Been looked after, has he?'

'He's been well looked after, Mr Drew. He's been staying with a friend from school. I think his friend's mother thought he had permission to stay for a few days.'

Dennis, fishing in his raincoat pocket, triumphantly produced a paper bag and held up the well-wrapped cake, now slightly battered.

'Deta's mum sent you this, Dad. There's enough for the two of us for a few days. She said it's a peace offering. Shall I make us a cup of tea? I ain't forgotten how to do it.'

As soon as normality was restored, Kemp prepared to leave.

'I think you should maintain better contact with the school, Mr Drew. They can give you some good advice, including the suitability of any time spent staying with other pupils.'

He looked meaningfully at Drew.

'I expect you get a bit bored with your old dad,' Drew said, correctly interpreting Kemp's look. 'You can go and stay with your friend, maybe once a week. Thursdays are best for me and I want you home for weekends.'

He was rewarded by a brilliant smile and an embrace from Dennis.

'I'm glad you're me dad. We're not allowed to be out

on the street there either. It's ever so nice there. I like it, but I like coming home.'

He showed his delight in rediscovering the things his father had bought him, obviously intent on making up for the distress he had caused.

Kemp, deciding not to mention Rashida's connection with Mrs Drew, made a move to the door.

'I'm off.'

'Bye, Mr Kemp!' Dennis shook his hand.

His father merely nodded, but came to the front door with him and kept the door open until Kemp's car was out of sight.

Driving back to the office Kemp found himself in reflective mood. Threatening clouds lay overhead. A loud roll of thunder sounded close by, drowning the sound of the car's engine, and then rain began to fall, spattering against the windscreen. He pondered about Drew, Rashida, people in general, society and his place in it.

It had been an interesting insight into belonging, and he grappled with the insularity of always being on the outside looking in. Yes, he was tired of not having close friends, but how could it be otherwise when the job came first?

A proverb came to him. His mother had repeated it to him when she thought he had been cosseted with his books for too long: 'All work and no play makes Jack a dull boy.' Well, he would surprise his pals and encourage one of them at least to meet him in town tonight. One way or another they would have some fun. As his colleagues had implied, there was no future in being a perpetual rescuer.

He looked in an old diary for telephone numbers, but after three calls to old friends, he gave up on the idea. They all had girlfriends and prior engagements, although each readily asked him to join them as threesomes. One had also suggested finding a partner for him to make up a foursome. He declined the offer and, putting the phone down, hoped he hadn't sounded forlorn.

McGovern had said that it was possible to be alone but not lonely. As far as his personal journey was concerned, he thought it fair to admit that the outcome of this particular call for help had made him feel it was a distinction without a difference.

8

The police visited Colin Foreman's home in Dalston after he was caught burglarising one of the affluent houses in Stamford Hill. They found it full of stolen goods and were initially prepared to charge his single mother with possession, but Gladys Foreman vehemently denied any complicity and refused to accept responsibility for Colin's thieving, declaring him out of control.

Her complete lack of interest in her son convinced the court that she wasn't an accessory to his actions. The police had an extensive record of their dealings with him and supported this view. Sent to an approved school, and under the control of the Home Office, the lad responded very well to the strict discipline; so much so that the management of the institution again supported his application for weekend home leave.

Kemp had denied the two previous requests but McGovern was now laying in front of him an opened envelope with a Home Office frank. It contained a third application.

'I'd love to see Colin rewarded for his change of attitude by a period back in his home,' Kemp said, 'although I fear going home to his mother won't be a good experience for him.'

'Is that why you've denied the applications?'

'No. In fact I would have been willing to allow each of them, even though I believe that reuniting him with his mother will be disastrous. Sooner rather than later it will produce bitterness and retaliation.'

'I don't understand.'

'I've had to reject the applications because his mother has given up on him. The trouble is, according to the school superintendent, Colin hasn't given up on his mother and no amount of delicately telling him she isn't interested in him will change his view. He has to learn first-hand that she doesn't want him.

'If Colin were to have weekend leave, my plan is that I take him to and from the station. It would give me the opportunity to build on any change of attitude towards returning home, and maybe get him to aim in a fresh direction.'

McGovern's brow furrowed.

'Very sound, but that would be another of your weekends gone, wouldn't it, and he's not even on your case load?' He shook his head in admonishment. 'Why is the plan not working?'

'His mother has shown no interest whatever in having him home.' Kemp ran his fingers through his hair in exasperation. 'It's very frustrating.'

McGovern leaned back in his chair, his hands clasped behind his neck. He was thoughtful.

'You seem to know her well.'

'I called one afternoon when she was out. A man living in the flat upstairs opened the door. Once he knew I was from the local authority he didn't stop talking. He said she's a disgrace to the neighbourhood and that she only comes alive at night when she meets her friends at the Blue Boar. He alleges that place is practically a brothel.'

'That's rather strong. Is this place a pub?'

'Yes. I asked if he was saying that Gladys was a prostitute and he said, "Not unless you call the price of a drink a payment." He went on to say that when she comes back at night is the worst – a lot of noise and screaming.'

'Surely the police would help?'

'He told me she was too wily for that – she never has anyone in the house. They go over to the cemetery opposite, where it's dark, and leave the evidence along the path by the wall for the dog walkers to find in the morning.'

McGovern raised his eyebrows.

'He could be a jealous suitor.'

'Hardly. He's a happily married pensioner. Besides, my experience with her tended to reinforce what he said.'

McGovern looked startled.

'You mean she tried to seduce you?'

'No, but as the pensioner implied, she's not shy. When I first met Gladys she didn't see me as a threat and said saucily, "A bit of the other can round off an evening's entertainment lovely can't it, Mr Kemp?" '

'What did you say to that?'

'Very little, Mr McGovern,' Kemp smiled. 'Very little.'

Moving to the door McGovern asked, 'Do I gather you'll be trying once more to get her to have Colin?'

'Oh, yes, I'm not inclined to give up yet.'

'When you come back, could you pop in to see me?'

Winding his way through an area of grimy flats and terraced houses, Kemp stopped the car outside a particularly dilapidated building. The house was without a number, and the brown paintwork on the windows and front door was peeling. Any stranger who was interested in finding the house would have to do so by checking the numbers of the houses on either side.

Since it was not yet twelve o'clock, the drawn, dirty, grey curtains at the window of the ground floor flat were an indication that Gladys would still be lying in bed. Getting up before midday seemed a problem for her.

The first time Kemp had called on her, he had gone through the formality of pulling at her front door bell. She had peered through the curtains. On this occasion it was raining and he lacked the patience. Tapping on the window he watched for the familiar twitch of the curtain, although the wet surface of the grubby glass made it difficult to see. Within a minute or two he heard the lock released on the front door and it opened slightly.

He gave Gladys time to get back to her room, which she had made in to a bed-sit: the second room had served as Colin's bedroom. The bathroom, toilet and kitchen were shared with the other occupants of the house. Kemp had ascertained that she hadn't made use of Colin's room since the boy had gone – a decision, he was sure, made from laziness rather than sentimentality.

As he entered her bedroom a stale powdery scent of body odour, talcum powder and cheap scent assailed his nostrils and he tried to make his breathing shallow. Gladys Foreman's pallid face stared coldly at him before she climbed back into bed. He was well aware that she would have preferred to ignore him.

As she adjusted herself, the pillow became trapped beneath her and she caught against the curtain. A ray of light lanced across the bed revealing the remnants of a pretty face and tired folds of thirty seven-year-old flesh. The crumpled grey-white satin slip fell away to reveal a sagging breast, and she made an exaggerated attempt at decorum.

In the semi-darkness Kemp was able to see two soiled army overcoats on the bed, heavy with fluff. Items of clothing hung randomly across the only chair. As he bent down to move them he caught the smell of urine. It seemed that she chose to use the chamber pot rather than visit the communal toilet.

Waiting for Gladys to settle gave him time to wonder what benefits there were for Colin in coming back to this hovel, with its minimal space and maximum indifference.

'Nothing's changed, Gladys?'

'Life ain't worth living sometimes, Mr Kemp. Since you was here last I ain't been well at all.'

'Your son's doing well.'

'Yes, it's good ain't it?'

'How would you know if I didn't tell you?'

She smirked. 'Well, you would tell us if he weren't, wouldn't you, Mr Kemp?'

'Kevin's developing very satisfactorily, has a large circle of friends and I'm told is particularly good at sport. It's possible to watch him every Saturday. Why not go and see him at one of the matches? You'd be proud of him.'

'He's better off where he is than being here, that's for sure. He'd only get into trouble.'

'You haven't been to see him at all, have you?'

'I can't go all that way, Mr Kemp. I don't travel well. I always get sick after a few miles. I don't know what it is.'

'Colin's anxious to see you and has again applied for home leave. Are you going to let him come?'

'I would if I could.'

She moved a little, as though she wished he would go and she could sleep.

He ignored the signal.

'What's stopping you?'

'I ain't strong enough yet. I don't want to spoil things for him by him having to look after us.'

'I bet you haven't even written to him, Gladys.'

'I'm no good at writing, am I?'

This time she made a very deliberate move to adjust the pillow. He tried just once more.

'You realise Colin's time will be up in a year from now? Coming home on leave for a couple of times would be a way of getting him to adjust to being back here.'

Gladys glared through half-closed eyes. Beneath the overcoat he saw the shrug of her shoulders.

'Think you should go now, Mr Kemp.'

'If you don't want him to come back, it's better he knows now,' Kemp said, offering one last piece of advice. 'You don't want it to go wrong again, do you? Can I give him a message from you?'

'You tell him it's better for him where he is, Mr Kemp. He'll listen to you. Best hurry now. It's pouring.'

Back in the office he reluctantly ticked the box on the form, 'Home leave denied'. He needed Colin to see that returning home was a poor option. If that were resolved the Home Office could release him under licence and monitor the situation through a probation officer.

Kemp wrote a note explaining the futility of Colin expecting hospitality from his mother. He suggested the superintendent might arrange some counselling and clipped the note to the form denying home leave.

He thought how lucky he had been that his parents had always wanted to see him. Even though they had been thousands of miles away their contact had been such that he had always felt they were close by.

Remembering that McGovern had asked him to call in to his office, he went along the corridor. As he walked into the room he saw the bulky file on the desk and guessed what was coming. On top of the file was the familiar green form from the juvenile court, indicating that yet another youngster had appeared before the magistrates and been placed in the council's care.

McGovern laid down his fountain pen.

'A successful visit?'

'I'm afraid not.'

'That's sad.' McGovern looked uncomfortable. 'I'm afraid I've another problem for you.' He motioned to Kemp to sit down and tapped the file. 'In all my time attending juvenile courts, I've never known a magistrate be so lenient.' He began to read, 'Harry Weston. Seven convictions for breaking and entering. Violent when apprehended.

'In spite of this the magistrate said, and I quote, "Because of your unfortunate past, I'm going to refer you to the council's officers for one last chance".

'It's the usual story. Harry's parents separated when he was three. She was on and off the streets when they were together and now she's a seasoned pro. The father took up with a single mother. Harry's been shuttled backwards and forwards most of his life. He's now seventeen.'

'That's awful,' Kemp said. 'What impression did you get of him, sir?'

'You mean did he look particularly appealing?' McGovern shook his head. 'One would have understood the magistrate being soft with Harry if he'd looked helpless. Far from it. He's an ugly brute and he's got a nasty temper.'

McGovern leant back in his chair, preoccupied.

'Something bothering you, sir?'

'I'm reluctant to give him to you as your caseload is heavy enough already, but there's no one else.' He shifted uncomfortably. 'Harry's not very bright. You could leave him in the Stockwell hostel. He's got less than a year to go before he's eighteen and out of our care. The probation service can take over then.

'Anyway, there's the file. You'll have to see him the nominal once every six weeks. Sorry to do it to you and now you'll have to excuse me – I've a meeting to go to at County Hall.'

Kemp took the file back to his office, surprised at McGovern's readiness to suggest a means of abdicating responsibility. He randomly opened it and his eyes fell on the first paragraph of a social worker's comment:

Harry Weston is seventeen years of age and of low intelligence. He seems unable to avoid becoming involved in disruptive behaviour. He's had numerous jobs and was dismissed from the last one for fighting on the shop floor, close to dangerous machinery.

Intrigued by the court's unusual leniency, Kemp began to read reports that reached back to Harry's early childhood. Living apart, it was evident that each parent had taken turns in accepting and rejecting him. In the struggle to survive, a regard for people's feelings and a respect for private property had clearly become irrelevant – in their place came vandalism and contempt for authority. Pleading for attention had given way to demanding it. Having no rights and owning nothing had led to the perceived right to take anything.

Harry was homeless, unemployed and without any form of funding. On course to be a full time thief-cum-thug, he was, from necessity, currently serving an apprenticeship for this.

As Kemp read report after report, the mental picture of a violent tough began to fade from his imagination. In his mind's eye it was replaced by an image of a wan child, surely with haunting eyes, searching for affection and finding none. Caseworkers collectively described the suffering and gradual destruction of any sense of morality as Harry learned to fight for a place in a world that offered him nothing but humiliation.

While not ready to accept the option that McGovern had offered, he thought it valid to take into account the fact that Harry must, by now, be more or less fixed in his ways. It would require a massive breakthrough to bring him back from life as a criminal.

He stretched his legs and walked over to the window. Across the road, in the nearest block of flats, a woman was negotiating the stairs with a child in a pushchair and a large bag of shopping. She didn't look harassed by the effort.

Idly he mused that this woman, like so many others, would put up with a lot as long as she felt needed. But for a child, to have each of your separated parents turn you out of their homes, to have them shout that you were useless and that they wished you had never been born, would break the sturdiest heart. No wonder Harry had built an almost impregnable wall of indifference.

Kemp returned to the file, searching for a way that might be used to get through to the youth, and found a surprising twist in the story. It was in a report dated almost ten years ago:

Harry Weston has turned up again. Twelve months ago his mother met someone and they lived together. She gave up prostitution and gained a job as a waitress. She descended on her sister, Mrs Glenn, who was looking after Harry and demanded he be returned to her. After trying to reason with Laura Weston, Mrs Glenn reluctantly gave way. Harry responded to his mother's sudden interest in him and went to live with her. The new partnership lasted only six months, his mother's job still less and Harry is before the court again.

This was the first time a Mrs Glenn had been mentioned. Kemp turned back to the beginning of the file, delving deeper, searching for the time when Harry had been living with his aunt. He found it. The same social worker, writing again, reported:

Mr and Mrs Glenn have four children, all boys. The eldest joined the army. Mrs Glenn, aware of Harry's plight, asked for the responsibility of looking after him. The arrangement lasted two years. He was happy here and his aunt was sorry to see him go.

Reading the rest of the file confirmed that it was the only favourable reference to Harry in the whole of the document. Kemp went back to those pages. From his personal experience, rare happiness like this would be unlikely to be erased from memory. Thinking of the aggression he expected when he met Harry, it occurred to him that there was a chance to avoid this if, in some way, he could be associated with that happy time in the boy's life.

Kemp needed to talk to the Glenns urgently, but when he rang the housing department he found that as a result of heavy bomb damage, everyone in the street had been re-housed, many of them to a new estate in Essex.

'There aren't any records here,' a clerk explained. 'The transfer to Essex was an LCC project. You could get on to County Hall but they won't give you any information over the phone. You'd have to write in stating who you are and why you want that information.'

On an impulse he checked the pocket on the inside back cover of the folder and found an envelope with an Essex postmark. It was addressed to Harry Weston and was still sealed. He had no qualms about opening it.

Groups of words seemed to leap off the pages:

How are you dear? . . . We like it in the country . . . We've quite a big house . . . Your uncle has been promoted to general foreman at the local engineering works . . . we've got a telephone because his job's important . . .

His eyes went to the top of the letter. To his dismay he found that Mrs Glenn had failed to include either her address or their new phone number. It was an extraordinary omission and made no sense.

Picking the envelope up once more he put his hand inside and smiled delightedly as his fingernail encountered something. He drew out a business card: 'Jack Glenn, General Foreman.' It had the company's address and, underlined in ink, the Glenns' home phone number. He saw it as a small affectation on Mrs Glenn's part – and he had nearly missed it.

Kemp was excited. If the number was still in use it could be the means of achieving a break through in Harry's seemingly impenetrable shield of indifference. If he could say that he knew Mr and Mrs Glenn, better still if he could give a message from them, it might get under Harry's guard and make progress possible. He might be willing to talk.

He dialled the Glenns' number, waited a very long time and was about to put the phone down when a woman's voice, with the familiar accent of the East End, came over the wire.

'This is Mrs Glenn speaking. Who's that?'

'My name is Kemp, Mrs Glenn. I'm a friend of Harry, your nephew.'

There was a long pause.

'What is it you want? I think you should talk to me husband.'

'Certainly, Mrs. Glenn.'

'Is Harry in trouble?'

'Well, yes, and no, Mrs Glenn.'

'What do you mean, yes and no? Either he is or he ain't.'

Kemp felt he was handling the call badly. Attempting to extricate himself he said, 'I don't want to worry you, Mrs Glenn. Could I speak with your husband please?'

'You've already got me worried so you'd better tell me what he's supposed to have done.' She made a wild guess. 'Is he in hospital?'

'No, a hostel, and I want to help him.'

'I think you'd better tell me who you are, what you want and what kind of friend you're supposed to be.'

'All I want, Mrs Glenn, is some information. I work for the council and Harry's in a bit of trouble. I want to research his background a little before I decide what action to take.'

'Why couldn't you say so at the beginning?'

Kemp stalled. Mrs Glenn clearly liked straight talking.

'He's been before the court but, because of his unhappy background, he's being given another chance to avoid a period of detention.'

'What do you want to know?'

'I want to know about those early years when he was with you and your husband.'

'Why them?'

The information exchange was too rapid. He could think of nothing but to tell the bald truth.

'It seems it was about the only time when Harry was happy.'

'When do you want to come?'

Her words took him by surprise.

'As soon as possible.'

'You can come tomorrow, after two o'clock. Me husband will be home then. You got the address?'

'No, I'm afraid I haven't,' he answered hastily.

He wrote it down and thanked her. There was an immediate click as she put her phone back into its cradle – decisive to the last.

Kemp frowned, feeling distinctly wrong-footed. Had he unearthed a gold nugget or a landmine?

9

It was a pleasant drive to Loughton, along the edge of Epping Forest and through farming country. After miles of countryside the sudden emergence of a large housing estate took Kemp by surprise. The streets of fresh-bricked council houses were identical, each with a front garden – surely a pleasant improvement on living in the heavily bombed East End. Few people were about.

After a few detours he pulled up at his destination and sat, for a moment or two, preparing himself. He wanted to avoid a repeat of the disjointed conversation he had experienced over the telephone.

Walking briskly up the path he rang the doorbell and saw, almost immediately, a small shadow through the opaque glass of the front door. The silhouette bobbed up and down before opening it.

Kemp was greeted by a woman who was slightly built, and appeared less formidable than he had imagined. Her frock had short sleeves, revealing thin arms, and grey strands streaked her mousy coloured hair. In her late forties, he thought, competent and a little careworn. He felt clumsy beside the diminutive figure.

She stepped back and indicated a door immediately to the right. There was a smell of lavender and a bundled apron and duster lay on the bottom shelf of the small hall table, explaining the bobbing up and down he had seen through the glass.

He walked in to the sitting room and noticed flying china ducks on the wall, assorted memorabilia in a china cabinet and tassels hanging off a central light fitting.

'Have a seat,' she said, placing her hands on the back of the sofa.

He sank into the large matching armchair while she remained standing. He wondered if she had deliberately reversed the difference in their heights.

'How's Harry?'

It was the worst of opening questions. He did his best to hide the fact that he had never met the lad.

'I'm sorry to say that Harry has appeared before the juvenile court, and not for the first time. He was particularly lucky not to be sent to an approved school and detained for a fixed period, but he'll not get another chance.'

'He deserves all the chances he can get. What did his mother say?'

'She wasn't present. I'm afraid Harry's parents have given up on him.'

'What sort of trouble has he been getting in to?'

'I regret his background has got a lot to do with it.'

Mrs Glenn's mouth tightened and he realised his gaffe: she had come from a similar background herself.

He hastened to explain how he had gone through Harry's case notes and how it had made depressing reading until he had seen the words, 'He was happy here.'

'This was the period when he was with you,' he said, 'so I thought if I could meet you I might gain some little insights about him which would help to build a decent relationship with him from the outset.'

'You mean you ain't even met him?' she asked incredulously.

'I want to get behind the tough front and all that aggression,' he said passionately.

The stony face mellowed, encouraging him to press on.

'Harry's been before the court seven times since you last saw him. There are many reports about him and, unfortunately, none of them are favourable.'

Mrs Glenn shook her head. Had he painted too black a picture? She was looking upset, but his previous experience of her suggested that he had better stick to the facts.

'I'm sorry, Mrs Glenn. By all accounts he's a big problem in more ways than one.'

'Poor little bleeder . . . beg your pardon.'

He waited, confident that she did, indeed, care.

'Harry's mother's not really bad, just wild. I should've helped more but I had me own kids to bring up. I got fond of little Harry while he was with us. Although he's not my child I've always felt responsible for him, because of the life she leads. I would've liked to have kept him but you can't do anything with Laura once she's made up her mind.'

As she described her nephew as 'little', Kemp could see that she might have difficulty relating to the hulking figure McGovern had described. Still feeling his way tentatively, Kemp completed Harry's history.

'Mrs Glenn,' he said with scrupulous honesty, 'the last two convictions involved violence. I'm afraid you've got to understand that Harry's no longer little now.'

'Course he is! I've been sending him a card every year for his birthday but he's never replied. I sent them to his mum's address so perhaps he's never got them.'

Mrs Glenn had evidently kept alive a strong affection for Harry, brusque though her manner was.

'Is Mr Glenn joining us?'

'No, he's at work. I only said that on the phone because I didn't know who you were and I was being careful. But me hubby and me had a talk last night and we've agreed.'

'Agreed?'

'If we have him back we can't have Laura come to take him away again. I couldn't stand that. Once we get used to having him around again we don't want no interference from her. If he comes here he's got to belong to us this time.'

Kemp was stunned.

'I'm sorry, Mrs Glenn, that's not what I'm here about.'

'Well, you've no objection have you? I mean, you said you'd no plans for him. Well, me hubby and me want him. After all,' she added pugnaciously, 'you ain't even met him yet.'

'That's true, Mrs Glenn, but . . . '

'The boys are looking forward to Harry coming back and he's going to share a bedroom with George. Me eldest son Mark is now married and living in Doncaster so I've only got the three younger boys at home. There's room for Harry.'

Kemp tried to interrupt but she played her trump card.

'Do you want to see his room?'

Without waiting for his answer she marched out to the hall. He stopped her before she mounted the stairs. He was lost for words but was duty bound to tell her that her plan was far too risky to contemplate.

'This is not a good idea, Mrs Glenn,' he said firmly. 'You've no idea how Harry has changed. He's guilty of seven break-ins, and in two of them he used violence when he was apprehended. I can't support this in the short term. Given a little time and a few visits you could reconsider this idea. You'd then be in a much better position to consider whether he would fit in.'

She would have none of his faint-heartedness.

'Oh, don't you worry, Mr Kemp. I know he'll have changed, but we'll soon have him back to his old self. Trust me, he'll be all right with us.'

'Sentiment's one thing, Mrs Glenn, but the reality would be something quite different. We can arrange that you can visit him regularly over, say, a six month period, and we can make an assessment after that.'

'That's not what me husband and me have decided. Are you going to let us have him or not?' She marched up the stairs before he could say another word. 'Come and see his room.'

He followed her, repeating, 'Six months, Mrs Glenn, then we can decide on the basis of sound evidence.'

She led him into a bedroom with two single beds. It was neat and adequate, as he would have expected.

'Look!' she said. On one of the beds, propped up against the pillow, was a piece of card with the words, WELCOME HOME HARRY written large in red ink. Underneath the words was drawn a smiling face. Mrs Glenn was smiling, too.

'The boys did that last night.' She turned to him. 'Are you going to let us have our Harry or not? After all, he's family.'

For the first time, Kemp allowed the idea to linger. Yes, it would be wonderful for Harry for he was homeless and he had lived with them before.

'Mrs Glenn, he's not used to any kind of discipline. Trying to get him to adapt to a normal home life could easily lead to quarrels and break up your happy home.'

She was silent for a moment.

'For all your confidence and experience,' he said, 'I don't think you can appreciate how much he's changed and what you'd be taking on. For your sake, and the rest of the family, let's take it in stages. Remember this is a lad with a criminal record. Wait . . . '

'That's the past,' she interrupted him.

'Wait for six months and in that time you can have him at weekends. I'll see that he is placed somewhere near you.'

Mrs Glenn was adamant.

'You said yourself he's homeless,' she smiled. 'Well, he's coming home, Mr Kemp.'

He turned away. To deny her would be to alienate her, and she could be valuable as an intermediary with Harry, if nothing else. An insistent voice in his head told him that unconditional love was beyond price and for Harry to have a place he could call home, after ten years of being homeless, could transform the lad.

'Well?' she said, fiercely.

'I'll have to visit on a regular basis until he's eighteen.'

'I think we can put up with that, Mr Kemp,' she said saucily, leading the way down the stairs. She was happy, obviously anticipating being able to pick up where she had left off so many years ago.

'I do hope your faith is justified.'

'You'll see. When can he come home? He needs to be out of that place and with us as soon as possible.'

Mrs Glenn was in command and Kemp thought of the advice 'When in a torrent go with the flow'. Swept along by her conviction he now had to get down to basics, and there was no time to lose.

'I do need your husband to confirm his cooperation.'

'You can speak to him now.'

She went towards the phone in the hall but Kemp stopped her. It was time to be practical.

'Let's sort out all the detail first. Harry will need to pay his way, of course. We can pay you for his keep for three or four weeks while he's finding a job. It will make him feel more secure if he's in employment. I'll get in touch with the youth employment service immediately.'

Mrs Glenn shook her head.

'None of that's needed. Me hubby has spoken to his firm and Harry's going to work with him starting Monday, so he'll be able to pay his own way. If,' she added artfully, 'that's all right with you?'

'For the last time, Mrs Glenn, are you clear that he's not a little Harry anymore? He's a very big lad now.'

'Not inside he ain't.'

'And he's got a bad temper.'

'Well, he'll just have to learn to control it, won't he? Anyway, once he's with us he won't have no reason to be bad tempered.'

Kemp was silent. The comment in the depth of that gloomy case-file, 'Harry was happy here,' echoed in his mind. Perhaps this remarkable lady would be able to tame him?

'Now, are you ready to speak to me husband?'

Mrs Glenn dialled a number and after an affectionate interchange she passed the phone to Kemp.

Glenn was affable.

'Yeah, we've agreed, Mr Kemp. The sooner Harry joins us the better. I've got a job waiting for him here. I've told the boss all about him and he trusts me judgement. Harry can start on Monday if you can arrange it. I'll be keeping an eye on him, so don't you worry.'

In spite of his caution Kemp could not deny his pleasure at the initiative shown.

'Then I'd better bring him on Friday, so he can have the weekend to settle in. Thank you, Mr Glenn.'

He put the phone down. Mrs Glenn nodded delightedly.

'That's better,' she said. 'Now, would you like some tea, Mr Kemp? I'm forgetting me manners.'

His first task on reaching the office was to phone the warden to ask how Harry was behaving. He was told the youth was moping about.

'He's not mixing with the other lads and it won't be long before he gets into mischief.'

'I'll come to see him tomorrow morning,' Kemp said, a strategy forming in his mind. Then he casually added, 'I'll be removing him two days later.'

He was pleased to be able to say it, but could claim no credit; it was a gamble yet to be played out.

'My word, that's quick!'

'Tell him about tomorrow's interview but,' Kemp paused, 'under no circumstances must he learn that he is leaving on Friday.'

Promising that the information would go no further, the warden rang off. Kemp spent the evening coaching Norman and was relieved to find him still motivated and impatient to learn.

At nine o'clock the next morning Kemp arrived at the hostel. It was a large, three-storey building, somewhat forbidding but not very different from the tall tenements that clustered around the run-down neighbourhood. Big double gates were locked after him with a huge padlock.

The warden greeted Kemp cheerfully and was talking to him when his deputy interrupted them.

'The lad disappeared the minute he saw the car pull into the yard.'

'That's fairly typical behaviour,' said the warden. 'He's showing you he's not at your beck and call. He's not going to be easy.'

Kemp shrugged. It was no more than he had expected.

Harry was found in the corner of the basement games room. Kemp's first sight of his new charge was not encouraging. Harry was six foot tall, and from the stubble on his chin it appeared that he didn't bother shaving regularly. He wore a belt with a large brass buckle, of which he seemed proud for he had a habit of placing his left hand on his waist and polishing the buckle with the side of his thumb. Kemp wondered if it doubled as a weapon. On his feet were battered boots, while a blue shirt hung loosely from his shoulders. He looked resentful and his eyes avoided those of his new supervisor. He had made no effort to spruce himself up for the interview.

'I'm not keen on you remaining here,' Kemp said, 'so my first job is to find somewhere for you to live.'

There was no answer.

'You've an unpleasant record. I've been looking through your case notes, which go back a long way. Have you got anything to tell me that might be useful?'

'You can read, can't you?'

Giving Harry a prolonged stare, and leaving him standing, Kemp turned over earlier pages of the file. The silence grew. He stretched it as far as he dared then said off-handedly, 'I see you spent some time with a Mrs Glenn when you were a child?'

Harry looked surprised but answered aggressively.

'What's that got to do with anything? She's only me aunt.'

'I'm simply noting that you lived with her.'

'Well, me aunt don't live there anymore and I ain't going to live in any old place.'

Kemp looked at him sharply. 'How do you know she doesn't live there?'

'I called there once.'

'Why did you do that?'

'It was something to do.'

'When you said you weren't going to live in "any old place" did you mean you didn't think much of their home?'

'No, I didn't. I told you, she's me aunt.'

'I asked you if that's the kind of place you'd like to live and you said it was only your aunt. It sounded as if you didn't think much of it.'

'What you on about, anyway?'

Kemp pursed his lips and said thoughtfully, 'I wondered what they were like?'

'It ain't your business,' Harry said, raising his voice. 'Ain't seen 'em for years anyway. Don't even know where they live now.'

'Oh, I know where they live.'

Harry's expression changed from insolence to curiosity.

'You ain't thinking I could go and live with 'em?' He laughed derisively. 'That was years ago. They wouldn't have me now.'

His voice tailed off, expressing the rejection that had dominated his life. Kemp said nothing, feigning a shrug and began to gather his papers together.

'Perhaps you're right.'

Harry searched for words and failed, then tried again.

'Why did you ask me about 'em?'

Kemp hesitated very deliberately.

'It's just that the notes here say that you were happy with a Mr and Mrs Glenn and I thought it might be worthwhile seeing if there was any chance of you living near them, but I forgot about your record.'

Harry's face was a study in emotion. Thank heaven, Kemp thought, he had checked with Harry's aunt first. To witness this rise in hope, only to have to tell Harry later that his aunt and uncle had given up on him, would have been dreadful. The important thing now was that this tremendous offer of a home for Harry mustn't be seen to come too easily and thereby be undervalued.

'Do you really know where they live, Mister?'

'Yes.'

'How do you know?'

'There's a letter on the file that they sent to you but you never got it.'

'Can I have it? It's mine.'

Carrying on with the charade Kemp said, 'What? Oh, the letter? That was years ago.'

'It's still me letter, ain't it?'

'I can let you see it now if you want, but for the time being I need to keep it on the file. Understood?'

Kemp gave him the letter. He had removed the business card earlier. Harry read very slowly, as if consigning each word to memory. Then he turned it over, looking at each page again.

'It ain't got no address on it.'

'No, they put it on a card.'

'Where do they live now then?' He clearly doubted that Kemp had visited. 'Like I said, they don't live round here anymore.'

'No, they live in Essex.'

'Would you really go and see 'em?'

'It might be a worth a visit,' Kemp nodded, placing the letter back in the file. 'I could give it a try.'

He stood up, face-to-face with Harry, and said sternly, 'I'll be back in a few days. In the meantime, you'd better keep out of trouble!'

Harry, who had chosen to hide when Kemp arrived, now anxiously followed him to his car. Kemp was inwardly ecstatic: it was a moment of affirmation. Close behind him Harry appeared to be searching for the right words and finally managed to blurt out, 'Do you have to tell 'em what I done, Mister?'

Harry was not a finished product. Despite his rough appearance, surly manner and violent temper he wasn't yet lost – he could still be malleable in the right hands.

Kemp was beginning to believe that those hands might be on the end of Mrs Glenn's spindly arms.

10

Could ten years of delinquent behaviour change overnight? It seemed highly improbable but Kemp knew that he had to keep faith with the Glenns. That was what took him to Hackney High Street, where he bought a large green canvas bag at a knockdown price. He needed to kit Harry out from the council clothing warehouse.

'I'm moving Harry Weston from his hostel on Friday,' he told Mrs Boulton on his return to the office. 'It's imperative that no one knows beforehand.'

'I'm not in the habit of discussing the action of field officers with anyone,' she said waspishly.

'Sorry, Mrs B. It's just that it's a key part of my plan that Harry mustn't know.'

She shook her head, clearly displeased that he could imagine she would discuss confidences entrusted to her.

'There was a phone call for you,' she said. 'It was a young woman's voice. She wouldn't give a name or say what it was about. She said it was private and that she'd ring again.'

She couldn't prevent herself.

'Is it a new girlfriend?'

'You'd be the first to know, Mrs B.'

He wondered if the mystery caller might have been Linda Simpson, wanting help with Michael Grant, but he quickly discarded that idea: she had been briefed to talk, in particular, to Mrs Boulton.

'You'll be going to that conference on Monday?' she persisted.

'Yes, I'll be going straight from home. Registration's at nine-thirty.'

He came across the booking confirmation while going through the contents of his in-tray and spent a short time reviewing the programme. It was aimed at 'Practitioners in the field of Social Services'. He was impressed with the calibre of the speakers.

His thoughts turned to the impending reunion between Harry and Mrs Glenn. How would she react when she saw the kind of person Harry had become? The years had dealt harshly with him. On the other hand, if the rather brutish exterior was ignored, Harry did have a kind of lost streak that could tug at the heart-strings.

On Friday morning, after confirming his identity to the lodge keeper, Kemp walked down the hostel's dark corridor, confident that Harry wouldn't be playing hide and seek with him this morning.

'He's barely been out of the dormitory since Wednesday,' the warden said, 'except to undertake the chores he's been given.'

'So there hasn't been any trouble?'

'None at all, and frankly I'm astonished. Often the new boys are a prime target for the lads who've been here longer, but they've steered clear of Harry. I think his size and manner warned them off.'

'Good,' Kemp said, knowing that he was about to push the boy to the very brink in order to make him truly value this opportunity to be part of a family. Aware that his strategy carried a high degree of risk he asked anxiously, 'He doesn't know that he's leaving?'

'No. I don't think he's come to terms yet with what's happening to him.'

'It's going to be a challenge for him,' Kemp said.

'Apart from anything else, he'll have to learn to control that vicious temper of his.'

'The best of luck.' The warden smiled. 'My deputy's bringing him down now. He's vacated his office for you so that you can have a private interview.'

Harry was brought in. Kemp occupied himself with his papers, leaving the youth standing. It was a minute before he glanced up briefly.

'Ah, Harry,' he said off-handedly, 'have you been getting on all right?'

'Yeah.'

'Oh well, that's something,' Kemp said, in a tone that indicated the intimacy of their previous meeting had been forgotten. 'Well now, we've got to think about your future. We can't have you hanging about doing nothing, can we?'

Harry stood silent.

'Can we?' Kemp repeated the question, his tone a little harsher.

'No,' Harry murmured, shuffling his feet. His face expressed disappointment and resentment.

'Have you given any thought to what job you could do?'

Harry didn't answer but, almost imperceptibly, began to assume his more accustomed slouch.

'You won't get far unless you speak up for yourself. What sort of jobs have you been doing?' Kemp flicked open the file and read aloud, 'Found fighting on the shop floor, adjacent to dangerous machinery.' He put his hand to his mouth and blew air through his fingertips. 'That sort of behaviour won't help you get a decent job, will it?'

Harry fidgeted, but Kemp continued to push him to the edge.

'I'm asking you about the work experience you've had.'

It was clear that the fragile element of trust that had surfaced at the end of their last meeting lay like a dead thing between them.

'I take your silence to mean none to speak of,' Kemp said relentlessly, surprised that he had got this far without an outburst. Opening the file at the history of court appearances, he shook his head in apparent disbelief as he counted out loud: 'One, two, three, four, five, *six* previous convictions before this one, for heaven's sake.'

His anger clearly rising, Harry's eyes narrowed and he looked around the room. Reasoning that the youth was making a choice whether to fight or take flight, Kemp calculated that he would soon choose to run. He rose from the desk, discreetly checking that the door behind Harry was closed. The silence became oppressive.

Harry's shoulders were tensed, one hand made into a fist, the other thrust deep in his pocket, presumably trying to hide the fact that it, too, was clenched. No doubt he was trying to hold back the rise of that ungovernable temper. Kemp knew he could provoke him no further.

As casually as he could he said, 'I suppose we'd better make this decision first about where you're going to live.'

Stopped for the moment from any intended flight, Harry produced the now familiar sneer. Believing that a second later would be too late, Kemp half turned away from the lad.

'You can't go to Mr and Mrs Glenn, who care about you, unless you're prepared to make some major changes.'

'But I ain't going to them, am I? You must . . . '

'Oh! So I've been wasting my time, have I? You've decided you don't want to go there now?'

'You ain't even been there. You must think I'm a f—.'

'Oh yes I have.'

The blast of profanity was halted. Harry stared searchingly at Kemp. Apparently working things out he said insolently, 'I know what you done. You told 'em about me and they're not interested.'

His words had slurred together with a disappointment he could not quite suppress. Once again he was face to face with a rejection that had dogged him all his life. Kemp's own interest visibly abated.

'That's just the trouble,' he said. 'They know, and they still want you. Your aunt says . . .'

'Don't give me all that!'

Eyeing him, Kemp finished the sentence, 'you should come back because you're family.'

He pronounced the last word firmly. Harry was unable to hide its impact. Despite experience that told him there was always a catch somewhere, he searched Kemp's face.

'Have you really been to see 'em?' he asked at last.

'Of course I have,' Kemp replied curtly. 'I don't make promises I can't keep – and neither should you.'

Harry's eyes showed his utter confusion and Kemp could see the lad was almost in his grasp, and, importantly, that his uncontrollable temper had been checked.

'Sit down.'

Harry obeyed and Kemp stood over him, reversing their relative heights. He spoke softly, as if to himself.

'I admit I'm worried.'

Tortured eyes stared up at him.

'What about?'

Kemp remained silent.

'What about, Mister?'

'Listen carefully, Harry.' Kemp moved a little closer. 'This is a chance in a million for you, but Mr and Mrs Glenn have had a hard life. It wouldn't be right, when they've done so well for their kids, for you to bring trouble into their lives now.'

He turned and looked out of the window. Harry got up and placed himself in front of Kemp, his fists clenched and his body tense, but he no longer looked menacing. His words indicated he was nearer surrender.

'I won't give 'em no trouble,' he said.

Kemp looked at him with what appeared to be new interest.

'I must say you've just proved to me you can control your temper.'

He let the message register then went quickly to the desk and picked up the charge sheet.

'What about this rubbish?'

'That's the past.'

'Damn it!' Kemp exploded. 'That's exactly what your aunt said.'

He replaced the sheet on the table. It was crass melodrama, but he was playing for high stakes and Harry wasn't a critical audience. He searched the youth's face.

'It seems you want to go to them as much as they want to have you back.' He feigned a sigh then walked to the door and opened it. He gestured Harry through. 'Go and get your things then.'

The lad was totally bemused.

'What for?'

'We're going to Essex.'

Harry remained still.

'To see me aunt and uncle?'

'You're going to live with them aren't you – in their new house? It's a long way to go, so we'd better leave soon.'

In a daze, Harry moved to the door. He paused, obviously wanting to ask questions but unable to utter one. Kemp was elated at the outcome so far, particularly the evidence that the youth could control his temper. Harry was walking very slowly towards the stairs, but Kemp was determined to allow no such reserve.

'Hurry up,' he called. 'I promised I'd get you there by lunchtime.'

Harry looked back for a moment then broke into a gallop. Leaping up the stairs, pulling on the bannisters, he took two steps at a time.

Kemp allowed himself the luxury of a deep breath and a moment's respite. He felt not a little mean at the ordeal he had put the youngster through. It had been dangerously close and he might have reaped a very different harvest. He returned to the car, picked up the green holdall and followed Harry up the stairs.

Inside the dormitory he saw a poor collection of items lying on the bed. He handed Harry the holdall but few of his clothes looked fit for anything other than the bin.

'You'll need some new things if you're going to make a new start.'

Harry stood still, half bent over the empty bag on his bed. Kemp went over to him.

'We'll buy some clothes on the way,' he said kindly,

'so pack only what you really want to keep. You need to dress up for them because they haven't seen you for a long time.'

As if in a trance, Harry followed instructions. Kemp could almost smell his fear that it might be a huge confidence trick and that shortly the world would be laughing at him. He thought of making light of it – of saying in a cockney accent, 'It's like Christmas, ain't it?' – but what did Harry know about Christmas? For over a decade of his young life Christmas had been for other people. During that period he had probably never had a family birthday party, never been rewarded for coming first and never been praised for trying. Nobody had rated him as special or kissed him for just being Harry. Well, maybe it was going to change. Maybe love, genuine love, was his for the taking.

Signing Harry out was done in front of a few other lads who were helping the warden. Kemp made a point of making the most of the moment by saying to the warden, a little louder than necessary, 'Harry's off today. Sorry it's short notice but his aunt and uncle want him with them as a member of their family.'

'You're a lucky man, Harry,' said the warden, picking up his cue. 'Where are you going to live?'

'In Essex.'

'That's a long way away. What's it like?'

'It's in the countryside. They've got this new house.'

'Sounds good.'

'I use to live with 'em once.'

The way he spoke betrayed his eagerness and the warden responded.

'It's like you're going back home then?'

'Yeah,' Harry said. 'That's it.'

While Harry exchanged a word with one of the boys from his dormitory, the warden quietly commented to Kemp that this was the longest conversation he had shared with Harry.

They stopped twice on their journey, the first time to buy underwear and socks. Kemp placed the bills safely in his wallet, alongside the letter he intended finally to deliver to Harry. It might serve to comfort him if he grew apprehensive on the journey. The investment in clothing would pay dividends, not only in eliminating the cost of keeping a young offender in an institution or prison, but also in terms of community safety.

'That's if it works,' he thought, closing his eyes.

Their next stop was as at the clothing depot. Among other things, Harry needed to select a suit and shoes. Kemp engaged the assistant in conversation well within Harry's earshot, explaining that he would be starting a new job and wanted to look smart. The youth's appearance began to improve markedly, but he was more comfortable in the loose jacket and trousers that he chose without help, rather than in the suit.

'Good here, ain't it?' said Kemp, making an attempt to set Harry at ease.

'Great!' Harry grinned.

Obviously beginning to believe his life was really changing, Harry began to show his excitement. He went into the changing room and emerged dressed in the self-selected jacket. His fancy belt had been fed through the loops on his trousers and he was wearing new socks and shoes. His other new clothes were packed into the canvas bag and he self-consciously paraded in front of Kemp for approval.

During the early part of the drive Kemp questioned

Harry about members of the family and added his own positive comments about Mr and Mrs Glenn, but as they drew closer to their destination Harry became ominously quieter and his answers stilted.

Kemp could feel the movement next to him as Harry's fingers nervously rubbed at the bright brass buckle on his belt, as if he were trying to summon up some protective genie. He was clearly getting agitated and the action was acting as a kind of therapy.

In this mood the surly looking hulk could easily be misunderstood. Kemp tried to think of a distraction. To his relief, on the fringes of Loughton they came upon a flower stall by the side of the road. He drew into the verge and pulled some money from his pocket.

'Go and buy some flowers for your aunt,' he said.

While the lad was gone, Kemp hastily reached for his attache case and took out the letter from Mrs Glenn. He carefully placed it on the dashboard in front of Harry's seat.

Returning, Harry laid a bunch of tulips carefully on the back seat. His face was difficult to read as he said, 'There's no change.'

He slid into the front seat and spotted the letter with his name on the envelope. His eyes darted to Kemp.

'Can I have it now?'

'Of course. It was meant for you.'

They rejoined the main stream of traffic. There was silence as Harry read and re-read the letter.

After a while Kemp said, 'Your aunt sent you a birthday card every year. I suppose you didn't get those either?'

'No, I didn't get none.'

'We're about to come in to Loughton, Harry. The

estate your aunt and uncle live on is actually in Debden. Can you look out for the turning please?'

They found the house easily and Kemp drew up, briefly touching his hands together on the steering wheel as he summoned help. He could think of no advice to give so got out of the car quickly.

'Don't forget your flowers.'

Harry left his holdall in the car, and as they walked up to the door he clutched the tulips as if holding a shield. Before Kemp could ring the bell the door opened and Mrs Glenn appeared. Smiling delightedly she hurried past Kemp and up to Harry, the top of her greyish hair level with his chin.

'Hello, love. Are these for me? They're beautiful! Thank you!'

She held the blooms for a moment before thrusting them in to Kemp's hands. Taking Harry's limp right arm she ducked her head beneath it, squeezing into him. With his arm over her shoulder she looked up into his face.

'We've missed you,' she said. 'Give your aunt a kiss. It's been a long time.'

Kemp watched in amazement as Harry dutifully put his head down and awkwardly planted a kiss on her upturned forehead. It was an amazing sight: the big youth entirely powerless in the hands of so tiny a figure.

Discarding sentiment, Mrs Glenn let go of his hand and went around the back of him, appraising him.

'My, ain't you grown!' she said. Placing both hands in the small of his back she urged him through the doorway and into the hall. Harry was unable to avoid her intent.

'Down there, love. Your Uncle Jack's waiting for you.'

The kitchen door was open. There were three young people sitting around the table. Kemp guessed that these were Harry's cousins. At the end of the table, his back to the door, sat a well-built man. Although large plates of food lay in front of them, no one had started to eat. One chair was vacant. The whole thing had been obviously and gloriously stage-managed, right up to the last moment.

Standing inside the doorway Harry was unsure, but not the family for with one accord they chorused, 'Welcome home, Harry,' and drummed on the table with the blunt end of their cutlery.

As soon as the noise ceased they began to eat, except Glenn. Going to the empty chair he pulled it out and turning to Harry said, 'Take a seat, mate. Your aunt's going to eat later. She's got to talk with Mr Kemp first.'

He was a tall man with the air of one used to being obeyed and Harry did as he was instructed. Glenn stood over him, dishing out the largest helping of shepherd's pie Kemp had ever seen. Wordlessly, Harry picked up his knife and fork.

From the doorway Kemp watched mesmerised, admiring what the Glenns had done. It was something he could never have duplicated. The emphasis was upon family and it was the corner stone of their welcome – a sense of belonging that he envied. Having seen the boy's reception, Kemp collected Harry's holdall from the car.

Mrs Glenn had placed Harry's flowers on the hall table. She returned to Kemp, closing the kitchen door so he could no longer see or be seen.

'I'm sorry, Mr Kemp. I had to get him settled first – his dinner was waiting for him.'

She tried to lead him into the sitting room but he declined to join the flying ducks.

'You don't mind waiting till he's got some grub in him, do you? You can talk to him then.'

'What do you want me to say to him, Mrs Glenn?'

It was her turn to look surprised.

'Nothing, but I thought . . . '

'He must look very different to you, Mrs Glenn?'

She looked confidently back at him, shaking her head.

'He ain't changed.'

'I'm going to leave him to you then.'

'Don't you want to talk to him?'

Certain that Harry's aunt wanted to get back to her long-lost nephew, Kemp felt privileged and oddly choked as he replied, 'I don't want to interrupt his meal. Will you say goodbye to him and your husband for me?'

She went outside with him.

'Are you sure you don't want to see him privately?'

Her accent was made more noticeable by her surprise. Kemp took out a card from his wallet.

'There's my office number if you need me. I'll drop you a line to make all this official. I'll have to call on you, on and off, just for a little while. It's a formality. I promise it won't be too often.'

'Harry would like to see you before you go.'

'I doubt it. I think you'll find that he's seen quite enough of me today.'

Now that things had gone well he was aware of how hard a time he had given the lad, but he couldn't bring himself to feel sorry. Mrs Glenn mistook his thoughtful look and hastened to reassure him.

'We'll look after him all right. Don't you worry.'

'I know you will. He's all yours now. It won't be easy but you've already made him feel he's wanted.'

He gazed at her. Could she guess how beautiful he found her, this spare, thin-faced cockney sparrow with so much wisdom at her fingertips?

'As a matter of fact,' he confided, 'Harry thinks you're wonderful.'

He paused before adding, 'But then, so do I, Mrs Glenn, so do I.'

'Now go on with you, young man!'

Mrs Glenn was suddenly confused. The colour rose at her thin, straggly throat and spread over her neck.

Kemp loved her for it. He hastened back to the office, eager to recount the day's events to people who could empathise.

'I've just seen a miracle,' he blurted out to Mrs Boulton and Jennifer Bowlby.

He told them Harry's entire story, lingering on the boy's reception in Loughton.

'What a wonderful way of making him feel he belongs,' remarked Mrs Boulton. 'Let's just hope that Harry won't feel too confined.'

'He won't miss the kind of freedom he's enjoyed,' Jennifer said prophetically. 'After all, it's been the freedom of the hunted.'

'What do you mean?' Kemp asked.

'When they've been rejected by their parents,' she said, 'it doesn't take long for them to feel that everybody's against them, does it?'

Her colleagues nodded. Perhaps, Kemp pondered, it wasn't extravagant after all to be optimistic about Harry's future. Perhaps, for him, the hunting season was over for ever.

After dealing with the papers on his desk, he dropped in on Mrs Boulton.

'I'm off home, Mrs B. I'll see you a week on Monday.'

'Do come back. . . . refreshed,' she said enigmatically.

Packing his suitcase on Sunday evening, Kemp felt that he might find the people at the conference rather tame after the drama of Harry and the lesson of unconditional love that Mrs Glenn had so wonderfully demonstrated.

As for his own journey, he remained far less optimistic about being able to find a special someone. That, however, was before he met Helen Townsend.

11

He had noticed the girl straight away – he guessed most people did. Small, shoulder-length fair hair, attractive face, she was worth more than a second glance. Kemp added 'stylishly dressed' to his initial assessment.

Looking about restlessly, she caught his eye upon her. He stood back, encouraging her to join his group which was being moved to an adjacent lecture room, where they both edged to the back. The lecturer rapped on his desk for attention.

'I'd like you all to pair up with the person sitting next to you, but don't speak yet. We're going to practise co-counselling, using open behaviour as a means of getting to know each other. After you've worked together for a while, I want each of you to move on to make a new pair, and so on, until you've all met each other.'

'Hello!'

She seemed unusually ill at ease. There was a considerable shuffling around them and the hum of conversation grew louder.

'I'm afraid I don't understand the terminology – co-counselling?' the girl whispered to him.

'There's nothing to it. Imagine we're hard working colleagues. We need to have some reassurance from time to time, so we use each other as a counsellor. Open behaviour is the best way to co-counsel. Each person shows complete trust, speaks honestly and freely and hides nothing. Then we do role reversal.'

She looked helplessly at him.

'I'm sorry, that's jargon,' he said, puzzled by her

obvious lack of understanding. 'It means that we take it in turns to counsel each other.'

'I don't know where to start.'

Kemp hid his surprise.

'Start with your name and background, and then think of a problem that you'd like to share.'

He smiled encouragingly.

'Oh dear, I'm not sure I could do that!'

She put her hand over her mouth.

'I'll go first and keep it short then you can try. We should be facing each other as maintaining eye contact is important. Unfortunately these desks are not designed for this so we'll have to swivel.'

They did, and he looked into smiling blue eyes.

He introduced himself and spoke briefly about his background.

'My problem is that I get too involved in my cases,' he said. 'Perhaps we could discuss that later.'

He leaned forward, encouraging her to do the same.

'Now, why don't you have a go? Name, please!'

Looking uncomfortable, she swallowed before saying, 'My name's Helen Townsend and my parents live in York. I went to a convent school there. I now have a flat in Kensington, and that's about it.'

Still leaning towards her he said quietly, 'What did you do after leaving school?'

'Oh, I went to finishing school and did some secretarial training.'

'Now you're supposed to share a problem with me.'

She sat back and was silent.

'No problems?'

'I do have one. It's not easy to share. I don't want everyone to know.'

'I'm not everyone. I'm your co-counsellor.'

She looked at him doubtfully, then at the couple nearest to them who were talking earnestly, and leant forward.

'I've come here under false pretences,' she whispered.

He said nothing, not understanding.

'I saw a notice advertising this conference in my local library in Kensington. I'm not involved in social services of any kind. Do you think I'll be exposed straight away and make a fool of myself?'

'No, it won't be like that – but why did you come?'

'I had some time on my hands and felt the need for fresh company. This seemed quite adventurous.'

'I don't know about that,' he said, hoping his astonishment didn't show. 'People are here to learn new techniques and polish up old ones. I'm not sure it'll meet your expectations – but this bit's working out, isn't it?'

'Are you going to tell anyone?'

'I wouldn't be a counsellor if I did that.'

'Do we have to do any more? It's a little scary.'

'The alternative is to sit here, looking at each other.'

Kemp entwined his fingers and rotated his thumbs. He put his head on one side and looked at her.

'Go on then, but don't expect too much. I don't want to talk about me any more, except to say that life's been good to me.'

Some people were changing partners already.

'Can we stay together please?' she asked, hurriedly.

Kemp smiled broadly.

'I don't think I'd find that a hardship.'

Her face brightened.

'I hope I'm not spoiling things for you?'

'I think you've made a good attempt at open behaviour, but we haven't reached a solution, have we?'

'Do you think I should leave the conference?'

'I think that would be a pity,' he said, speaking for himself. 'Sit and take notes and if anyone asks you a question, admit that you don't have any experience to call upon. In the unlikely event that you're publicly pursued, repeat your answer. If you're spoken to privately, disclose what you've told me but don't be defensive. It's not an indictable offence.'

'That's not a bad idea,' she said, relieved. 'I don't want to lie.'

One or two individuals came up to partner but went away. When the lecturer announced that the session was over they slowly moved outside, standing apart from the crowd. Helen seemed in no hurry to leave him so they went to the dining room together.

Yes, she was very attractive. Part of him would be very happy to abandon the programme he had selected to coach her, but instead he said rather brusquely, 'I've put my name down for something a bit more demanding next, so I'd better go. We'll no doubt meet again.'

'Yes please,' she responded, clearly disappointed.

They met briefly in the hall the following afternoon. She was in a small group but turned towards him as he approached.

'How's it going?' he asked quietly.

'I don't think it's quite lived up to my expectations.' She smiled. 'The first session was the best.'

'Hopefully it will get better. I'm on a learning curve and trying not to slide off it. See you later.'

It was good that she wasn't tamely following him –

she would be a distraction. He would keep her at arm's length.

For the rest of the week he saw her only occasionally during breaks, certain that she would have no difficulty finding a companion. He convinced himself that he was simply being professional, wanting to follow chosen subjects. Later on, with the seminars completed, he had no excuse for not responding to the feelings Helen had awakened in him. He decided to gamble by reserving the seat next to him at the winding up session the following morning. If she arrived without companions and came to sit beside him, he would try to build on the opportunity.

'You're early,' one of the organisers greeted him as he walked into the hall that morning. 'Have you enjoyed the conference?'

'Very much, it's all been very useful. I'm early because I need to reserve a seat.'

Kemp placed his notepad on the chair next to him and sat half-turned, ready to catch Helen's eye if she arrived unaccompanied. When she appeared he thought she looked stunning in a pale yellow suit. This positive appraisal was not lost on her. Neither was it lost on the organiser who had spoken to him, for he grinned knowingly at Kemp.

She picked up the pad he had placed on the chair and held it out to him.

'I hope this seat is reserved for me'.

'Indeed,' he said.

'I'm glad you're here,' she murmured. 'Everyone else is so intense. Shall we lunch together?'

Her forthright manner surprised him.

They lunched and he offered her a lift home. Since neither was in a hurry, they stopped at the Thames Embankment, parked the car and walked to St James's Park.

Flowerbeds appeared on fire as orange and yellow tulips moved in the breeze. The fragrance of the wallflowers was intoxicating, and blossom rained from the trees. Sunshine sparkled on the lake, reflecting the blue sky and the numerous shades of green around the water's edge. It was a heady mixture.

Kemp held Helen's hand as they walked, astonished by the emotions churning inside him. It had been a long time since he had a girl by his side. They found a bench away from the crowds and sat, and after a while he put his arm along the seat at the back of her.

'Don't get too involved, Peter,' she murmured. 'I'm not wanting that.'

He quickly removed his arm.

'I'm sorry. I thought we were getting on well.'

'That's not quite what I meant. Do you mind putting your arm back? I rather liked it.'

'I don't understand.'

His voice was clipped and his arm remained by his side. She looked at him intently.

'I've been thinking about that exercise we did on open behaviour and feel that it requires one to be confident and take a risk.'

'That's true.'

She leaned forward and kissed him lightly on his cheek, then moved back to look at him. Completely taken aback by her behaviour, he was aware that away from the somewhat academic atmosphere of the conference she appeared a different person.

'Well, thank you,' he said belatedly, 'but I'm a bit overwhelmed at the moment.'

'Good,' she giggled. 'It's my turn to be in charge.'

Excited by her behaviour, he abandoned any attempt to understand.

'Can we perhaps carry on with that exercise in co-counselling?' she asked impishly.

'Of course,' he said, mesmerised by her initiative.

'Is this where I tell my problem?'

'Indeed.'

Suddenly she was serious, and silent. Then she asked, 'You are acting as my counsellor?'

He nodded

'My problem is that I've stopped seeing someone whom I've been sleeping with for about a year. He's been a good friend and I'm very fond of him, but in terms of anything else it's been rather one-sided. There's been no one else.' She gazed into the distance. 'How's that for open behaviour?'

'Courageous.'

He looked at the bold, confident Helen and was intrigued. She had a mind of her own, was challenging convention and stirring emotions that had lain dormant within him for a long time.

"But I'm not sure what the problem is.'

'Are you playing hard to get?' she asked.

'Certainly not.'

For the first time, she looked embarrassed. He gently touched her face, as if needing to be sure she was real.

'That's nice,' she whispered. 'It's to do with the relationship I had. Physically it was one-sided. I told you I don't want to become emotionally entangled, which is true because I want some time to myself. But . . . but my problem is that I do want to know that I can respond properly to a man I'm physically attracted to.'

He was silent. Neither of them moved. For a short while she kept eye contact, then dropped her gaze and stared at her hands.

'Please forget what I said.' She turned away. 'I've made an awful mistake.'

'No, you haven't.' He caught her arm. 'I'm delighted to be of service.'

Too late, he realised his unfortunate choice of words. Unable to hide his chagrin he said, 'I'm sorry, that wasn't meant to . . . '

But Helen giggled at the Freudian slip and in seconds they were laughing together. It was a perfect moment that completely removed any remaining awkwardness.

With her scent assailing his senses, he held her close, his right hand following the contours of her arched back into the small recess between her shoulder blades. She shivered and they kissed hungrily.

They raced to the car. On the way Kemp thought that the whole thing might have been a dream were it not for the hand that lay lightly on his knee. They were close to her flat when he pulled up.

'I won't be a moment,' he said.

She was puzzled but guessed his purpose when she saw him enter a chemist's shop. When he returned she kissed him.

'Thank you for being so thoughtful.'

Her flat was on the second floor of an imposing four-storey block. From the lift a short corridor led to her apartment. Helen showed him into a small hall and then to the drawing room where they removed their shoes before stepping on to a thick green carpet that was soft underfoot. The room was snug and expensively furnished.

He reverently touched the attractively carved Moroccan table that held centre stage. A crystal vase held a vast number of yellow roses. She saw him glance at them and said, 'My cleaning woman must have put these here. They'll be needing fresh water.' He glimpsed a greetings card but attached no significance to it.

She disappeared through a doorway in the far corner of the room. The flowers were returned a few minutes later, without the card. She gently tweaked the blooms, her head on one side as she did so, before looking at Kemp.

'I'm sure we need a celebratory drink. Be patient and have a seat.'

She went back to the kitchen and he wandered over to the fireplace where ornaments from different countries were on display, but no photographs. He stood with his back to the hearth, marvelling at the turn of events. It wasn't beyond his imagination that sooner or later they might have ended up in bed, but to confront this prospect so clinically beforehand was an extraordinary experience. Given his exposure to the seamy side of life he found it incredible that he wasn't questioning Helen's morals. She had told him that she had known only one lover, and an unsatisfactory one at that, and he believed her.

She emerged from the doorway carrying a tray with two glasses and a bottle of champagne.

'Will this do?'

She placed the tray on the table and showed him the label.

'Perfectly, thank you.'

He thought it a flamboyant gesture. She handed the bottle to him to open and as the cork popped said, 'I like being with you, but you will accept, won't you, that we walk away from each other tomorrow morning?'

He raised his glass and gave a toast. 'To tonight's togetherness.'

Lifting her glass to his she giggled and said, 'I like that. It describes perfectly what I want at the moment.'

'This is a comfortable place, Helen.'

'Don't get too comfortable.'

Picking up her glass she held her hand out and pulled him into the small hall. She opened a door to a large and comfortable bedroom and flung herself on to the bed, tugging Kemp down beside her. They helped each other remove their outer clothing. Leaning over, she touched the side of his nose as if to admonish him, before kissing him carefully on his lips.

'You'll have to curb your impatience,' she said. 'I want to shower. The bathrooms at the college were so awful that I didn't linger in them, and there was never enough hot water. You mustn't follow me. You can shower after me.'

Her hair fell about his face and her scent stirred him, but he lay still. She was beginning to take control.

Gathering up the clothes from the floor, she hung them tidily on hangers. From his reclining position Kemp watched, making no move, but it wasn't easy. He pondered about the shower. These were expensive items and this was certainly a luxurious apartment.

The sound of running water broke his reverie as he lay on top of the bedspread, and he looked about him. A dark red carpet contrasted with pale wallpaper. Wardrobes spanned the length of one wall and he wondered if they were all in use. Helen's dressing table held several cut glass bottles and scent sprays. Four amateurish watercolours hung on the wall above the bed, striking a slightly incongruous note.

He squinted at them. They were all by the same hand and elegantly framed. The artist's signature was indecipherable. Again, there were no photographs on display. He rose, removed the rest of his clothes then pulled a sheet across himself and lay back on the bed. Helen returned wearing a loosely wrapped, maroon silk dressing gown and, he guessed, nothing else.

'You'll find all you need in the bathroom, Peter,' she said, tossing a large towel on to his chest. 'Don't be long!'

Showering quickly and drying vigorously, he returned to the bedroom with a fresh towel tied round his waist. The champagne bottle was now on Helen's bedside table. She had fetched his glass from the drawing room and it was on the table by his side of the bed. The sheets had been turned down and Helen lay propped up on her pillows.

'Hello,' she said softly.

Reaching up, she pulled at the towel around his waist. As it fell away she appraised him from head to toe then held out her arms. He removed her dressing gown and they kissed hungrily. Their movements were hasty, as if they were gladiators preparing for a naked battle.

Once she pushed him away but he lightly resisted the movement. She remained tense and soon it was his turn to move away. They continued caressing each other, but with much less urgency. The outcome was inconclusive for both of them. They lay quietly in each other's arms, aroused enough to know they were just at the beginning of an adventure.

After a time, Helen sat up.

'I'm hungry, Peter. Let's go to a restaurant I know in Beauchamp Place.'

'Won't we need to have booked?'

'I'm known there, so I think we'll be all right.'

When they walked in to the restaurant the manager saw her and immediately came across, bowing to her then to Kemp.

'We came on the off-chance,' Helen said. 'I'm afraid we haven't booked but we don't intend to stay long.'

'Of course. Just a moment please, madam.'

He beckoned to the head waiter and whispered for a moment. The waiter turned to them, giving a half bow.

'This way madam, sir.'

The reserved plaque on a table was removed then he and another waiter, who had suddenly appeared, drew back their chairs and flourished napkins on to their laps.

Kemp didn't understand why they were allocated a reserved table as, a few minutes later, he saw an additional table being erected in another corner of the restaurant.

'Such service,' he murmured to Helen. 'You must dine here often.'

She made no reply but studied the menu. He was startled to see dishes listed that hadn't been available for many years. The prices were high and he discreetly checked that he had sufficient money in his wallet.

They were totally engrossed with each other during dinner, and when they left the manager again bowed low over Helen's hand.

Back at the flat, Helen made a pot of real coffee. For years he had been drinking a chicory and coffee essence, real coffee being difficult to obtain.

Returning to the bedroom, they lay touching each other. This time there was no haste to remove their clothes. Each garment was removed slowly, as part of the lovemaking. Kemp was gentle and Helen responsive.

Gradually she became more excited. Her mouth was hungry, open and seeking his. She was possessed and possessive. Her breathing grew rapid and she gasped, pleading for release yet demanding that he stay with her. Finally her quickening breath rewarded him and she gave a long, half-strangled moan.

Kemp's control was lost. He jerked and spilled air from his lungs and lay still. Sleep overtook him but Helen continued to cling to him. It was a long time before her grip lessened.

They woke simultaneously.

'You were wonderful,' she said, her eyes sparkling. 'You don't think I'm going to let you go now, do you?'

Her words seemed prophetic. Surprisingly, Kemp didn't feel threatened.

Disentangling herself from his arms she got up and knelt beside the bed. Placing the tips of her fingers together, palms touching in a typical eastern gesture, she bowed her head in mock supplication.

'What would my lover like to drink?'

Her teasing delighted him and he reached for her from his prone position but she evaded him. She struck an artistic pose, her hand on the back of her head, elbow pointing upwards. She tossed her blonde hair up and around her face and struck another pose, then another. It was spontaneous. He loved her switches of mood.

'You're beautiful,' he said, aroused by her golden hair, proud neck, shapely breasts, flat stomach, small waist, white thighs and curls of darker hair. 'Exquisite!'

With one of those giggles he found so endearing she jumped back into bed, pulling the coverlet over their heads. Kemp nuzzled her ear, whispering, 'And now you do know you're a beautiful and complete woman.'

She snuggled tightly beside him as he gently traced the curves of her lovely body. They made love again and sleep overtook her, but it was a long time before he fell asleep – and not before he accepted that he was bewitched.

Waking first, he gazed with pleasure at the woman beside him, idly wondering what options she would take if he woke her. Would she immediately want to make love again? Would she suggest breakfast? Or would she want to go back to sleep? He decided not to disturb her and drifted back to sleep himself.

A whispering in his ear awoke him. He lay still as she repeated, 'Peter, you've only twenty-five minutes.'

'Sorry?'

'Twenty-five minutes to shower, dress and take me to a nearby hotel for breakfast before they stop serving.'

Within fifteen minutes, ignoring the drizzle of rain, they were running hand in hand to the hotel at the end of the street where they hungrily consumed a full breakfast. Nothing seemed ordinary for Kemp and, for the moment at least, he forgot a cruel past from which he had learned never to become dependent on anyone.

Later, they sat languidly on the sofa in the flat. Helen began to talk about the exercise in co-counselling that seemed to have worked so well for them.

'We never did get to deal with your problem, did we?' she said, her eyes twinkling. 'I remember you told me that your colleagues say you get too involved in your cases. Tell me more.'

He couldn't keep the passion out of his voice as he spoke briefly of the damaged lives he dealt with and how every second seemed to count, but he was unable to tell her the truth of why it had been so important to fill his life in this way.

He stopped when he realised that Helen's eyes were no longer soft, but sharp and probing.

'I see I've a rival,' she said.

Her voice was challenging and he looked at her curiously. She seemed almost offended.

'It's my role as your co-counsellor to make the rules, Peter. As you have this obsession you can't take meeting me regularly for granted until you've rid yourself of it.'

'Obsession?'

It was an unpleasant description of his commitment. She continued, very much in control, 'We'll meet once in midweek and perhaps at weekends. They're the rules. You're not allowed to ring me. I'll ring you.'

'You're not serious!'

He looked at her delightful retrousse nose and saw beneath, her lips in a thin line.

'You can be sure I'm serious. You wanted a solution and I've given you one.' She stood up, impatient of him. 'I want you to go now,' she said. 'I've had a wonderful time and I want it to continue, but I won't be second best.'

He followed her from the room without speaking.

'Give up your obsession with rescuing,' she told him, 'or you'll end up needing to be rescued yourself – but it won't be by me!'

Helen kissed him very delicately. Looking at the indomitable figure in front of him he found himself bemused. He was convinced that she wouldn't be swayed from the stance she had taken, and he was not prepared to risk trying.

'I'll ring you,' she said, and closed the door on him.

He walked slowly to the lift and out of the building and sat for several minutes in his car, unwilling to start the engine that would take him away from her.

He was sure that she would get over her annoyance. What was really disturbing was that she had made the same prediction about his long-term future as his colleagues.

12

The night passed in a succession of nightmares. He was isolated, lost, unendingly travelling towards an unknown destination. He awoke several times, hot, sticky, perspiring – and unable to define a destination that remained elusive.

In the morning, things looked much better. In spite of their blip, as he called it, the excitement of the weekend occupied his thoughts. Even if Helen persisted with the rules she had imposed, seeing her only one evening a week and every weekend would mean that he could get on with his job. Neither was it any real hardship that he must not ring her. If that were all it cost to appease her resentment at any thought that she was second best, there would be no conflict.

He arrived at the Hackney office buoyant, dealing eagerly with the work that had accumulated in his absence. Everyone who saw him was aware that something out of the ordinary had boosted him and assumed that the conference had been a great success. Mrs Boulton, of course, was particularly pleased.

'Did you see the note I left on your blotter?' she asked, coming up to his desk. 'That girl's been on the phone again – the one who phoned before you went away. She rang once during the week and again as I was about to go home on Friday. I asked for her contact details so that you could get in touch with her, but she wouldn't give any or leave a message. She sounded very young, and this time she sounded upset.'

While she talked, Kemp found her note in his in-tray. Mrs Boulton said crossly, 'The cleaners must have moved it. I left it tucked in your blotting pad so that you'd see it first thing this morning.'

Kemp frowned.

'You say she wouldn't give a name?'

'No. Although, come to think of it, she may have said her name was Lydia at the beginning of the call.'

He drew a deep breath.

'It wasn't Linda by any chance, was it?'

'Yes, that's it. Linda. Do you know who she is?'

'Yes, I'm afraid I do. You said she sounded anxious?'

'Upset, I said. I thought she sounded upset.'

Kemp went down the steps two at a time. He hadn't followed up on Mikey because he had complied with Linda's request to give him time to settle down with her and Geoff. Nevertheless, she had the names of all the officers and that of Mrs Boulton, who had answered the phone to her three times. Why hadn't she declared herself before this?

He drove to the Simpsons' address and hastened up the stairs to their flat. Receiving no answer to his knocking, he assumed it to be a morning when Linda was working. He went back to the office but was unable to concentrate. Hoping that Linda would come home at lunchtime he returned to the flat, arriving soon after midday. There was still no answer so he decided to wait throughout the lunch period, positioning himself so that he had a clear view of the entrance to the flats.

Shortly before one o'clock he saw her coming across the courtyard. He got out of his car and she hurried over to him, but there was no welcoming smile.

'He's gone!' she said abruptly.

Kemp tensed.

'Where? How long's he been away?'

'Since I first phoned. I don't know where. Mum says he's not with them, and he's hardly been here except at the very beginning. Geoff's furious, because he began by waiting up for him. I don't think he's going to put up with it any longer. I'm sorry, but me marriage comes first.'

'But how could you have left it so long before telling me?' Kemp demanded, a sinking feeling in his stomach.

Linda bridled.

'I called three times,' she said.

'But you didn't speak to anyone – or give your name!'

'Geoff said I wasn't to leave me name in case it would get out about Mikey. He's afraid for his job if it gets out.'

'If what gets out?'

'What Mikey's been up to.'

Kemp ran his fingers through his hair.

'I need to know, Linda.'

'I'm sorry, but Geoff said I wasn't to say. I wish you'd come when I first called your office.'

'I would have, but you didn't talk to the people I suggested. I didn't know it was you.' He stopped pursuing this issue and softened his tone. 'Where is he, Linda?'

'I don't know.' She looked around as though conscious of being observed and repeated uncomfortably, 'I phoned straightaway. I thought you'd know it was me. Do you want to come up?'

'No. I'll go to your parents and then I'll come back to you.'

'Be best to come about six when Geoff's in.'

Arriving at the Grant house, with its corrugated front window, he found that the door was ajar. He banged on the door panel and Mrs Grant appeared.

141

'Oh, you've finally come, have you, Mr know-it-all? I knew it wouldn't work, you and your grand idea of a bedroom to himself.'

Kemp ignored the rebuke.

'Is Michael here?'

'No, he ain't,' she scoffed. 'Buggered off, ain't he? I don't blame him neither.'

'Where is he?'

'I dunno. I thought you'd have all the answers. You and your fancy ideas.'

She was obviously enjoying her moment.

'If he's not with you, why aren't you worried about him?'

'Because Bobby's looking after Mikey now. That's all right, ain't it? After all, he's older than Linda.'

She leered triumphantly.

'No, it isn't all right. Mikey was assigned to the care of Linda and Geoff and it's not for anyone other than the Children's Department to alter that arrangement. Where's Bobby?'

'I'd leave Bobby well alone if I were you. I don't fancy your chances if you interfere.'

'I'll be back to see him after six-thirty tonight.'

'You might be lucky,' she said. 'And then again, if he's in you might be very unlucky.'

She slammed the door.

Back at the office he rang the school and found the headmaster in a testy mood.

'I did have a visit from a Mr and Mrs Simpson a few weeks ago, asking if a Michael Grant could start on the following Monday. I made arrangements for him but he didn't turn up until a week later.'

Kemp needed to ask, but recognised the answer would expose his poor supervision. 'Has he been attending regularly?'

'For one week – and we haven't seen him since,' the headmaster continued dismissively. 'I don't think he's the sort of boy we want in this school.'

'I understand. I'm sorry you've been troubled.'

The headmaster promptly rang off, leaving Kemp feeling very uncomfortable.

A distant church clock chimed six as he parked his car outside the Simpsons' block of flats. He saw Geoff arrive and gave him time to settle before going up to see him.

The young man was in low spirits and made no attempt to curb his language.

'I've been buggered about too much by that little bastard,' he said. 'I'm not having him back. If I'm not careful he'll have me out of me job.'

'Tell me about it.'

Kemp was growing more anxious by the minute.

'Well, when you left us they all got on to me about Mikey having to go straight to school after having been put away and not having time with them. They said it wasn't fair. I didn't want to fight with Mikey immediately so I let him off for a week then took him to school every day the next week.

'I expected him to continue by himself the following week but the little bugger never turned up, did he? Not here, nor at the school, so I went round to his mum's, didn't I? She said she'd no idea where he was but she thought he was with Bobby G. Said I was to forget about it.

'I didn't believe her, of course. If she really didn't

know where Mikey was she'd have been worried sick. She's a nasty piece of work – sorry, Linda love, you know damn well she is – but if Mikey was really missing she'd have been having her say. I told her I thought she did know where he was and she lost her rag and slammed the door in me face. I ain't going to be treated like that by her nor no-one so I left, and I ain't stepping foot in that house again. She needn't think she's coming here neither.'

'It's been bad for you,' Kemp said. 'I'm so sorry it didn't work out. I'm afraid there are too many bad influences at work on him.'

Shrugging his shoulders in a gesture of resignation Geoff continued, 'Mikey ain't been back here since but I've heard what he's been up to and I want no part of it. I ain't trying no more.'

'Where do you think he is now, Geoff?'

'I'm sorry, Mr Kemp. It'd be best if I didn't say no more, and Linda's got to keep out of it too. In the shop she hears all the local gossip. Me job at the bank would be on the line.'

'But what kind of trouble has Bobby G got Mikey into now?'

'I can't tell you, Mr Kemp, except to say it affects the local shops and it's criminal. If it gets into the local paper and the bank hear about it, then maybe bang goes me job and maybe Linda's.'

Kemp stood silent for a moment in the face of their anger. His regrets were an inadequate response to the problems they had endured.

'Perhaps we should've guessed things would go wrong with those two evil bastards in the family,' Geoff said. 'And I don't mean Mikey and his dad.'

Linda followed Kemp outside.

'Mikey's staying with one of Bobby's gang,' she whispered, half closing the door behind her. 'I don't know the address. They're all in it together. They get Mikey to go in to a shop first to ask for protection money – that way, if he's trapped, he's to pretend it's just a schoolboy lark. While he's talking the gang drift into the shop, as innocent as you like, applying the pressure, and Mikey leaves. I'm sorry he ain't learned nothing, Mr Kemp.'

'Thanks, Linda.' He squeezed her arm. 'I'm afraid I'll need to send him away again. We can't allow him to get another conviction on his record.'

'I know.'

The door was pulled out of her hand and Geoff stood behind her. Realising that Linda had opened up to Kemp he nodded, then held her close as she began to cry.

'You can't say where you got the information, Mr Kemp,' he said.

'Of course not, you have my word. Thank you both for trying to help. I'm so sorry it turned out like this.'

He shook hands with Geoff and went to his car. There was no point in having words with Bobby G, but he was loath to let the thug imagine he had intimidated him. He would confront Bobby again, no matter how challenging the encounter might be.

It was a quarter to seven when he walked into a row between Mr and Mrs Grant. He could hear it as he approached the door. Mrs Grant answered his knock.

'Not here,' she snarled.

Kemp put his foot in the door.

'Who? Bobby or Michael?'

'None of 'em – and do you mind not cluttering up me doorstep?'

'I'm recalling Michael's licence, Mrs Grant.'

'A good thing too!' shouted her husband from indoors.

Mrs Grant let go of the door to aim a blow at him. They continued fighting as Kemp drove away.

By the time he reached the Montgomery Estate it was almost seven thirty. He let himself into the empty building, went straight to his office and rang McGovern's home number. His wife answered. It was obvious from the background noise that he had interrupted their meal.

'What's up, Kemp?' McGovern asked.

'I'm sorry to phone while you're having dinner sir, but I need your help with Michael Grant. I'm afraid my arrangements for him have failed and he needs to be returned directly to a place of safety. Can you help with a police issue that's arisen, please?'

'I thought you were a bit optimistic with that crowd,' the dour Scotsman replied. But as he heard the details he picked up the disappointment in Kemp's voice and added in a kinder tone, 'You canna win 'em all, laddie! I'll have a word with my police contact and ring you back.'

While waiting, Kemp regretfully removed Michael's name from his caseload, making a recommendation that the boy should go to a secure unit where he would receive psychiatric help. He then began a laborious report that would accompany the lad as soon as he was apprehended. He cited the unsuitability of the parents to have their son back until he was more mature, and emphasised the unsavoury influence of his elder brother. The telephone interrupted him.

'I've tipped off a detective I know about the protection racket Bobby G and Michael are involved in,' McGovern said. 'It confirms what they've already suspected. They're mounting surveillance immediately.

'I've told them that Michael's home trial has been abandoned. The plan is that once Michael has been picked up coming out of a shop, they'll let me know and I'll arrange for him to be taken to a secure unit. You keep out of it, but let me have your full report. They'll then proceed to apprehend Bobby G and his cronies and charge them. What a joyous moment that'll be.'

'Thanks for your help sir; it's much appreciated. My apologies for disturbing your evening.'

'Don't you worry about that, laddie. Now you get off home and relax with a good Scotch whisky. And, Kemp – don't be too hard on yourself. You're doing a grand job and proving the worth of the Department, which is new to many people.'

Kemp replaced the phone and turned his attention once more to the report. Acknowledging his failure to counter the boy's hero worship of his lawless brother, he wanted at least to make sure that Bobby G's visiting rights would be denied: with any luck his hours of freedom would soon come to an end. Reading his report through he was disappointed that it wasn't optimistic for Michael's future. He placed the completed document in his out-tray, locked the building and went to his car.

It was a miserable journey home. He ran through the many things he could have done differently. He should have personally introduced Michael to his new school. He should have realised the burden he was placing on Geoff and Linda. After placing the boy with them, he should have refused her request to delay the follow-up.

Once home he took McGovern's advice and poured a measure of whisky into a glass. He put on a record, sunk into the sofa and let his mind wander to Helen. He wished he could gain a little solace by talking to her but her words when they parted yesterday made that impossible.

No, there would be meagre comfort from that source. He felt he had taken a step backward in terms of his own personal journey.

13

Torrential rain beat down as Kemp arrived at the office. He raced into Reception and was surprised to find McGovern and Mrs Boulton waiting for him.

'Mrs Boulton phoned you just after eight o'clock, but you'd apparently already left,' said McGovern. 'Then she phoned me in case you didn't appear. I'm afraid it's serious. I know you don't like to involve the police if it can be avoided so I've been hanging on for you.'

'What's up, sir?'

'One of our clients you placed on a farm when you first joined is on his way here with a shotgun. Oscar Bridges. He's looking for you!'

'That's nice,' said Kemp facetiously, for he disliked dramatisation.

'It's no joke, Kemp. The farmer phoned. It seems he gave the laddie a roasting, first thing this morning and he ran off saying he was coming to London to see you. He's nineteen, isn't he? Unfortunately, it took a while before the farmer realised his shotgun was missing. He drove to the station but the train had already left. It's due in at Liverpool Street Station at ten-thirty. We should have police waiting.'

'Certainly not! I'll meet him. Oscar Bridges is deemed educationally subnormal. He'll have become confused about something. It's only then that he behaves irrationally. It's important to avoid panicking him.'

'He was before my time, Kemp, so I'll go along with your assessment of him. But you're not going on your own to the station to meet a young man with a shotgun, and that's final. I'm afraid I'll have to call the police unless you let me come with you. There's the safety of the public to consider.'

Recognising that his boss was determined, and conceding the point about public safety, Kemp said, 'Come with me if you must, sir, but please stay out of sight when I meet him.'

Kemp put his hand on Mrs Boulton's arm to soothe her.

'Will you ring Gerry Thompson and tell him that I'm meeting the train and that I'll be bringing Oscar straight back? You have his number?'

She nodded and watched while the two men got in to Kemp's car, then hurried to make the phone call.

On the way to the station McGovern's unease was apparent, so Kemp filled in the details.

'Oscar's an orphan. He's a gentle boy who went out of care soon after I was appointed. As I said earlier, when he gets confused he can become unstable but in that state he's more likely to hurt himself than anyone else. There's really no harm in the lad.'

McGovern looked unconvinced.

'Oscar's always wanted to work on the land and this excellent farmer and his wife agreed to take him into their home and to employ him as a farmhand. He's normally very happy. He hates towns. Busy streets, cars and crowds make him feel insecure.

'I last saw him about six months ago when visiting Gerry, who's very good with him. Gerry and I've become friends and the only problems we've had have been when Oscar gets muddled. He then merely becomes obstinate.'

Kemp stopped at traffic lights and faced McGovern.

'He's actually a gentle giant.'

'I hope you're right.'

The tone in McGovern's voice caused Kemp to raise his eyebrows before letting in the clutch.

'I've no doubt it's a storm in a teacup.'

'Does Oscar know how to use the gun?'

'Oh yes! He's been involved in a number of rabbit culls while on the farm. There's no chance of him shooting himself in the foot, if that's what you're thinking.'

'It wasn't exactly what I had in mind.'

They arrived at the station in good time and settled for a cafe overlooking the platform as a vantage point.

'I'm going to get a platform ticket in order to meet up with him straightaway,' said Kemp, trying to ease his boss's concern.

'I'm glad you have a plan, Kemp, if only for the sake of innocent bystanders.'

McGovern nodded, indicating his trust.

The train was a few minutes late. Kemp was watching from behind a pillar and quickly spotted Oscar. He stepped off the train, halfway down the platform, one arm against his chest, carrying a raincoat that was obviously concealing something. Kemp gave thanks for knowing what was being hidden. He waited until the youngster was past him, then he came up behind him on the gun side, matching pace with him.

'Oscar. I was looking out for you.'

Startled, Oscar made as if to stop but Kemp linked arms with him, the shotgun held between them, and kept the young man moving.

'My car's over there,' he said. 'What've you got to tell me?'

'I've had a bust-up, Mr Kemp. It's about them lambs.'

Oscar stopped, anxious to tell his story.

'Let's get to the car and then you can tell me all about it – but you shouldn't have run away.'

'I want you to help me, sir.'

'Of course I will.' Kemp pointed to the front seat and took the shotgun off Oscar to help him into the car. He put the gun in the boot. 'By the way, what did you bring this thing for?'

Oscar looked cunning.

'I don't like coming to London. I wanted it to keep meself safe. I thought if they saw I had a gun, the bad blokes won't come near me.'

McGovern had appeared from nowhere, and was sliding into the back seat. He must have heard Oscar's explanation because Kemp heard him expel breath. Kemp introduced him.

'This is my boss, Oscar. I'm going back with you to the farm but I'm dropping Mr McGovern off at our office first.'

'Hello, mister.' Oscar twisted round in his seat and gave a toothy grin.

Kemp let in the clutch and moved out of the parking bay. He handed his ticket to the attendant at the barrier.

'You can tell me all about it on the way, but I'm surprised that you're letting Mr Thompson down like this,' Kemp said. 'He's your friend, he's good to you and he knows what's best for the farm.'

'I don't like killing lambs, sir, and this was me favourite.'

'If you asked Mr Thompson, I'm sure he'd tell you that he doesn't like the lambs being killed either, but it's part of what farming is all about. If farmers didn't send their animals to the abattoirs, their farms would soon go out of business. You do like all the other things you do in farming, don't you?'

'Yes, sir. I like growing things and feeding the animals. It's smashing. I gets up a bit earlier these mornings and goes to the fields to check on the wheat. It grows at night because every morning it's a bit taller. Harvest time is good because you can see what all your hard work's been for.'

'That's good. You must talk with Mr Thompson about things that upset you, Oscar. Will you promise you won't go running off to town again? I won't always be here to meet you.'

'It was me day off, Mr Kemp.'

A sound of choking that turned into a sneeze was heard from the back of the car. There was silence until they pulled up at the office. Kemp got out and opened the door for McGovern.

'Thanks for the company, Mr McGovern,' he grinned.

'Thanks for the ride,' replied McGovern dryly. He shook hands with Oscar.

'I'm not coming in. Oscar and I are leaving for his home now.'

McGovern strode indoors. Mrs Boulton was waiting anxiously.

'Young Kemp's got a hell of a way with him,' said McGovern in answer to her enquiring look. He failed to notice Mrs Boulton preening at the comment.

Continuing their journey, Kemp encouraged the innocent young man to talk about life on the farm. By the time they were halfway to their destination Oscar had forgotten his earlier distress.

'How long before we get there, Mr Kemp? I want to be back at the farm. I can use everything and Mr

Thompson says I'm indespesable now.' He stumbled over the word. 'Is that good?'

'You mean indispensable. Yes, that's very good.'

'Is it far now?'

'Not much longer, Oscar. Let's make the time go more quickly by singing. What songs do you know?'

'Do you know, "Old McDonald Had a Farm", sir?'

'That's a good one,' Kemp said, and Oscar joined robustly in many tuneless renderings of that song and others.

Some time later, and in good humour, they pulled up just short of the farm. Oscar looked enquiringly at Kemp, who reverted to being serious.

'You should say sorry to Mr and Mrs Thompson for the worry and the trouble you caused by leaving the farm in such a way. You're special now and you know where everything is. Mr Thompson relies on you so you've got to be there in case anything goes wrong.'

Oscar made no reply but puffed out his chest.

A rubicund Gerry Thompson was waiting at the kitchen door for them with his wife. They were not demonstrative people, but clearly both were fond of Oscar and pleased to see him. Kemp knew that because of Oscar's limited ability the Thompsons had not thought it practical for him to inherit the farm, but they had told Kemp that Oscar would be well looked after if anything happened to them.

Thompson immediately took the shotgun out of the car boot. He locked it away then came back to Oscar.

'You must never again take the gun off the farm. The licence only allows for the shotgun to be used here. You could have got into serious trouble.'

The boy looked downcast.

'We won't talk about it any more,' promised Thompson, 'but running away is not the best way to settle an argument.'

'Oscar now knows that he should talk to you about the things that bother him, Gerry. I think he's learnt a valuable lesson today,' said Kemp.

'I didn't like going to London,' Oscar admitted. 'The train was noisy and the engine's smoke smelt dirty. Not like the smoke when we have a bonfire. Honest, I don't want to run away again.'

'I'm glad to hear that.' Thompson smiled. He added jovially, 'You mustn't be so bolshie in future.'

'I like that word,' Oscar laughed. 'What does it mean, bolshie?'

Mrs Thompson intervened.

'It's when young people won't listen to the advice of their elders. I think you should be ashamed of yourself, Oscar. You had us worried out of our minds.'

Oscar looked shaken by this outburst from Mrs Thompson. Her husband put his arm round her.

'He's home safe now, love, and he's promised not to do it again.' He turned to the crestfallen young man. 'Take Mr Kemp and show him what you can do now.'

Looking delighted, Oscar took Kemp into the well-scrubbed yard, past the milk churns and the outhouses, to introduce him to each of the cows by name. They walked past the chickens.

'Mrs Thompson looks after the chickens,' Oscar said. 'They're good. We get fresh eggs every morning.'

They walked on.

'I help with all the animals and the milking and I drives the tractor and works the plough. The sheep is over there.'

'Well done. I won't see the sheep, Oscar. I must get on my way.'

'Thanks for seeing me, Mr Kemp. I know it's a long journey because we just done it, didn't we?'

Having avoided the animals that had initiated the upset, Kemp strode back to the farmhouse. As he was leaving, Oscar gave him a dozen eggs.

'Mrs Thompson said I was to say thanks for bringing me home safely, Mr Kemp. I ain't coming to London no more.'

He stood between the Thompsons. All three were beaming as they waved Kemp off.

On the journey back he couldn't help but wish he were not returning to an empty flat. He thought of Helen on her own in hers: their independent lives didn't make much sense. He had begun to worry about the routine of their meetings, so the last time they had met he had said he wanted to surprise her.

'I don't like surprises,' she had answered.

'I thought you might like a change of scenery?'

'What do you have in mind?'

'How about staying at a picturesque country pub for a weekend?'

'It's not my thing, darling. The emphasis is usually on the age of the establishment and the scenery around rather than comfort and sophistication.'

'How about I take you to the opera, or the ballet, or the theatre?'

'Is this a roundabout way of telling me you're getting bored with my company?'

'On the contrary, I want to . . .'

She had put two fingers on his lips.

'Shush!' she had said.

At lunchtime the next day Mrs Boulton rang. 'There's a young woman on the line for you, Peter,' she said sharply. 'I said I didn't know if you were free. Do you want me to put the call through?

Mrs Boulton had recently started to sound cold when she answered Helen's calls, so he knew who it would be. Helen's voice came on the phone.

'That little clerk is so protective of you, Peter,' she said. 'I found it amusing to start with but now it's irritating.' Not giving him time to respond she said, 'Shall we meet tonight?'

'Is everything all right?' he asked.

'Fine. I thought that since you wanted variety, we could go to the Royal Festival Hall. I've only been once since it opened last month.'

'I can't tonight, Helen. I'm visiting a young man who hopes to have a career in the Merchant Navy. He's had a very poor start to his life and he's trying very hard to make up for it. I'm coaching him.'

He hoped that describing the circumstance would touch her sufficiently to offset his failure to meet her wish.

'Oh, all right,' she said rather stiffly. 'I did think our romance would take precedence, but if you think him more important than me, do what you want.'

'That's not the reason. You know it isn't.'

'It sounds like it to me. Oh well, next Tuesday then.'

'What's the matter with the weekend?'

'I'm committed.' She offered no explanation, merely adding, 'Tuesday then. My place – usual time,' and the phone went dead.

One of the things Kemp had learnt about Helen was that she did not like to be thwarted and while being far from pleased with the interchange that had taken place, he decided he wouldn't risk a quarrel. He wondered whether cancelling the weekend was a reaction to him not being available tonight, then discarded that idea because she always enjoyed them as much as he did. He thought her work was probably responsible, then realised with a start that he had no idea what she did for a living.

It was noticeable to the rest of the office that his spirits had taken a dip. Having taken the call, Mrs Boulton was the one person who knew why.

The weekend, when it came, dragged for Kemp, but it was natural that it would compare unfavourably with the passionate weekends that followed the conference. He chose to be industrious rather than mooch about, but didn't go out in case she rang.

On Tuesday evening they met at her flat. She was happy to see him, if still a little subdued. She surprised him by suggesting they eat in.

'I'm not the best of cooks Peter, but if you promise not to be too critical I'll do this chicken dish that's in my recipe book.' She waved a book at him and gave one of her attractive giggles. 'You can relax.'

'Marvellous!'

'By the way, I've bought you a present.'

She reached behind the sofa and handed him a large, well-wrapped parcel.

'It's a Kenwood Chef – it's a wonderful food mixer. I saw it at the Ideal Home Exhibition last year when it first came out and bought one for myself. As you have to cook for yourself, I thought you might like one too. Don't open it now. You can read all about it some time when you're on your own.'

She placed it on the small table by the door, looking pleased with herself.

Kemp was delighted at her thoughtfulness and pulled her on top of him, kissing her vigorously as she struggled to get away from him.

'No! No!' she said. 'You mustn't interfere with the cook – not until after the meal.'

'Can't I watch you demonstrate the mixer?'

'No, I'm attempting a special dish that I had in a restaurant. You mustn't come near the kitchen.' She left quickly, only to return with a gin and tonic. 'This is to curb your impatience,' she said. She had put a frilly white apron on over her blue frock.

He took the glass, admiring the back of her as she walked towards the kitchen. He was content as he relaxed back on the sofa, well pleased with the change of plan. The truth was that Beauchamp Place was proving expensive for him.

A little later, she called for him to open up the leaves of the corner table. He did do so and then set out the cutlery. It was a long time before the meal was ready and it was passable only, for which she apologised.

'I wanted it to be so much better. I wanted it to be perfect for you,' she said with a pout. Her belief that she had failed affected her mood and she was downcast. She hung on to his shoulders and he held her tight. 'It looks so easy when it's placed before you in the restaurant. I shall have to go to classes.'

She was slurring her words and he became aware that she was slightly tipsy. He noticed a whiff of something more than her scent. He laughed, sat her down on the sofa and cleared the table. In the kitchen he found an almost empty gin bottle.

Going back to her he said, 'I'm sure you could be as good as any chef one can find, but I don't think you're supposed to keep drinking while you're cooking.'

He smiled down at her. She had curled up on the sofa and she looked up at him, holding out a languid arm.

'I was upset because I ruined the first attempt and had to throw it out.' She snuggled in to him. 'It's so infuriating. I had this lovely simple meal in Bruss . . .'

She stopped suddenly, biting her lip. Holding her shoulders, he was able to look directly in to her eyes.

'Where, Helen?'

'Brussels,' she said, defiantly. 'I had this lovely simple meal. The shops there are full of wonderful things and the restaurants are superb.' In an exasperated tone she continued, 'The Belgians have managed to put the boring war behind them and are enjoying life. They aren't constantly having austerity measures drummed in to them, as we have here.'

'When were you last in Brussels?'

She shook free from him, her face a little flushed.

'Oh, some time.' She leaned away from him then stood up, swaying slightly. 'It's hot in here. I think you're right – I've had too much drink for my own good. I'm going to splash cold water on my face.'

A little later she returned, outwardly composed and carrying two cups of coffee. Sitting opposite her, he asked about her weekend. She was evasive and said breezily, 'Well, we don't want to see too much of each other, do we? Or do we?' She lifted the corner of her skirt provocatively, exposing a silk-clad knee.

'The weekend passed dreadfully slowly for me,' he said.

She smiled but did not reciprocate. Instead, within minutes, she announced that she was going to tidy up in the kitchen. It was, he thought, an attempt to curtail further discussion.

Towards the end of the evening, more and more disturbed by her excessive secrecy, he mentioned the weekend again and it sparked off their first tiff.

'We're so close sometimes, Peter, and I find it wonderful, but I don't think that gives you the right to keep asking me questions about what I'm doing.'

'Helen, I only keep asking because I want to be with you in spirit as well as in person, so that when we're not together I can picture where you are and what you're doing.'

'Well, I find that stifling. I don't want to feel watched.'

'Helen, be fair. It's not unreasonable that I want to know what it is that's preventing us meeting.'

Colour had risen in her face and was spreading down from her throat.

'And I'm not inclined to tell you just because you're pursuing me.'

The impasse upset them both. They parted quietly, agreeing that they had come too close to spoiling a loving evening. She handed him the gift she had bought him.

'This proves I think of you when we're not together.'

He made to reply but she put her fingers to his lips in an all too familiar way.

14

Knowing no other remedy for introversion than to immerse himself in his casework, Kemp looked at his diary. It was the day of the summer fete at Wellington Residential School, and an opportunity to keep his promise to the superintendent to review whether Eric O'Reilly should return to his father. He rang Wellington and spoke to Ben Sears' secretary.

'What's the latest on Eric O'Reilly?'

'I don't know much other than that he went home during the break. The superintendent's still very doubtful about releasing him to his father. He thinks the man probably has an eye to the lad's potential to earn.'

'It's not an unknown inducement,' Kemp agreed, 'and one usually doomed to failure.'

'You've had your invitation to the fete. Will you see Eric today?'

'I will, and I'm on my way.'

'I'll let the house parents know.'

While locking his filing cabinet he thought of Eric's feelings. If the return to his father was denied him and no attractive alternative offered, then the boy might become seriously upset by the vacuum. As a precaution Kemp made a short list of three possible foster homes to contact, then went downstairs to see Mrs Boulton.

'I'm off shortly to visit Eric O'Reilly. If you recall, I took him on as an extra and you dug out his file for me.'

'I remember.' She looked at the clock. 'You're going early. Will you be back?'

'Probably not. It's their summer fete and I may get involved.'

'Look after yourself then. You're looking a little pale.'

He attempted a smile but left immediately, unwilling to be subjected to further scrutiny.

Arriving at Wellington, Kemp went to meet the Nevins. Ben Sears had told him that they were childless and new to residential care. Richard Nevin was in his tiny office.

'Mr Kemp? My wife sends her apologies but she's involved elsewhere at the moment. She'll join us as soon as she can.'

Kemp sat down and took Eric's file from his attache case.

'Have you had much opportunity to talk to Eric about his plans when he leaves school?'

'I think you know that his father's been here and Eric's expecting to go to him.'

'If that's the case I needn't bother to take any further interest in him ahead of his leaving date.'

Nevin looked doubtful. 'Well, it's your decision of course but I've a feeling something's not quite right.'

'Can you explain?'

'There's nothing tangible. It's just that, well . . .' Nevin leaned back in his chair. 'The prospect of going to his father isn't raising enough enthusiasm.'

'Have you met him?'

'No. We were away when he turned up. He arranged to collect Eric at the gate and the superintendent confirmed his identity.'

'It should be a desirable placement on the simple basis that blood is thicker than water,' Kemp said.

'I agree, but shouldn't it produce some anticipation? For example, Eric was supposed to have a long weekend with his father but came back a day early.'

Kemp sat bolt upright.

'What reason did he give?'

'That he was missing the boys and there was the first cricket match of the season in which he wanted to play.'

'He must have known that beforehand.'

'He did. He'll be coming in soon so I'd better keep a look out for him.' Nevin left the door ajar and returned to his chair. 'I can't find anything tangible to support my unease. I've casually talked to the other boys but Eric hasn't confided in any of them, either about his father or what it was like in his home. Nothing.'

A capable looking woman hurried into the room. Kemp stood up.

'Hello, Mr Kemp,' she said breathlessly. 'I'm Mrs Nevin. Phew! Excuse me while I get my breath back. I've run from one of the other buildings and I'm obviously not as fit as I thought I was.'

She pulled a face at her husband as she closed the door.

'No, leave it Rosemary. I'm looking out for Eric O'Reilly.'

Nevin pulled a chair closer to the desk for her.

'This is about Eric coming back early, isn't it?' she said, sitting down and smoothing her hair. 'It must be unnerving for a youngster, who's used to living with friends of his own age, to have to adapt to a stranger who suddenly appears and announces that he's your father. His dad probably looks and acts completely different from the person he might have imagined.'

'You've a point,' said Kemp, 'but I'm surprised he hasn't talked to anyone.'

Mrs Nevin looked disappointed. 'We haven't got his confidence yet but Eric spends a lot of time in the kitchen with Mrs Burns, our daily help. I don't know if he talks to her. She's about seventy and a doddering old dear.'

'I'd like to find out,' Kemp said. 'Can I make my own way to her rather than be introduced?'

'Of course.' Mrs Nevin rose. 'I'll point out the way.'

'And can you hold on to Eric for me, if you please? I wouldn't want him interrupting us.'

He went to the kitchen where Mrs Burns was rolling pastry. She wiped her hands on her apron and looked apprehensively at him.

'Good morning. I'm only looking round,' he said. 'Mrs Nevin said I could, but is it all right with you?'

She summed him up.

'There's a chair over there if you want to sit down.' She sprinkled flour on the pastry board and turned the pastry over. Picking up the rolling pin she said, 'And who might you be?'

'I keep an eye on some of the boys when they leave here. My name's Kemp, Peter Kemp – and you're Mrs Burns, I believe? Your reputation's gone before you. I've heard the boys say you're a smashing cook.'

She smiled, her cheeks rosy.

'Do they indeed?' She deftly lifted the pastry and placed it on top of a pie dish. 'I've known a lot of boys in the last few years. Some of them come in and talk to me. You know – tell me all their plans. They're lovely boys, even though they time their visits for when I'm having my break, in the hopes that I'll give them a biscuit or a bit of cake.' She chuckled. 'Always hungry they are, growing boys.'

Picking up a sharp knife she quickly trimmed the excess pastry from the edges of the pie dish.

'I'm sure you're right,' he said.

She peered over her glasses.

'You here for anybody special? Is anyone leaving?'

'I'm looking in to one lad's prospects for going home.'

Her busy hands were suddenly still.

'You don't mean young Eric, do you?'

'Yes. Is he one of your biscuit boys?'

'He don't want to go there,' she said, twisting her apron. 'He shouldn't be made to, you know.'

'But he's chosen to go there, Mrs Burns.'

'That's only because he's afraid of being on his own and is trying to make the best of it.' She showed her agitation by moving pie dishes around unnecessarily.

Attempting to soothe her Kemp replied hastily, 'He won't be made to go there, don't you worry.'

'You won't tell him I talked about him, will you?'

'Of course not. I've delayed you enough so I'd better be going. Perhaps Mr Nevin will invite me to lunch one day – that pie promises to be very tasty.'

Mrs Burns smiled, her anxiety seemingly forgotten.

'You do look as though you could do with a bit of fattening up.'

Back in the office Mrs Nevin was writing.

'My husband's keeping Eric company,' she said, looking up. 'Was Mrs Burns able to help?'

'I think you should hear from her. You might have to go slowly at first but she has Eric's confidence. I don't think she would expect me to tell you what she said to me, but I'm sure if you reassured her that's she's a part of your team, working for the benefit of the boys, she'll provide you with some interesting disclosures from time to time.'

Mrs Nevin was thoughtful.

'I'll talk to Richard.'

'Anyway, what I can tell you is that Eric doesn't want to go to his father so it remains for me to get that information from the lad first hand.'

'I'll take you to him.'

She left Kemp waiting in the small library while she went to fetch Eric. He was scanning the bookshelves when he heard a knock, then the door opened. Turning, he found a small, wiry, red-headed boy standing in front of him.

'I'm Eric, sir. I was told you wanted to see me.'

The lad had the faintest of Irish accents.

'Hello, Eric. Come and have a seat.'

They discussed sport before Kemp subtly steered the conversation to the purpose of his visit.

'I hear you returned early from your holiday. Home sickness is supposed to work the other way.'

Eric stared at him.

'I suppose,' Kemp added casually, 'you came home early because you got upset. It's often difficult at the beginning of a new relationship, isn't it?'

Again Eric failed to respond.

'It must be awkward for your Dad too, after all this time. He has to get used to you, just as you've to get used to him.'

'He spent more time having a laugh with this other bloke.'

'Who was that?'

'This other bloke that lives there,' Eric said.

'I'm sure they made a fuss of you while you were there?'

'It was all right until Sunday.'

'What happened on Sunday?

'They were both drunk, weren't they?' Eric exploded.

'What – falling all over the place?'

Kemp kept his tone light.

'No, but he swore at me. For nothing!'

Eric avoided Kemp's gaze.

'Is that all?' Kemp said disparagingly.

'No! He threw a plate at me head. Said if I was any good I'd have got a meal ready for 'em. Blooming cheek!'

'That was bad.'

'I weren't going to stand for that,' Eric said indignantly, 'so I come back. Mr Sears had given me the money and directions in case I didn't like it there.'

'That was your long weekend break spoilt. It sounds as if you did right to come back – that was a bad experience.'

'Yeah!'

Eric glowered at the memory. Kemp leaned towards him.

'Are you going to give it another try?'

'No I ain't!'

'Perhaps you should?'

'No! You can't make me.'

'I wouldn't want to do that, but you lost your weekend break.'

Eric was silent.

'I'll tell you what! Why don't I arrange a special weekend to make up for it? It won't be long before you leave this school and you need to have a good experience away from here to let you know what it's going to be like.'

The boy was shaking his head, about to refuse, but Kemp headed him off.

'It's a bit like riding a bike, Eric. If you take a tumble,

you've to get back on the bike to keep your nerve. I have some friends with whom you can have a weekend so you can see what it's really like out there.'

'But I won't know them.'

'You're right, but I hear you're playing cricket for the school next week. I'll get them to come and watch you. If you don't like each other then you don't have to go. That's fair enough, isn't it?'

Eric shifted his feet, his head down.

'They'll no doubt want to take you for tea in the village after the match. I think you'll find them easy to talk to.'

Eric smiled weakly.

'My friends are huge sports fans. Show them a bit of real talent during the match. I've heard you're a pretty good all rounder. Okay?'

'Yeah! I don't mind,' Eric said doubtfully.

As soon he had gone Kemp made a call to one of the prospective foster parents, and in the afternoon he took a small group from the house, including Eric, to the fete. They bumped into another group led by Kathleen Ashley, the teacher he had spoken to about Eric on his previous visit.

'I feel like the Pied Piper,' she said.

He smiled at her. The children were noisily challenging one another.

'We seem to have a conflict here,' she said. 'I suggest we have a contest.'

The children cheered. The two impromptu teams used the activities of the various booths to compete, the final event being the most popular. Kemp and then Kathleen put on hooded waterproofs to enter the stocks and be pelted by wet sponges. They retired soon after, ready for refreshments.

'When we spoke the other day, Kathleen, you gave me the impression that you knew Eric O'Reilly quite well,' Kemp said, as he handed her a lemonade.

'I do, or rather I did. He was in my class during his last year at primary school. He's a sociable boy. Plays football and cricket for the school. I watch all their matches. He'll be playing next Wednesday.'

'I know. Do you think you could introduce a married couple to Eric for me when he comes off the pitch? His long-lost father recently came on the scene not too happily. I'm asking this particular couple to meet Eric immediately after the match, with the aim of getting him to spend a weekend with them.'

She stared at him quizzically, then nodded.

'I'll get the Nevins to give you the details,' he said, 'and we could tell Eric now what you'll be doing, if it's all right with you?'

She laughed. He liked the way she tossed her head on one side as she did so.

'If it's important for Eric, I could do that.'

'I'll give you my telephone number in case you experience any difficulties. Could I get a message to you if needed?'

'You can always leave a message in the staff room.'

He looked at his watch.

'It's later than I thought. I'm going to have to leave. I'll see you at the next battle.'

She looked puzzled.

'The Staff Open Day. I've already had my invitation.'

'Oh yes!' she said, her face clearing. 'I'm working in the kitchen that day.'

'I'm sure you'll get some time off.'

'Yes, perhaps.'

Somehow the relaxed atmosphere was lost and the parting awkward, but he felt sure she would play her part. He told Nevin of the plan before he left.

Two more weeks passed without a call from Helen, then he received a postcard with a view of St James's Park. On the back of the card she had simply written: *Take care. Will phone soon. H.*

Kemp was pleased but felt that the message might have been a bit more affectionate. He willed himself not to question her in the future and paid the price in restless nights.

Almost at the same time he received a message that Eric's hosts had enjoyed having the boy and wanted to continue with the relationship. Deciding that he needed to check Eric's reactions for himself he left for Wellington, arriving just before the school day ended. Nevin took him into the lounge.

'There's been quite a change in the boy since he stayed with those prospective foster parents.'

Eric came through the front door before he could say anything more.

'Hello sir!' he said chirpily.

'How did you enjoy your weekend, Eric?'

'It was good, sir. The man took me to see a cricket match and he showed me where Arsenal play. They live in Highbury.' His eyes sparkled. 'They've got a smashing dog. I had me own room.'

Kemp was delighted to see the boy's eagerness and asked for more details of how the weekend was spent.

'I helped with the garden.' And after a pause he said, 'It ain't half a smashing dog. I took it for walks and it kept chasing this stick.'

Eric became guarded when Nevin joined them. Guessing that the man had barely had time to get to know the boys, Kemp decided to ease the situation.

'Have you got time for a game of corners, Richard?'

It was a popular game in the house, but Nevin admitted that he hadn't had chance to learn it.

'Eric and I will show you,' said Kemp, leaving most of the explanation to Eric. Half an hour later the two of them were much closer.

'What did you call those people you stayed with, Eric?' Kemp asked afterwards.

The boy looked anxious.

'Well, the lady said I could call her aunt if I liked and I called him Uncle Bob when we went to play cricket near Highbury. His football team is Arsenal, the same as mine.'

'I shouldn't worry about it,' Kemp said. 'There's plenty of time to sort it out if you're going there again.'

'Can I, sir? She said I could – if you'll let me, Mr Nevin?' he added tactfully.

Nevin smiled and looked at Kemp for confirmation.

'It's fine by me, too,' Kemp said. 'You should write to tell them you enjoyed yourself. They'd appreciate that.'

After a long pause Eric said, 'I think I'd like to do that now. Would you help me, sir?'

Nevin fetched pen and paper and left them to it. Kemp sat down beside the boy.

'See how far you can get with the letter on your own. I'm sure Uncle Bob and Auntie Kay would prefer that.'

Eric began to write laboriously: *Dear Uncle Bob and Aunt Kay, I had a good time . . .*

While Eric was writing, Kemp reflected that the last time Bob and Kay Greening had looked after one of his charges for a few days, Bob's favourite football team had been Tottenham. Bob had obviously switched his allegiance to suit his young guest. He grinned as Eric looked up. He had been sucking the pen and blue ink was on his lips.

'How do you spell alsatian, sir?'

'D-O-G,' replied Kemp without hesitation.

Eric gave a hoot of laughter then returned to his writing, eager to build a relationship with his new family.

Watching his intensity, Kemp marvelled at the power and importance of a sense of belonging. The irony was all too obvious. He was constantly encouraging the youngsters he was responsible for to develop close ties, yet he had spent the years since his own adolescence avoiding relationships. Helen's behaviour might well have reinforced this original belief that erecting barriers to intimacy was wise, but his young charges were continually proving the reverse.

'You're sure to get a reply soon,' he told Eric when the letter was finished. 'And another invitation.'

The irrepressible youngster beamed.

The following morning Kemp answered the telephone to Jennifer Bowlby. She had been duty officer the night before and needed his help.

'I received a three year old girl named Julie Fleming into care,' she explained. 'Neighbours think that her mother has deserted her father, leaving Julie with him. They've been living in a flat in a private house in Clapton and appear to have no friends. Nothing is known of their history.

'Last night Mr Fleming left Julie alone in the flat when he went to the pub. According to a neighbour it's not the first time he's done this. Before leaving he had tied a cord from Julie's ankle to the cot to keep her safe – at least, we assume that's why he did it.'

'Good heavens!'

'I suppose he wanted to prevent Julie from reaching the window and falling out.' She sighed. 'Apparently he didn't consider that she might panic on waking or that the cord might tangle around her neck. Whatever his reasoning, Julie awoke to find herself tethered to the cot. She screamed and threw herself about. The commotion persuaded other tenants to break in to find the child wild-eyed and covered in perspiration.'

'How did we get to know about this?'

'Neighbours called the police, who asked us to help. I've spent a harrowing time calming the frantic child and Margaret spent hours in the office trying to find a vacancy for her. It was very tricky at such a late hour but she succeeded and we took Julie to the home last night.'

'So how can I help?'

'We've not seen or heard anything of Mr Fleming. Peter, would you mind calling on him? We need to tell him his daughter's been removed to a place of safety.'

'Of course! Off you go. I'll tidy up that side of things.'

'Mrs B has the details. You'll need to assess whether he should be allowed to have access to Julie. I confess I'd have great difficulty being objective with him, Peter. I think you know that?'

He heard the catch in her voice as she rang off.

Mrs Boulton supplied him with the address and he left for Clapton. He had no idea what type of man to expect and resolved to reserve judgement. Entering the large house he found an abject figure in clothes clearly slept in.

'What do you want?'

'I've come about your daughter.'

Long hair hung about Fleming's unshaven white face and his cheeks were hollow. There was despair in his eyes, which did not once focus on Kemp as he confronted him.

'We're going to have to take Julie away from you at the moment, Mr Fleming.'

The man did not react. Kemp asked to see where Julie had slept, for the purposes of his report. Fleming showed him the cot, which butted against a wall. He saw something unusual and bent closer to inspect it. On the wall, beside the cot, was an arc of small, dark red blotches. The design fanned out like a child's version of the rays of the sun.

Fortunately he was not squeamish for on closer inspection it seemed likely that the marks were made by the child squashing bed bugs. Aware that details would have to go to the sanitary inspectors, he hurriedly left the room and spoke sharply to Fleming, who was loitering aimlessly.

'The police know about the situation here. They know Julie's been left without adult supervision. May I suggest you consult your doctor, Mr Fleming? If you're not well, that might help you with the police, who may press charges.'

Fleming became alarmed, waving a hand in Kemp's face.

'I don't want no police here. They got no business meddling, they ain't.'

'But they will be here, Mr Fleming, believe me. The only way to protect yourself is to get a doctor to pronounce you as sick.'

Anxious to avoid the police, Fleming gave his doctor's name. Together they went out to a nearby phone box. With Fleming listening he advised the receptionist that an emergency had arisen and Fleming was on his way. He then bundled Fleming out and rang the number again. It was engaged. He pressed button B and collected his coins. Re-inserting them, he was relieved to hear a voice and hurriedly pressed button A.

He managed to persuade the receptionist to put him through to the doctor. He described the emergency and suggested that Fleming might need to be encouraged to enter an institution as a voluntary patient, or even need sectioning.

He badly wanted a wash and joined the queue at the Hackney Slipper Baths, hoping not be recognised. He pictured a suitable headline for the office meeting – COUNCIL OFFICIAL ADMITS NEED FOR CLEAN-UP – before pushing his way through the turnstile, treasuring a small tablet of soap handed to him with the towel.

When he got to the office, Kemp wrote a report for Jennifer Bowlby. He included his opinion that, subject to more information about the disappearance of the mother, little Julie's reception in to care might well be deemed to be 'long term'. It was an important statement for if the Children's Department could assume that the child was destined for a long stay in their care, they would make immediate plans to introduce Julie to 'aunts and uncles' who might become satisfactory substitute parents.

Jennifer and Margaret approved the recommendation. Mrs Boulton, taking the report, said, 'When the parents are shadowy figures, randomly dropping in and out of a child's life, it's almost impossible to obtain a stable foster parent relationship for them, isn't it?' She paused before adding, 'That's why it's so important to choose a partner wisely and cherish them for as long as you're given the opportunity. Every day's a bonus.'

Kemp looked up sharply, unsure whether she was talking about her past or his present, but her face was a mask of innocence.

15

'Everybody seems to be in today,' McGovern said, entering Reception. 'Shall we have a meeting at two-thirty to have a look at progress and problems? We'll begin with any good headlines to share.'

'That would be helpful,' Jennifer Bowlby said. 'Concentrating only on adoption isolates me.'

Kemp smiled at her. They were friends and guardians of intimate information about each other. Jennifer lived with a female friend and he had been invited to the house they shared in Wembley. No-one else in the office knew that it was unlikely that the tall, attractive, thirty-eight year old would ever marry.

She had an inkling of his secret too. She had said one day, 'It's so important that these adopted children have a sense of belonging immediately. I guess we all need that.'

In an unguarded bitter reply he had said, 'Belonging is for others.'

She had looked up very quickly and had seen the anguish in his eyes. He had little choice but to tell of the tragedy that had befallen his parents. She had cried for him but their secrets were never spoken of again.

In the group discussion with McGovern, Kemp was asked to give a progress report on Harry, and then Margaret told one of her cases. A knocking on the door interrupted them. Mrs Boulton came in, looking furious. Going straight to Kemp, she whispered in his ear. With the meeting suspended, her whisper carried, so that everyone knew that she had taken an abusive phone call.

Outside the room she stated tartly, 'The man on the other end of that line is no gentleman, and he has a quaint way of putting his views across. He's demanding to speak to you.'

Kemp picked up the phone and introduced himself.

'Eh! Ye'll be the black hearted villain.'

Amused by the archaic terminology, Kemp said, 'Who is this?'

'Ye might well ask, ye blackguard!' said the voice, which had an unmistakable Irish brogue to it. 'Me name is Mister O'Reilly. Ye've been dealing with me son.'

Kemp's spirits plummeted. From being relaxed about the telephone call, he now felt distinctly uneasy. He hadn't contacted O'Reilly since his visit to Eric but it appeared the youngster hadn't been so lax.

'Listen to this from a slip of a boy. "I don't never want to see you again."' There was the sound of apoplectic coughing at the other end, followed by a bellowed curse. 'Ye'll go to hell for your sins!'

Kemp winced, holding the phone away from him as the Irishman continued to call the wrath of God on to his head. Laying the blame squarely on Kemp's shoulders, he punctuated the harangue with other phrases from Eric's letter.

'What do ye think to this? "Me welfare officer has got me a good home and he says I don't have to come to you." What kind of letter is that for a loving father to receive, I ask ye?'

It was an indictment. He should have known that his preoccupation with Helen would affect his efficiency. The man had genuine cause for complaint and he obviously intended to take full advantage.

'Ye'll pay for this,' O'Reilly continued relentlessly.

'Ye'll regret you interfered with me and mine. Poncing about, interfering with kids. I know your game.'

Not wanting this theme to develop, Kemp interrupted him.

'I'll come and see you tonight, Mr O'Reilly.'

'Not before seven ye won't. Not before seven – and be ready!'

His tirade was now reduced to a mutter but the menace was unmistakable.

'Confirm your address, Mr O'Reilly,' Kemp said firmly, 'and I'll be with you at seven.'

Cursing, O'Reilly gave his address.

'Seven o'clock now see. It ain't no good ye coming early – I'll not be there. Ye'd better come or I'll be after ye, ye blackguard!'

He banged down the telephone.

Mrs Boulton, catching the drift from a distance, looked concerned.

'Are you sure you should go? Perhaps you should take someone with you?'

Kemp was too depressed to reply. Why had he allowed this to happen? He read the O'Reilly file again but there was nothing further to gain from it. True, he had no legal obligation to keep the father informed, but there was an ethical one that he had failed to honour.

He was concerned that if O'Reilly persisted in his complaint, the case could drag through the courts. The local newspaper coverage could stir up a reaction that would cause misery. He envisaged the headline: SON TORN FROM FATHER BY ARROGANT BUREAUCRACY.

It wasn't at all amusing: the happiness of his charge was at stake. While he was sure that Eric would be better off away from his biological father's home, there shouldn't be any dispute over where and with whom the lad would reside. He didn't return to the meeting but caught up with his reports until it was time to visit.

Mrs Boulton came to bid him goodnight and reiterated that he shouldn't call on O'Reilly unaccompanied.

'I can think of no one better to do battle by my side than you, Mrs B,' he said, 'but there's no point in testing Mr O'Reilly's patience more than is necessary.'

'Be it on your own head.'

He heard the outer door slam as she left the building.

Kemp carried on with his work. A while later a tap on the door startled him. Mrs Boulton carried in a tray of sandwiches, a pot of tea and a custard tart, which she knew was a favourite of his. She interrupted his thanks.

'I've got to be off. My friend will be wondering where I've got to, but you can't go to see that awful man on an empty stomach. It's a dreadful.evening, Peter, so you'd better leave enough time to be at Mr O'Reilly's for seven.'

'Bless you, my wonderful T.O.B,' he said teasingly. 'You really are a marvellous person to have on one's side.'

'Don't waste your charm on me, save it for O'Reilly. He'll need rather a lot of it, I fancy.'

He cautiously touched the back of her hand, wanting her to know he appreciated her concern. Mrs Boulton knew what T.O.B. stood for. He rather thought she took pride in it.

'Now you be careful.'

She hurried away.

Kemp drove through the ugly streets and houses of a part of Shoreditch currently under demolition. The low clouds had trapped the smoke from nearby factory chimneys and smog swirled about, making visibility difficult. This was an area where the street lighting hadn't been improved and it didn't augur well for his visit.

Searching for numbers on the doors of the little box-like terraced houses became impossible from a distance and he left his car. Before getting out he reached under the dashboard for his torch: it was often needed for finding an address in the back streets of the East End. The two-storey terraced houses abutted straight on to the pavement. There were rows of the grim dwellings.

After about a hundred yards Kemp guessed that he had found his destination. He checked the door for a number by the light of his torch but could find none. His wristwatch showed that it was just after seven. Standing in front of the door he could see a dim light through a tiny crack in it, indicating that there was life in the house.

Shining his torch over the door again he saw a shoebox top covering an area of missing glass; a nicotine-coloured stain creeping up from its lower edge. He couldn't find a bell or knocker. There wasn't a letterbox either, only a cut-out with bolt-holes either side. Finally he located a tarnished number plate dangling askew on the wall. Switching off his torch he was plunged into semi blackness again. The smog closed in about him, as if drawing a shroud over what was to take place.

He thought he could picture Eric's father as a hulking Irishman with beetle brows, wearing a leather belt with a brass buckle round his navvy-type trousers. Working in the strike-ridden docks, he would roll his own cigarettes. His rolled up shirtsleeves would reveal muscular arms displaying tattoos and his horny hands would be huge.

Kemp sought for a suitable newspaper heading, perhaps something to do with a barrage of plates hurtling down the passage as soon as the door was open: FLYING SAUCERS LAND ON COUNCIL OFFICER. He grinned.

The luminous hands of his watch pointed to five minutes past seven as he banged on the door. He imagined Popeye-like arms reaching out for him, pulling him in and bouncing him off the ceiling.

The door did open suddenly, and in the gloom of the passageway he could see very little. Then he dropped his gaze. He was peering at a small, bald-headed man with a rotund figure.

'Come in,' growled the diminutive Irishman, his unmistakable accent more menacing than musical. Kemp followed him into a poorly lit hall.

'I'm Mister O'Reilly and ye've got questions to answer, ye blaggard.'

He thrust a stubby finger at Kemp and then pointed in the direction of the pale light coming from a room at the end of the passageway. Despite his size the menace was obvious and Kemp went meekly past him. The Irishman closed the door with a bang.

A single light bulb hanging in the centre of the room produced dark shadows on the walls, intensifying the threatening atmosphere. It was totally inadequate for reading – but Kemp thought it unlikely that reading was what O'Reilly had in mind. Directly beneath the lamp stood a table and three wooden chairs. At one side of the room, where the light just penetrated, was a washbasin with half a dozen tiles above it as a splash-back. Against the opposite wall was a wardrobe. There was a low-slung, grubby sofa in front of it, while a heap of discarded clothes lay in the far corner.

O'Reilly pointed to the sofa with his stubby finger and Kemp guessed that the clothes had been tossed from it to ensure that he would sit there. He chose to misinterpret the signal and sat instead on one of the chairs. Not only was it more hygienic, it guaranteed ease of movement should the odd plate fly about.

Observing O'Reilly closely, Kemp saw he was wearing corduroy trousers, an open-necked shirt and a waistcoat. He did have beetle brows, which were now drawn together in an unpleasant grimace. He had a curious way of squeezing his eyes, as if he continually needed to refocus. It went well with the impression of concentrated venom. The degree of suppressed anger was obvious, for his voice was harsh with malice and every action was darting and violent.

'I've got no time for the likes of ye. I'll swing for one of ye one of these days, so I will!'

O'Reilly spat the words out, clearly working himself up for another barrage.

'Have ye got nothing better to do than make life difficult for the likes of us?'

Not getting a reaction, O'Reilly raised his voice and launched into a tirade against a vast army of civil servants and, in particular, council officials like Kemp. He listed every injustice that had ever been heaped upon him, including a recent rate demand for the premises, and he ended on a high note of exasperation: 'They're going to be pulled down anyway, so they are.'

Drawing breath quickly he continued, 'What do ye think ye are going to be doing with me boy, the ungrateful bastard?'

There was a more sinister edge to his voice now. Kemp, with limited options, decided to be firm.

'Well, Mr O'Reilly, let me tell you that in the first place you've no legal . . . '

He broke off as the man moved with lightning speed to the tall cupboard.

'Careful what ye say,' O'Reilly cautioned. 'I've got a witness here.'

He triumphantly swung the cupboard door open to reveal a little man standing inside. A slightly younger edition of O'Reilly, he was blinking sheepishly in the unexpected half-light.

As if regretting the premature disclosure of his ally, O'Reilly closed the door on his unfortunate helpmate. The humour of the incident pricked at Kemp's well-developed sense of the incongruous. No newspaper headline could quite match this situation, which had surely swung the initiative his way.

Frowning, Eric's father lowered his brows even further and for the first time he was silent, seemingly aware of his error. The old-fashioned clock ticked loudly. Kemp broke the silence.

'I don't mind having a witness, Mr O'Reilly. In fact I think it's a good idea. Why don't you let your friend join us?'

O'Reilly didn't reply but went over to release his companion. The significance of the Irishman's insistence on not arriving before seven was now apparent: the two men had been setting the scene to entrap him. The offer to sit on the sofa put the cupboard out of sight. The forty-watt bulb and the timing had all been part of their plan to intimidate.

'Why don't we sit around the table to talk?' Kemp

asked, subtly taking charge. He had guessed that the Irishman would be a smoker and might respond to a peace offering so had bought a packet of Woodbines and a box of matches. He laid them in front of him. A non-smoker himself, he was prepared to take an occasional puff for the sake of authenticity.

'Do you mind if I smoke?'

Without waiting for an answer he opened the packet and offered it to O'Reilly. The ploy was not welcome and the cigarettes were ignored. Fortunately the cupboard man leaned forward eagerly.

'I'm gasping for a fag,' he croaked, taking one gratefully. 'Me name's Sean. Thanks.'

His accent was not quite as broad as O'Reilly's.

'He does his own,' he added, pointing his thumb at his friend.

O'Reilly extracted a pouch and a packet of Blue Rizla cigarette papers from his waistcoat pocket. He proceeded to roll a cigarette, slowly and meticulously, watched in admiration by Sean. After several minutes he put the misshapen object in his mouth. Both observers relaxed when the straggly cigarette lit successfully.

The performance had reinstated O'Reilly to centre stage and he took his time before resuming hostilities. He drew smoke and watched it curl upwards.

Kemp slowly lit his own cigarette, knowing his attempt at a polished performance fell far short of O'Reilly's. He smiled at Sean, wondering how best he could use the man's more amiable disposition. It was obvious that he was the 'this bloke' Eric had spoken of, and that the two men shared the house. Under those circumstances he was unlikely to want Eric join their partnership.

A smoky haze enclosed the three men, almost

companionably. Kemp guessed that the Irishmen lived in a little world of their own that they didn't want disturbed so he began to stress, ever so slightly, the responsibilities involved in having Eric at home. He gave no indication that he intended to resist any claim from O'Reilly but tactically sought to know the reason for the man's reawakened interest in his son.

He didn't have to wait long. Sean started talking about waiting to move and, slowly, O'Reilly added his comments, letting slip that if Eric lived with him they would be placed higher on the housing list and thereby be re-housed sooner.

'We'd like one of those flats near the Horse an' Hound,' said O'Reilly. 'Sure it'll cost us a little more, but with the boy going to work soon that would cover the extra rent. Mind you, I'm not so sure now that the young wretch would hold a job for five minutes.'

Showing that he was considering their plans, Kemp pointed out that if Eric returned to his father's care early enough to affect the re-housing programme, his schooling needed to be sorted out.

'One of you will have to take him to school for a bit and collect him. He's not used to London. But of course, you can probably find a neighbour who could help.'

O'Reilly reacted predictably to the ludicrous idea.

'I'll not be beholden to any neighbours,' he said, scowling.

'I can understand that, but you don't want any truancy officers on your back.'

Sean shook his head vigorously at the prospect.

Careful not to expose his hand too obviously, Kemp said encouragingly, 'I daresay you would find a way of managing it between you?'

Sean now looked decidedly unhappy.

'You'd do well to help select a job where you can keep an eye on him when he finally does leaves school,' Kemp encouraged. 'Be firm and make sure he keeps at it. You don't want him to become a liability. Adolescence is a difficult age and, as you said, he's a bit headstrong.'

'Don't I know about that?' O'Reilly said. 'The little demon.'

Busy with their own thoughts, the three of them smoked in silence. After several minutes Kemp made an insincere offer.

'Would you like me to help arrange a meeting with the lad? I could be present and help keep him in line.'

'That I would not,' said O'Reilly. 'Ye know, I think that might be a bad idea. We'll let him stew, so we will.'

Sean nodded sagely. Kemp idly wondered how long he would keep up his silent agreement and whether it would be worthwhile getting him to speak out, but decided it wasn't weighty enough to have an impact on O'Reilly.

'I'm sorry I didn't notify you about the plans for Eric to leave the residential school,' Kemp told O'Reilly, 'but as you'd not been in touch with him for so long and his last visit had failed . . . '

O'Reilly accepted the apology and ignored the reference to the failed visit.

'I think maybe I was a bit hasty with ye.'

'I don't think the little bugger would settle in at all,' chimed in Sean, evidently delighted with the prospective outcome that would leave their friendship intact.

Kemp offered him a cigarette. He took one and O'Reilly followed suit.

Deliberately leaving the cigarette packet on the table Kemp said, 'I must be going. I'll be seeing young Eric again. Do you want me to try to get him to apologise for his letter?'

'No!' O'Reilly snapped. 'The little bugger's had his chance. I'll have nothing more to do with him.'

Sean looked at O'Reilly with glee, apparently confident that his friend was already adjusting plans that would affect the two of them only. Kemp stood up, inwardly very relieved for Eric's sake.

'So be it,' he said.

They shook hands amicably but O'Reilly had the last word.

'I don't know why you're working for that lot in the council. You don't seem like one of them at all. I'd give it up if I were you, so I would!'

Kemp saw it was intended as a compliment and thought it best not to comment. He was in good spirits as he drove home, replaying the image of O'Reilly acting like a magician and producing Sean out of a cupboard like a rabbit from a hat.

It had been an amusing as well as a successful evening, but in hindsight he recognised it could have all been avoided and he could take little credit from it. The evening was an example of brinkmanship. If he had done his job properly it shouldn't have been necessary. He had placed Eric's future in jeopardy. It had been totally predictable that O'Reilly would react to his son being snatched away from him, upsetting the plans he had made to which Eric was central. But for the action taken tonight, it could have resulted in a very unpleasant court case. Even if the verdict had gone against O'Reilly, it would have been a disastrous experience for Eric.

His thoughts turned to an earlier failure – Michael Grant. He compared it with the risk he had just taken with Eric's future. What did the two cases have in common? What must he learn to avoid another potential failure, one that might end with tragic consequences for one of the youngsters placed in his care?

His car idling in an impatient queue, he saw the answer in the traffic lights. There were times when he should slow down, even stop and wait. He needed signals on his personal journey. He needed the caution to listen and the stop to reflect. Perhaps he should add a speed limit. He remembered McGovern saying after the Michael Grant case, 'You need to slow down, Kemp.'

He arrived at his garage rather chastened, and hadn't been in his flat long when the phone rang. It was Mrs Boulton, apologising for ringing at a late hour.

'I know you're not going to be in tomorrow and I wondered if you wanted a letter to go to Mr O'Reilly?'

Her excuse for ringing him was so obviously to check on his welfare that he felt a rush of affection for her. Irreverently, in his mind's eye, he pitted the indomitable Mrs Boulton against the wild Irishman and decided that the Irishman would be no match for her.

'Thanks for calling Mrs B, but the correspondence can wait for a day. I'll deal with it when I come in.'

'And you're all right?'

'Oh, Eric's father's not really a bad chap, you know. He asked me to apologise to you for being rude on the telephone.'

'I should think so too!' she retorted.

'Actually, I don't blame him. I should have been in touch with him earlier.'

'You're not letting the boy go to him, are you?

'No, but that's not the point. He had the right to be advised properly of what action we proposed to take.'

'I believe you're right. Well said, Peter. Goodnight. Sleep well.'

He heard her put the phone down and replaced his receiver, wishing that it had been Helen rather than the T.O.B. who had shown such concern for his welfare.

16

Deviating from his normal route to Hackney to call at the premises of a commercial company in nearby Clapton, Kemp was warmly welcomed by the general manager. Two of the youngsters on his caseload were employed in their large warehouse. He was told that the company was well pleased with the two lads and he spent an official tea break with them. It confirmed his view that an interesting job and caring foster parents combined to create a simple and effective formula for many of his homeless youngsters.

Realising that he had parked his car close to where the Drews lived, he decided to make an impromptu follow-up call. Dennis would be at school but there was a strong possibility that Drew might be home as he did shift-work.

The dour man was not only available but surprisingly positive and forthcoming.

'Mrs Bannerjee said if I saw you I was to thank you for sorting out the visiting arrangement.'

'Is it working well from your point of view?'

'Yeah, Rashida's like a mum to him and makes up for me. I'm not very good at that side of things.'

Kemp took a few seconds to recover from hearing Drew refer to Mrs Bannerjee as Rashida.

'You've got to know Rashida Bannerjee well, have you?'

Drew looked sheepish.

'She collects Dennis from school on Thursday with her son and brings him back on Saturday morning. She gives him breakfast here and cooks one for me too. I insist she uses my food, mind. She says she'll cook me a curry one day but I'm not sure about that foreign food. But she's a very fine lady and says she loves looking after Dennis.'

'She's a very interesting lady,' said Kemp, deliberately repeating the words the police sergeant had used. It was clear that it was not only Dennis who was benefiting from Mrs Bannerjee's intervention into the male-only household. He was sure that Drew would have no knowledge that she had been a close friend of his wife. He left for the office fascinated by the riddle that was Rashida Bannerjee, but determined not to get involved.

He was half-way up the stairs when he heard Mrs Boulton calling his name. She sounded distraught.

'Thank God you're here, Peter. It's an attempted suicide – Mrs Stevens, that elderly lady you said should come and talk to me about her grandson.'

Kemp was incredulous.

'Mrs Stevens has attempted suicide?'

'No, no! It's her son. Jamie's mother's gone. A neighbour's been here, sent by Mrs Stevens. It's Jamie's father who has apparently attempted suicide. I don't know his condition. The flat is number 204. The grandmother's waiting for us.'

'How long's the wife been gone?'

Mrs Boulton was holding the door open.

'She's been missing several days. Margaret's duty officer. She's phoning for a residential vacancy for Jamie. Hurry!'

Kemp raced past her. Within minutes he was sprinting for the concrete stairs of the large block, climbing them two at a time. The door of 204 was open and Mrs Stevens was in the doorway. He remembered her as the hunched figure immobile at the bottom of the steps.

'Oh, it's you!' she cried. 'Please help me.' She was holding her side, as if in pain. He made a move towards her. 'No! Please help me son Charlie, sir. Me neighbour Thelma is with him. She's a nurse. I managed to pull his feet so his head come out the oven.'

She broke into a spate of coughing then, recovering a little, added with a sob, 'I turned off the taps. I couldn't do no more!'

Her voice mounted to a shriek as he hurried in to the kitchen. A blanket still hung down from the top of the gas oven, its door open. There were pillows on the floor, and although the window was open wide the smell of gas was strong.

The nurse was kneeling beside a man lying full length on the linoleum floor. His face was ashen and his head lolled sideways. White liquid drooled from his slack mouth. Several empty packets lay nearby, indicating he had taken a quantity of pills. He began to retch and more liquid spilled from him. The nurse signalled for help to turn his body so that gravity would assist in emptying his mouth. She was too engrossed to ask Kemp's identity.

Stevens was heavy but between them they managed to re-position him half upright. He continued retching into the bowl she was holding until there was nothing more to come. When the bowl was removed saliva slid down his chin and reached his open shirt. It clung there before dripping on to his half-open trousers, from which his belt had been removed.

While Kemp steadied the man, Thelma went to the bathroom to empty the bowl and came back with a damp flannel to wipe Stevens' face. She sat back on her heels, taking a well-earned rest.

'That's the best we can do until the ambulance arrives.'

'I'm Peter Kemp from the Children's Department. You look exhausted. Would you like a glass of water?'

Too weary to speak she nodded and checked Stevens pulse. His mother stood in the doorway.

'Is he going to be all right?' she sobbed.

Kemp handed Thelma the water and went over to Mrs Stevens. He put his arm around her shoulders.

'Thelma thinks so. You mustn't give in now.'

She stopped crying and broke away from him in an attempt to show she was in control. He kept his eyes on her.

'How is Jamie, Mrs Stevens?'

'Me friend's looking after him. What can I do?'

'Has the doctor been called?'

She nodded, her eyes fixed on her son.

'And the police?'

She nodded again.

'Where's Jamie?'

Clutching at his sleeve she said, 'Upstairs in me flat. Tell me what I've got to do.'

Two people appeared at the kitchen door, whispering.

'Please get rid of the spectators,' Kemp said angrily. 'I'll have a word with Thelma.'

Mrs Stevens ushered the two onlookers to the front door, where several more stood. Kemp turned to Thelma.

'Will you be all right?' he asked the nurse. 'I should look after the child.'

The siren of an emergency vehicle sounded nearby. She checked Stevens' pulse again.

'His pulse is irregular. Help me move him again please, and that'll be enough. The ambulance will be here in a moment.'

Stevens' eyes were half-open but not focusing and his head kept falling on to his chest. Kemp did as Thelma directed, moving a chair to ensure that his head was supported.

'You've done a great job,' he told her, helping her to stand as they heard a rush of heavy feet.

Two ambulance men came through the door. They immediately took charge, asking questions of Thelma at a rapid rate.

Mrs Stevens stood distraught in the doorway. Kemp joined her, knowing that he mustn't allow her to let go of herself.

'Your son's going to be okay,' he said crisply. 'We should look after your grandson now.'

Ignoring the small crowd on the landing he led her out of the flat. As they climbed the stairs Mrs Stevens gasped out the details.

'It was about half an hour ago – it seems so much longer. Jamie ran up to me on the fifth floor screaming his head off. Well, he'd woke up and found his dad, see. Oh, poor little mite!'

She paused for breath after mounting only a few steps.

'Me neighbour heard him and came to help. She said she'd look after him. Thelma lives next door and she came with me. When we were going down the stairs we met another of me neighbours and I asked her to call you people. I got into his flat first and pulled his head out of the oven. Thelma opened the windows else we'd all have choked.'

She was panting and wheezing, holding on to the

bannister with one hand and her right side with the other.

'You need to rest a bit, Mrs Stevens,' said Kemp, 'but I ought to check on Jamie as soon as possible. Will you be all right coming up on your own or shall I go and fetch someone to be with you?'

'I'll be all right after a few minutes rest. You go see to Jamie.'

'What's your friend's name, the one who's looking after him?'

'Mrs Thomas.'

'I'll run on ahead then. Are you sure you don't need help?'

She shook her head, attempting a smile. Kemp went up the stairs two at a time and located the flat immediately because a small knot of women had congregated outside. The door was open and he pushed past the group and went in. Two elderly women were standing by the door of a room on the left. As the flat was identical to the one downstairs, it had to be a bedroom. Jamie was on the other side of the door, holding it shut. He was sobbing hysterically.

'Don't you go in there yet, mister,' advised one of the women, who seemed to be in charge, 'or he'll scream his head off.'

'You'll be Mrs Thomas?'

'Yes. He's going to do himself an injury, poor little beggar.'

Her companion muttered sympathetically, 'Poor little sod.'

The group at the door were edging in to the flat and muttering among themselves.

'Pity about his dad topping himself,' said one.

Kemp ignored them and addressed Mrs Thomas.

'Mrs Stevens said you were keeping an eye on Jamie for her. She's on her way now so we'd better get rid of these onlookers.'

She nodded but made no attempt to do so. Kemp went over to the group of women, his arms wide.

'Sorry, ladies. It would be better for the boy if we could avoid a crowd.'

He shepherded them all through the door and then returned to the two women in the flat.

Mrs Thomas said, 'I think we'd best wait for his Nan before we touch Jamie.'

'I agree. I'll go back and see how she's getting on. Can you manage?'

'Don't worry,' she said, now an ally, eager to continue her support. 'I'll look after him.'

The knot of women had re-formed around the doorway as Kemp hurried out of the flat. He met Mrs Stevens at the top of the stairs, breathing heavily.

'Jamie's all right,' he reassured her, 'but you'd be better at calming him than anyone. See if you can settle him down.'

'Yes, he'll be okay with me,' she gulped.

Gathering her breath she walked unsteadily to her front door, holding on to Kemp's arm. The group made way for them. Mrs Thomas put her arms around Mrs Stevens, who returned the hug but quickly moved away.

'I must see Jamie.'

The screaming had subsided and she tried the door. It wouldn't open, but the noise started again.

'Go away, I want me daddy.'

'Oh, the poor little darling,' moaned Mrs Stevens, guilty over her previous preoccupation with her son.

Mrs Thomas took Mrs Stevens' hands to lead her away but she pulled free and bent down by the keyhole.

'It's your Nan, Jamie,' she whispered in a voice just loud enough to penetrate through to the bedroom. 'Let me in, love.'

There was silence before the door edged open and then widened. The little lad rushed into her arms. She went into the bedroom with him, closing the door behind her.

'Could you keep the crowd away?' Kemp asked Mrs Thomas. 'I'm going back to his father.'

'Is he going to be okay?'

'He'll recover.'

She accompanied Kemp to the door and addressed the neighbours.

'Jamie's dad is going to be all right and Jamie will settle now his Nan's with him. Best you all go home.'

She went back inside and closed the door. Pausing at the top of the stairs it occurred to Kemp that Mrs Stevens, with her neighbourhood support, would probably be a better choice to look after Jamie than the vacancy Margaret was seeking. Margaret would also handle this situation here much better than he.

The police had arrived and were already inside Stevens' flat. Showing his credentials, Kemp told them all he knew and assured them that Jamie would be the Department's responsibility. He then hurried back to the office.

'Thank goodness you're back, Peter,' Margaret said. 'We've been wondering what was going on over there. I've only got one vacancy so far, but it's way out of London in Hertfordshire. I'll continue to ring round.'

'Margaret, I think you'd be better than me in dealing

with this situation. You might find that Mrs Stevens could cope with Jamie.'

'Is that your considered opinion?'

'You'd be the best judge. I haven't said anything to her - but, yes.'

'Right, I'll get over there and assess the situation. Give me an hour. I'll get a message back to you if I don't think it will work. If I don't return, you cancel the vacancy. It's only provisional and the number's there.'

She pointed to the desk and then swept out, obviously preferring to be where the action was. Kemp sat down, grateful for the rest.

When Margaret returned she had made up her mind.

'The grandmother will do a good job,' she said. 'We'll need to subsidise her and she'll need to visit her son. Her neighbour promises to help and is competent. The nurse has also agreed to keep an eye on things.'

Within minutes Mrs Boulton came bustling in with a pot of tea, which she began to pour.

'I expect you both could do with this while you make your joint report,' she said.

She stayed long enough to hear them speak of the wife whose absence had triggered Stevens' suicide attempt, and as she left the room she said wickedly, 'That's what happens when you get yourself a bad one.'

Kemp reacted angrily but she had gone - and Margaret was laughing at him. He was furious that all his colleagues appeared privy to his frenetic love life, but he managed a rueful grin.

'She's incorrigible,' he said.

Mrs Boulton heard their laughter and pursed her lips grimly.

'You may well laugh, young man,' she murmured,

'but you'll regret getting entangled with that stuck-up madam.'

It was agreed between them that Margaret would continue with the case and do everything possible to avoid Jamie entering an institution, although both thought he looked like a candidate for long-term care. They had almost finished the report when Mrs Boulton appeared again. She spoke stiffly to Kemp.

'It's a personal call for you. Do you want to take it?'

Her tone of voice spoke volumes. Kemp raced upstairs while, down below, Mrs Boulton and Margaret exchanged meaningful glances.

Helen greeted him briefly.

'A little notice this time, Peter. Are you free tomorrow night?'

He closed his eyes, overtaken by disappointment.

'I've arranged a coaching session with Norman tomorrow night, Helen.'

There was a hiss of irritation at the other end of the line.

'Can't you put him off? Say you're sick or something?'

For all his intense desire to see her this was not an option he was prepared to consider. He took a deep breath.

'I'm sorry.'

There was a deadly silence. When Helen at last spoke again her voice was flat.

'I thought we should meet as soon as possible, but if you can't make it, fair enough.'

'I miss you Helen but I've a commitment. Why don't we have the weekend together? We could go away somewhere romantic.'

'I had planned for tomorrow.'

She left a small pause for him to give in. When he didn't answer she said, 'I'll get back to you some time,' and put the phone down.

There appeared to have been no improvement in his topsy-turvy relationship with Helen. The suggestion of a romantic weekend had produced no reaction whatever. Could this break down of their courtship be only because of his refusal to let his commitment to his youngsters take second place? There surely had to be a more rational but personal explanation for her selective availability.

The following morning McGovern came into his office.

'I hear everyone had a very busy time yesterday while I was at court. I've just spoken to Margaret. You all did very well. I understand this was the old lady and grandchild you spotted some time ago, Kemp? Well done.'

He perched on the corner of the desk, polishing his glasses while he peered down at Kemp.

'You might also like to know that the police picked up Bobby Grant and three others for demanding money with menaces. I'm told other charges are pending.'

Kemp said nothing but glanced up thoughtfully.

'What are you thinking now, Kemp?'

'I was wondering what chance there might have been of preventing Bobby G going down this destructive route if the Children Act had come in earlier.'

'Difficult to say, isn't it?' McGovern shifted his position. 'Unfortunately, from what you've told me about his mother's behaviour, she will have been a persistent influence on him. A case of, If you're being stung every day, you're likely to become infected.'

He stood up and walked across the office, stopping at the door to look back.

'Are you all right?' he asked thoughtfully.

He didn't expect an answer.

Kemp spent an extra hour in the office to give Norman time to get home to his digs for the coaching session. He hoped the young man's enthusiasm hadn't waned but as Mrs Windsor opened the door to him, she gave a warning glance before greeting him. Norman was at the sitting room door, looking miserable. He gave a twisted smile and slumped into a chair. Kemp feared the worst.

'Is the job going all right, Norman?'

'It's bad, Mr Kemp. It's a real sweatshop. There are these big vats with boiling soapy water and I've got to use this great paddle to keep stirring the clothes. Scum bubbles round me paddle and there's this great roaring noise all the time.'

Kemp endeavoured to lift the boy's mood.

'Do I gather you don't like it?'

'It's hard work and it's bloody boring. I'm sorry for me language, Mrs Windsor.'

Mrs Windsor said, 'Never mind. It isn't for ever.'

He appeared to perk up.

'Best get on, Mr. Kemp. I ain't beaten yet.'

He got out his books and laid them on the table from which he worked, giving a half-hearted grin to indicate he had shaken off his ill will.

'What's Pythagoras? It says apply Pythagoras?'

'Pythagoras's theorem is a way of providing a solution to a mathematical problem. Look, you've got a reference there.'

He pointed at one of the books from the library.

'Oh yeah.'

He worked on his studies for two hours without respite, Kemp helping him whenever he could.

Afterwards they went for a meal at a Chinese restaurant. Experimenting with chopsticks, Norman spread quite a lot of his food over the tablecloth.

'I ain't never used these before,' he said. 'A bloke could starve to death trying to eat with these things. Good job they've got these oil tablecloths to just wipe over.'

'Try holding the chopsticks this way. Look, hold the first one like this.'

Norman spent the next ten minutes trying to pick up various items with increasing success. When the next course was brought to the table he gleefully announced, 'When I'm a seaman and go to them eastern countries, they'll think I'm an experienced traveller, seeing as how I can eat with chopsticks.'

He was engaging company and in spite of being dissatisfied with his job, he was pleased with the wages and determined in his aim.

'It really will help if I've got a regular work record won't it, Mr Kemp?'

'You need a good reference from your job to counteract the poor school record, Norman, and your academic marks must be at least comparable with other applicants. Your strength will be in demonstrating your potential, in short how positive you can be once you know what you want.'

'I understand.' he said, sighing. 'I ain't helped meself, have I?'

Thinking of all the well-meaning individuals who had tried to rescue him from his aimless mind-set, and how resistive he had been, Kemp could only hope that this belated understanding had come in time to allow him to achieve his goal. Norman was maturing fast and Kemp had a comfortable feeling that no matter how devastated he might be if he did not gain acceptance into the Merchant Navy, he wouldn't go backward.

As they left the restaurant the waiter bowed to them. Norman was intrigued.

'I suppose they do that to get you to come again?'

'I think it's a little more than that. It's a polite form of behaviour in their culture.'

'I think it's good.'

When they were back at the lodgings Mrs Windsor joined them. She had obviously become a great fan of Norman's. He had told her all about his dream and his enthusiasm had captivated her.

'Did you have a good meal?'

'Great,' said Norman. 'I can use chopsticks now and this waiter bowed us out like we was special.'

'So he should. You are special.'

'What both of us? Mr Kemp as well?' He flashed a mischievous look at his counsellor.

'He bowed at both of you, didn't he? Don't you be cheeky.'

She looked at Kemp and smiled.

'I've never been to a Chinese restaurant,' she said. 'I don't know if I would like it. I've read that there's been quite an influx of Chinese people.'

Kemp had been quiet throughout their exchange, watching Norman. He thought he could read what was in the boy's mind and guessed that with his new wealth the lad was thinking of taking Mrs Windsor for a Chinese meal one day. He was liking Norman more and more and was, for the moment, less worried that he was challenging him to take a step too far. There was, in any case, no conceivable half-way point – giving a lesser target would be unacceptable to Norman.

'I'd love to keep Norman as a permanent lodger,' Mrs Windsor said when he had left the room, 'but even more than that, I want him to fulfil his dream. Is it possible for you to influence the interview?'

'I'm afraid I can't. It's now entirely up to Norman.'

'He's so grown up in some ways and so innocent in others, and he's had such a difficult start to his life. There are times when I want to hug him. I don't know how his grandmother can let him go.'

'Well, he was a handful,' Kemp confided, 'but your support will mean a great deal to him. If you find him losing his way I'm sure you'll remind him that he's not without friends. As long as he gets reasonable marks his personality may carry him through.'

'I do hope so,' she said, as Norman came back into the room.

'You haven't been telling Mr Kemp about me bad bits, have you?' he asked with a cheeky grin.

'I didn't know you had any bad bits, Norman.'

He gave her a frank stare, a look that Kemp had never seen him use before.

'You trust me don't you, Mrs Windsor?'

'I do, Norman, completely. Why do you ask?'

'No reason,' he replied. 'I think it's lovely.'

For a moment Kemp thought he saw the boy's lip quiver.

Driving home, he reflected that his life was full of drama on the surface, but that beneath it there was an emptiness. It seemed to centre on the subject of trust. Helen appeared to have given up on him and, worse still, he didn't know why. And the more he wanted to know, the less she wanted to tell him.

Things had gone suddenly awry during their last meeting, which seemed a lifetime ago. In a way it had been his fault. He had suggested they should they go away for the weekend.

'Not this weekend, Peter,' she had told him. 'I've things to sort out.'

He had raised his eyebrows but she had only said, 'I'll explain some time.'

Exasperated at her continuing secrecy he had burst out with, 'For goodness sake, Helen! Are we lovers or not?'

'I don't like being interrogated, Peter.'

'You tell me nothing, Helen. You're demanding too much of me.'

'And you don't own me,' she had said angrily.

'Of course not. Nobody owns you.'

For some reason the reply seemed to add fuel to her ill-temper. Waving him away she had fled into the bedroom, slamming the door behind her.

17

He awoke early to a beautiful morning. On the road before the rush hour, he drove to Hackney in record time. By the end of the day, he thought, Helen would surely ring. She might even surprise him and apologise.

As he walked into the office Mrs Stevens came into Reception with Jamie in tow. She greeted him with pleasure.

'We've come specially to see you, Mr Kemp.'

He shook her hand.

'How are things working out?'

'They're good, Mr Kemp. Jamie's dad's recovered and since it got into the news what he'd done, some people wrote to him and yesterday he got a job offer. Well pleased, he is. I came in to say we won't want support no more because we can manage. I'm going to move in with me son and look after Jamie.'

She turned to Jamie.

'Say hello to Mr Kemp, Jamie. You remember him, don't you?'

She gave the boy a light push towards Kemp. He was looking well, and smarter than the last time Kemp had seen him. He took the hand Kemp offered but clearly had no memory of him.

'I wanted to say it was a godsend, Mr Kemp, when you stopped your car and came over to us on them steps. Things wouldn't have turned out so well but for that.'

'How's your son, Mrs Stevens?'

She threw her hands up in the air.

'You wouldn't believe! Such a changed man. I think he must've got a shock. He's not going to have his wife back. They never did hit it off from the very beginning, and now I can look after him. He'll not go wrong again.'

He could see that she wanted to carry on talking but Mrs Boulton was making faces in the background. He held the door open for them and waved as they disappeared around the corner.

'That's a good way to start the day, Mrs B,' he told his would-be guardian angel, and hurried up the stairs to avoid a waspish answer.

He spent the rest of the morning on visits to four youngsters on his caseload, all of whom were making good progress.

'Would you like some tea?' Mrs Boulton had seen his car arrive and contrived to be at the door when he returned. 'It's already brewed.'

Having no wish to be preached at he replied, 'Only if I can take it upstairs. I have to catch up on some admin.'

The telephone interrupted them. Mrs Boulton picked it up, listened for a second and handed it over to him without a word. He recognised Helen's voice and reacted with pleasure, but the smile faded at her opening words.

'Are you free this evening?' she asked.

Once again she was phoning on impulse. There were no loving words of greeting. Yes, he was free, but the immediacy made it clear to him that he was not an equal partner in their dating arrangements and never had been. He had accepted her rules from the beginning because he had felt guilty that she saw herself as second best to the demands of his youngsters. He should have made her see how important it was never to break appointments with these damaged children. After all, they had been worse than second best for most of their lives. It was a question of building trust, but Helen had turned it into a conflict of interest.

'Just a moment,' he said. 'I'm downstairs. I'll take this call in my office.'

He handed the phone to Mrs Boulton, who looked sourly at the instrument.

Dashing up the stairs he admitted to himself that he was pleased that she hadn't wanted the row to continue. As their conversation developed he suggested a change of venue.

'What about staying at my place this evening, Helen?'

'Why not?' she responded positively, 'I'm sure I could get to you.'

She didn't drive, but he resisted the temptation to offer to collect her. Instead he gave directions for her to come by tube.

'I'll pick you up at Woodford station. I'm looking forward to seeing you.'

'Me too,' she replied, adding, 'I'm sorry it went wrong last time. I'll get to you at about six-thirty.'

Tonight was going to be different, he decided. Perhaps being in his territory would work its magic and they could find a better understanding.

Later in the day he took a call from Mrs Windsor.

'It's worrying but not serious – I think,' she said.

His stomach tightened.

'What's happened?'

'Norman decided to run away. He actually left his job.'

'Well that's it – his dream is blown,' he said resignedly.

'No, it isn't. He went back.'

'That still won't do. They'd take him back because

they need the position filled, but they're the nominated referees. They're duty bound to mention it in their reference and that will end his chances. I'm afraid they were slim enough as it was.'

Mrs Windsor was getting excited at the other end of the phone.

'No, no, you don't understand! He clocked out and then clocked in again. They don't know about it.'

'They will when they see his time sheet. How long was he gone for?'

'Only about twenty minutes.' He could sense the excitement at the other end of the phone. 'It's all right to do that because of the conditions he works under – all that heat!'

'I think you'd better tell me all about it,' said Kemp, wanting to be sure no harm had been done.

Her voice trembled.

'It's such a lovely story really.'

'Please tell me what happened, Mrs Windsor. I hope he hasn't weakened in his ambition.'

'I'll try to tell it as he told me. He came home and sat down with me and said he'd become so fed up with the horrible job – all that heat and noise and looking at the scum settling round his paddle. He said he started shouting at the top of his voice to get rid of the frustration, knowing no one could hear him.'

She paused for breath.

'Then he said he felt so alone with nobody to hear him and nobody caring that he decided he was going to run away.'

'I stopped him there. I gave him a hug and said I cared and so did you, and then he said he wasn't sure about that.'

'What did he mean, Mrs Windsor?'

'I asked him that and he faltered a bit and said it was your job to come and see him. I said what about the extra coaching you'd given him, and he said you might get paid overtime or something, or maybe it was all part of some huge confidence trick to keep him quiet . . . I'm just telling you what he said.'

Her voice trailed off.

'Carry on, Mrs Windsor. It's all right.'

'He said you were funny at the beginning and told him to disappear because you couldn't be bothered with him.'

'He's quite right, I did say that.'

'But he said it was odd because later he saw you get very angry when he told you his Gran said he had bad blood in his veins. He said these things were going backwards and forwards in his head and he felt he shouldn't really trust you. That's why he decided to clock off. He thought he could always collect the money he'd earned when the chase was over.'

'How was he when he told you this?'

'That's the amazing thing, Mr Kemp – he was different.'

'How different?'

Kemp leaned into the phone, anxious to catch every syllable.

'Well, he looked different. Sort of purposeful, you might say. He said he got outside the works without being seen, looked down the road and wasn't happy. He stood there with all these thoughts churning inside him. He stuck his hands deep in his pocket and then . . .'

She was crying.

'Take your time Mrs Windsor. What went wrong?'

'Nothing, absolutely nothing! When he stuck his

hands in his pockets he felt a key in one of them. It was the key to the house. It made up his mind for him.' Her voice trembled. 'He decided he was being trusted and chose to go back to work after all.'

At the other end of the line, Kemp heard a sob.

'Norman said he wasn't going to run away any more because that was going backward and he was going forward. He thanked me and . . . oh, it feels wonderful.'

Kemp said goodbye to her with a lump in his throat.

That evening he arrived at the station car park twenty minutes early. It was full of homecoming commuters. Watching them as they came out of the subway in droves, he positioned himself so that he could assess Helen's reaction when she caught sight of him.

His spirits lifted as he saw that she was one of the first to alight– surely a good omen? As usual she was smartly, even expensively, dressed in a pale pink suit, her blonde hair drawn back from her face and held in place by tortoise-shell combs. As she walked through the barrier she drew the attention of others who were waiting. She was good-looking and knew it, but he thought she had a right to this conceit.

Seeing him, she quickened her pace even further and her face brightened into a smile. He stepped forward to embrace her.

'Hello, darling.'

He was happier than he had been for many days as he told her about the little restaurant he had booked.

'It has a limited menu but it's good food. Not up to Beauchamp Place of course.'

'It sounds good to me,' she replied, throwing a quick glance in his direction.

Later he was to remember that look but for the moment he was absorbed with trying to be the perfect host. They reached the restaurant and he watched with indulgent approval as she made her way to the table reserved for them. Following behind her, he was well aware of the admiring glances she drew.

While they were waiting for the menu he said, 'What work do you do, Helen?'

'I don't at the moment,' she said quietly, clearly wanting to resist his questioning. He was annoyed with himself.

'Fair enough.'

Wanting to avoid any mood changes, he trod carefully for a while. When they were eating he mentioned their first meeting.

'You've been very reticent about the conference, Helen. What did you really think to it?'

He had struck the wrong note – again.

'I found most of the delegates incredibly boring, totally involved in other people's messy lives and apparently completely unable to have a life of their own.'

Her face was flushed. He laid down his knife and fork. She had spoken unkindly and it had implications for him.

'Is that how you saw me?' he asked quietly.

'No. Well, yes, a bit, but you were different. You were alive. You weren't parading your commitment to the unwashed all over the place. It was one of the reasons I was attracted to you.'

He found her description of the underprivileged offensive, but gave ground on the assumption that she had felt belittled and was angry. He changed tack.

'How do you manage without a . . ?'

'Don't go on, Peter.'

She directed a cool glance at him. He ignored the warning.

'What's your particular interest? Are you . . ?'

'Peter, you have your interest in those young people and give them priority over me, so you can't be surprised if I deny you access to part of my life. Perhaps my interests and yours can come together, but they won't if you keep on at me, wanting to know everything I'm doing. I'm a private person and I don't want to be analysed. Try just being rather than doing.'

Ordinarily, if someone had spoken to him like this, he would have pursued the issue, but he was out of practice at being a lover and guessed he could be very disappointing in the amount of attention he gave to her. She wanted to be number one in his life but he couldn't give her precedence over the welfare of his charges.

The rest of the meal was a very tentative affair but back in the flat things began to return to normal between them and she asked to see the bedroom. Once there she lay down, pulling him beside her, and kissed his mouth. Evading his encircling arms she kissed his neck. Undoing his shirt she continued to plant kisses over his chest. Her lips slid down across his stomach, unhurriedly down and down. They were lovers again.

Sometime later she broke the silence.

'I'm sorry,' she whispered. 'It's so difficult and you don't make it easy!'

'But what's difficult?' he begged.

She shook her head.

In the small hours of the morning her hand crept through the coverlet and found his hand, bringing him out from a deep sleep.

'Love me, Peter,' she whispered.

Not for the first time that evening he misunderstood her. He turned to her and clumsily sought her lips.

'You're insatiable,' he said, moving to touch her.

Helen sat upright, disengaging herself. The action startled him. He struggled to peer at the luminous hands of his watch.

'What time is it?' she asked.

He groaned.

'It's one-fifteen.'

'I must go,' she said. 'I want to be up early this morning. Are you going to drive me back or shall I ring for a taxi?'

The words were unbelievable. Suddenly fully awake, he was aware that she was angry. Then he recognised that he had made a terrible blunder. For the second time this evening he had managed to humiliate her. Half asleep, he had misinterpreted her loving overture as a sexual invitation. He ventured a softer approach.

'Forgive me, I'm sorry!'

She stared coldly back at him, not bothering to answer. He could see that she had completely switched off from him, but despite his clumsy comment he wasn't about to plead. After all, they were supposed to be lovers. Surely a single thoughtless remark did not merit this degree of reaction? He shrugged his shoulders and spoke quietly.

'You'll need to wait while I get the car.'

He took his time putting on his clothes, all the time hoping she would change her mind. But when she returned from the bathroom she was preparing to leave.

'I'm going to the garage now,' he said.

She did not respond and continued to ignore him

when he went to the door. He felt he was in the presence of a different woman. He went outside, still moving slowly to give her plenty of time to relent. It was a moonless night. The street lamps had been switched off at midnight and it was a dark, unwelcoming world that he entered.

There was an edge to the contrition he felt, for she was behaving more like one of his clients than a lover. He did not want to see her in those terms, but her mood swings spoke of ambivalence.

With part of him still hoping that she would change her mind, he collected his car and parked in a spot that would be secure for the rest of the night. It was a waste of time, because he found her standing fully clothed by the door. He walked with her to the car and, perversely, opened the back door for her: he had no wish to have her po-faced beside him all the way to Kensington. As he drove the car's headlights picked out shaded trees and houses. The ratio of one to the other began to reverse the nearer he came to town. There was little traffic and few pedestrians, but there were shadows everywhere.

Arriving at her flat he went up with her in the lift and inserted her key in the lock. Moving inside she framed her face in the partially closed door.

'You won't mind that I'm too tired to be a good hostess. I won't be free at the weekend. I'll ring you sometime – but not immediately.'

She closed the door on him.

Kemp, unused to such irrational treatment, was nonplussed. Her behaviour was out of all proportion. He was furious with both himself and her. She wasn't merely dismissing him, but both of them as a couple.

It had been so good – why was she behaving like this?

Heading eastwards he tried to discard the emotional backlash of her extraordinary behaviour and put himself in her shoes, recalling her words on waking, 'Love me, Peter.' He now believed it to have been an overture to bond much closer. In the small hours of the morning this very private person had been ready to tell him all he wanted to know and, not unnaturally, had begun by asking him to love her for herself.

His interpretation of their early morning disaster made him feel guilty, but this was tempered by his disappointment at the way she had referred to his colleagues at the conference. Her criticism of the delegates – suggesting they were made whole only by their significance as rescuers – was a harsh assessment of some very fine people. It must apply to him also, implying that the commitment he had demonstrated for so long was no more than a prolonged search for victims to feed his need to be needed – in effect accusing him of participating in deep emotional experiences from a vantage point of safety.

The route he took back to his sterilised bachelor existence in Woodford took him through the familiar and relatively tree-less streets and houses of the East End. Within these streets it was true that he never paraded his emotions, for it was important that he remained detached from the melodrama in order to bring cold reasoning to bear. Inevitably his work gave him insights into the anxious, impulsive lives of many troubled people who moved effortlessly in and out of their relationships, without any of the agonising in which he was indulging. Some could be so casual in their intimacy, others so close.

He recalled meeting extremes in the same house. After several years of refusing to give her husband a divorce, an unforgiving wife had sworn to the Children's Department that the two boys of the subsequent union were in moral danger. He had visited and found a devoted partnership with two well-loved sons. On the floor below a husband lurked in the stairwell, waiting for the stranger he had propositioned in the local pub to finish using his wife. What could he learn from these conflicting examples of intimacy?

Had his preoccupation with the tangled emotions of others made him unable to respond naturally to the demands of an intimate relationship of his own? Was he nothing but a professional voyeur?

He had discovered much about the vagaries of human nature during the last few years, but he had always been the onlooker and the outsider. He had met harsh prudes and gentle prostitutes, the strong that were weak and the weak that were strong. He had seen beauty in dark places and dark places in people's hearts. He had learned so much in so short a time, but no golden rules about how to express love to someone.

Kemp garaged his car and made straight for the bed he and Helen had shared just a short while ago. He fell asleep, but in sheets still holding Helen's perfume he was repeatedly dragged back to the edge of consciousness, his body taut as a bowstring. His fingers clawed at the sheets, drawing them tightly around his knuckles. The sense of purpose and direction that had been his gift from boyhood seemed to have deserted him.

'My God!' he whispered into the enveloping darkness, 'I'm only half a page of Braille ahead of my clients.'

18

Nothing had been resolved but he knew that, whatever the interpretation of his motives, he was happiest doing what he did best: working with his young clients.

Mrs Boulton brought him a cup of tea.

'Thank you, Mrs B,' he said, gratefully. 'I did miss breakfast this morning.'

She shook her head, hesitating at the door. Apparently something else was on her mind. He looked at her encouragingly.

'Did you know that Norman almost ran away but changed his mind?'

'Yes, I did. Mrs Windsor told me. How do you know?'

'He rang here just after you left. He wanted to tell you but told me instead. He seemed very pleased with himself.'

'What did he have to say?'

'That I was to give you this message: "Would you tell Mr Kemp that Nomadic Norman decided to run away but changed his mind. Tell him it's me bad blood keeps coming out." Those were his actual words.'

'What was your response to that?'

'I told him he's a young rascal and he'd be getting me into hot water. I also said he could talk to me anytime if you were out. He seems a good lad.'

'He's a joy to work with and it's fascinating to watch him mature.'

She beamed.

'Is there any more you can do for him?'

'Norman clearly detests his job but it's important that he keeps at it if he wants to enter the Merchant Navy.

This incident could be construed as a warning. I'll visit him this evening.'

Kemp arrived at Mrs Windsor's house late in the afternoon, wanting to talk to her before Norman came home from work. He found her even more excited than she had been on the phone.

'I've been out most of the day but look what I've come home to!' She rushed him into her sitting room. 'Oh! I do wish Norman would hurry. Look, Mr Kemp! Did you know about this?'

She held up an envelope with MN printed in the corner. Kemp's brow furrowed.

'Oh dear, this could be awful timing.'

Mrs Windsor put her hand to her mouth.

'You don't think it's a refusal?' she said, looking alarmed.

Kemp shrugged.

'It could be. It's too late now to ring and ask my contact at the Merchant Navy office.'

They sat opposite each other, the envelope on the table between them. After a while Kemp said, 'I must admit I'm tempted to steam it open so that we can be prepared for the worst.'

Mrs Windsor was shocked.

'Oh, we mustn't do that! If it's bad news we'll have to help Norman get over it. But I hope so much that it's good news. He deserves it.'

She twisted her lace handkerchief in her lap and sighed, while Kemp paced the room. They heard a key in the front door lock. Mrs Windsor jumped up, wringing her hands.

'I'm home,' Norman called, approaching the kitchen.

'I'm in the sitting room, dear!'

Her words tumbled out in her excitement.

He came in, obviously surprised to see Kemp. He opened his mouth to speak, but Mrs Windsor held out the envelope. He saw the letters MN, then looked at their worried faces.

'What's it say?' he asked hoarsely.

'We don't know,' Mrs Windsor said.

'You open it,' he said abruptly.

'Oh no. It's your letter.'

'Perhaps it says they don't want to see me.'

'You should put it in the dustbin then.'

Norman was recovering his composure.

'Is that before or after I've read it?'

'For goodness sake open it,' she said. 'The suspense is unbearable.'

Kemp felt the same. The fingers of his left hand hadn't loosened on the arm of the chair since Norman had come into the room.

Norman turned his back on the two adults as he tore open the envelope and took out a single sheet of paper. He quickly scanned it then turned to face them, tears in his eyes. Mrs Windsor gasped.

In a strangled voice he said, 'It's an invitation to go for an interview for entry in to the Merchant Navy Sea Training School.'

Mrs Windsor clapped her hands, gave a little scream and rushed to hug him, tears streaming down her face. Norman lifted her up and twirled on the spot.

Kemp waited until the lad had set his landlady down before shaking his hand and clapping him on the back.

'Well done, Norman! Well done!'

'Can you stay and check my work please, Mr Kemp?'

'Of course.'

'You know I nearly threw it all away yesterday, sir? I was so bored with this job.'

His cheeks glowed but his bright eyes were thoughtful.

'The important thing is that you didn't run away,' said Kemp.

While they had been talking Mrs Windsor had slipped out of the room. She returned with three glasses and a bottle of sherry.

'It's a treat for a very special occasion, Mr Kemp.'

They drank a toast to a successful interview.

Norman wanted to study, infused with new energy. He was clearly thrilled with the opportunity and shaken by the ease with which he could have lost his dream.

After an hour and a half of checking his work Kemp said, 'I'll be off now, Norman. I'll look at what you're doing tonight the next time I visit. You know you must keep studying right up to the last minute? I'm sorry to be a Jeremiah but your chances of getting in are still slim.'

'A what, Mr Kemp?'

'It means a person who fears the worst.'

'I know me chances are thin, Mr Kemp, but whatever happens I'm going to keep going. Remember that stuff I told you at the beginning about wanting to be a master criminal – that was all kids' stuff. It seems ages ago now. Can you please come tomorrow?'

In his office the following morning Kemp studied his cactus. The tiny flames of a week or so ago were now more definite, but they still looked fragile. He never ceased to be amazed that such an uncompromising prickly plant could produce such delicate beauty.

Mrs Boulton knocked at his door, eager to hear about his meeting with Norman.

'He's been called for interview,' Kemp said, smiling at her.

'Oh, that's splendid news – and coming so soon after he nearly gave up! It's incredible! I'm so pleased for him, and glad he won his personal battle before he got the letter.'

'Norman's a cheeky beggar, but in spite of the life he's led he seems to be working things out,' said Kemp, feeling some satisfaction.

He rang the Merchant Navy office and spoke to Malcolm Wilkinson, the recruitment officer. He expressed his pleasure at Norman's letter of invitation, but Wilkinson responded a trifle scathingly.

'We'll need that reference from his current employer, and since his CV is a bit sparse, it would be useful to have the backup of a personal reference from you about the boy's character and his ability to bring credit to the service.'

There was the faintest of pauses while Kemp weighed in the balance the aspirations of countless other young people who might pass through his hands in the future. He remembered the sullen insolence when he had first met Norman; the train journey when the boy had walked away from him; the tears that he had refused to witness when Norman was first placed with Mrs Windsor; and the study hours he had spent trying to avoid exposing those wasted school years. It was a pause Wilkinson did not fail to notice.

'Mind now, Kemp, if he proves unreliable it's bound to affect your credibility as a sponsor of other young people in the future.'

Kemp spoke firmly.

'Norman's a good prospect – fit, intelligent and motivated towards a life at sea. I'm prepared to write a letter confirming this.'

Mrs Boulton, guessing the nature of the conversation, had held her breath and now breathed out slowly. Wilkinson accepted the assurance but was seemingly far from convinced.

'It can only go some way towards compensating for his limited CV,' he warned.

'The letter will be in the post tonight. You're going to see him for yourself soon. You'll like him. He's a great lad.'

'I accept what you say but I can't influence the tests. He'll still have to pass those on his own account.'

'Your intelligence tests give a prediction of potential, which is important. You'll see.'

Kemp rang off.

'Climb this hill, Norman, and you start level with the rest of us,' he said out loud. He turned to Mrs Boulton. 'I'll have to give him another coaching session tonight.'

She nodded and left the room.

'All I need now,' thought Kemp, mocking himself, 'is for Helen to ring up and for me to tell her I can't meet her this evening.'

He grimaced ruefully, sure that she wouldn't be phoning.

At the end of the day he went to see Norman. He found him nervous, and desperate to have his homework assessed. Mrs Windsor gave up the sitting room to them and promised to provide a meal.

Despite his apprehension about the quality of his

homework Norman asked, 'Can we take Mrs Windsor to that Chinese restaurant tonight, sir? I want to treat her. She doesn't go out much and she's been very good to me, Mr Kemp.'

'That's an excellent idea. I'll ask her to come back in here. She'll probably refuse, but you can persuade her.'

'There's no need to take me out, Norman dear,' Mrs Windsor said when she rejoined them. 'You need to save your money and it's no trouble for me to prepare a meal for us.'

'Are you turning me down, Mrs Windsor? I ain't having none of that.' Turning to Kemp he said with mock severity, 'This is the first time I've asked a lady out, Mr Kemp, and I gets rejected. Do you think Mrs Windsor could be doing long-lasting harm to me future love life?'

Not giving Kemp a chance to respond, Norman turned back to Mrs Windsor. Placing his hand on his heart he said cheekily, 'If you care even a little for me, Madam, please do me the honour of allowing me to take you to dinner tonight.'

'The cinema is having too great an impact on you, young man!' she said, clearly moved, although doing her best not to show it. 'But how can I resist when the invitation is so charmingly extended?'

She went over to where he was sitting and put her hand on his shoulder.

'Thank you, Norman, I'd love to be your dinner guest tonight. I'd better go and change so that I don't let my young escorts down.'

Norman stood up and bowed as the Chinese waiter had done.

'We're honoured, Mrs Windsor.'

She lightly tapped the side of his face.

'That's enough of your charm. Go back to your books.'

Blushing, she glanced across at Kemp as she left the room. What a find she had been, he thought, only to be brought back to earth by Norman holding out three notebooks. He hurried through them while the lad watched anxiously.

'What do you think of me homework, Mr. Kemp?'

'It's like the curate's egg.'

'What's that mean?'

'Good in parts.'

'Show me the bad bits,' said the determined youngster.

'We can't predict the questions, Norman.'

'We'd better do a bit more then.'

His absorption was complete for another forty-five minutes. It was unfortunate, Kemp thought, noticing the concentration on Norman's face, that the selection committee wasn't present to witness this remarkable level of commitment.

At the restaurant Mrs Windsor looked around curiously.

'This is all very exciting, Norman,' she said. 'I haven't been taken to dinner since my husband died.'

He looked at her affectionately.

'This is just the beginning, Mrs Windsor. When I comes home on leave, me and you are going to explore many new places.'

'It's always a good idea, Norman, to have a back-up plan in case you can't achieve the first one,' said Kemp.

He was careful to avoid saying 'failed', but anxious that the boy should face reality.

'I don't want to think about anything else. I've set me heart on the Merchant Navy.'

'But you can't just expect to pass, can you?' said Mrs Windsor. 'There'll be so many who want to get in.'

Kemp shook his head very slightly, indicating that they had best drop the subject.

'He knows the odds are against him, don't you, Norman?'

'Yeah, I know,' Norman said dejectedly, but a minute later he cheered up when the chopsticks were laid before them.

'Come on, Mrs Windsor, I'll show you how to use these.'

To Kemp's amusement Norman had brought three toffees, which he laid on the table. Under his earnest guidance Mrs Windsor practised using the chopsticks to pick them up. Her efforts were hilariously unsuccessful and when the food was brought to the table she used a spoon and fork, expressing her admiration from time to time at her companions' skill.

'By the way, Mr Kemp, Jeremiah's a character from a Dickens novel, "Oliver Twist",' Norman said.

'How do you know that?'

Wetting a finger and pointing it in the air as if testing the direction of the wind, Norman said, 'I asked for help, Mr Kemp. Do you remember telling me that's what I should do?'

'You amaze me,' said Kemp.

Mrs Windsor laughed, and patted her protege's arm. Norman looked pleased with himself as he spooned more rice on to his plate.

Singing enlivened the journey home. Mrs Windsor initiated it – she had a strong voice. To Kemp's surprise, Norman joined in without a trace of self-consciousness. Their duets seemed well rehearsed, and then Kemp remembered the piano in Mrs Windsor's sitting room and realised how some of Norman's evenings had been spent.

'You *both* amaze me,' he said, and merrily joined in the singing of a chorus.

It was not yet eleven when Kemp parked his car in his garage. Tempted by the balmy evening he walked for a while along the tree-lined avenue. As he breathed in the mild fresh air he reflected that his life was something of a roller coaster.

The upside was his work and the downside the void left by Helen. The shock of hearing her describe the under-privileged young as 'the unwashed' belatedly surfaced from his subconscious. It was offensive.

Mrs Boulton's suggestion that he had made a bad choice probably had less to do with intuition than with her speaking to Helen while transferring calls and observing his reactions following them. Either way, it did nothing to make him comfortable with the pearls of wisdom she continued to trot out, however much she had his best interests at heart.

He would shortly be duty officer, and Mrs Boulton was sure to continue her campaign. He considered writing down several of her trite one-liners and handing her the list the moment she came out with any one of them. Within seconds, however, he felt ashamed that he should consider allowing his distress to alienate him from an excellent colleague for whom he cared.

As it happened, his stint as duty officer proceeded amicably and without emergencies. He was able to plan for a number of statutory visits. One was to Harry. It wasn't enough that he had spoken to Mrs Glenn on the phone: he was required to call at the house, unannounced, and personally check the boy's well-being. He remembered, uncomfortably, that the only time he had delayed a follow-up had resulted in Michael Grant having his freedom curtailed. He had no wish to have a similar failure on his conscience.

He left the office before five, coolly telling Mrs Boulton that he was off to see Harry Weston.

'Good luck,' she said. 'Drive carefully.'

It was apparent that she wasn't deceived by his casual manner and he guessed that she sensed his unhappiness.

He calculated that Harry and his uncle would have returned from work by the time he reached Loughton. He was keen to see the big youth again and to discover whether any changes had occurred. Perhaps the Glenn household might bring a little warmth back to his own frozen heart.

Driving through the lovely Essex countryside he became increasingly eager to see whether Mr and Mrs Glenn's faith in themselves was justified. He pulled up in front of their house. Glenn answered the door, greeting him warmly.

'It's good to see you, Mr Kemp,' he said, shaking hands firmly. 'Come on in. Harry's upstairs changing his clothes. I'll tell him you're here but you go on in to the sitting room to see my missus.'

Mrs Glenn sat with a bag of socks beside her. She beamed a welcome and patted the seat next to her.

'Come and sit down, Mr Kemp. Don't mind me carrying on with me darning, will you? I don't know what you men do to socks.'

As she tucked the darning mushroom inside yet

another holed sock, Kemp was reminded of his mother who had done the same task for his father and himself.

He heard someone coming noisily down the stairs, as if taking them two at a time, then Harry burst in to the room. The sullen expression that Kemp had thought a permanent feature had disappeared, and in its stead was a beefy young man with an open expression. He grinned, offering his hand to Kemp, but didn't speak. Glenn came in a few seconds later carrying a tray laden with glasses, bottles of beer and lemonade.

'Will you have a beer, Mr Kemp, or would you rather have something else?'

Kemp accepted a beer. Glenn handed a shandy to Harry and lemonade to his wife. Raising his glass he said, 'Here's to you, Mr Kemp. We're very happy we've got Harry with us.'

Harry smiled self-consciously as he raised his glass.

The Glenns had an endearing way of seeking confirmation from Harry each time they spoke about him.

'He's doing fine, ain't you Harry?' said his aunt, looking fondly at the big youth.

'Yeah.'

Harry's eyes followed Mrs Glenn's every move. Looking on approvingly, Glenn added his weight.

'Doing all right at work too, aren't you boy?'

Not only did he agree with his wife's verdict on Harry but, that evening, he was taking him to his men's club.

'You'll have to excuse us, Mr Kemp,' he said, 'but it's time young Harry and I were off. We've entered a darts competition. Harry's me secret weapon and I'll be in trouble if we're late.'

Kemp stood up, saying he must leave also.

'Oh, must you go?' said Mrs Glenn. 'I'd like to talk with you for a while, unless you've got somewhere else to visit?'

'No, I haven't, but I don't want to take up any more of your time.'

'Well, if it's all right with you, I'd like your company while these two are out.' She kissed her husband goodbye and then Harry. 'But first I'm going to get you something to eat. You can't have had anything before you came here.'

Kemp began to protest but she had already gone, reappearing after a few minutes with ham, a slice of pork pie, salad and buttered bread. She had also made a pot of tea.

'Now, you eat up young man – and there's plenty more where that came from.'

'This is wonderful, Mrs Glenn, and very kind of you.'

'Nonsense. Now you eat and I'll talk.'

He learned that she was the eldest of a family of three girls. She went on to give details.

'Harry's mother, Laura, is the youngest. I always felt responsible for her but I couldn't control her. We had a decent life in the East End, you know. We didn't have a lot of money but as kids we was happy. Me dad was working in Covent Garden and at weekends he used to bring Ma bunches of flowers home. It was lovely.

'The house always smelt of flowers. At Christmas it was all holly and mistletoe, everyone kissing everybody else. Me dad used to love that – always hugging and kissing whenever he could get hold of me mum or us girls. Then he fell ill and passed away inside six months.

'The fun seemed to go out of the house when he went. Me mum refused to leave her room most days.

Molly's two years younger than me and between us we done all the shopping and washing and ironing. It was tough then because me dad's pension didn't go very far. Molly got out of the house as soon as she could, and I don't blame her. She married young. I only saw her a little after that but I think she's happy.

'I'm afraid me mum lost interest in life and began to stay in bed all day. It wasn't long before she passed away. I got a job and tried to look after the food and the bills and make ends meet. We used to get hand-outs from dad's old mates, but you can imagine that the house never smelt of flowers again.'

As Mrs Glenn spoke, Kemp thought of his own youth and identified with the feelings of desolation as she described how first her father, then her mother, slipped away, leaving an ultimate sense of being abandoned.

He couldn't help but ask, 'How would you describe how you felt?'

'Cheated,' she said without hesitation.

Kemp laid down his cup of tea, his hand trembling slightly. He knew that feeling. He could only marvel as she described how she had gone on from there, building a family of her own and a new life. He felt small beside this towering character.

'Laura lived with Jack and me for a while. She started dolling herself up when she went out. She was always coming home with new clothes she'd bought. I knew where the money was coming from but she wouldn't listen to me. She got pregnant and moved in with her friends. She seemed to cope with the baby when it first came and we didn't see much of her.'

Mrs Glenn went to the window but it was only a moment before she turned back to face him.

'Harry started coming round our house looking for attention. We could see he weren't being looked after properly. We'd give him a bite to eat and let him sleep in the living room. Laura would call round sometimes. I got her to let him stay with me and Jack else he would have been sent away.

'You know the rest. Harry deserves looking after. He's had a rotten life.'

Saying goodbye, Kemp offered his hand. When she took it he felt a desire to share his story, but resisted.

Once on his way Kemp reflected on Mrs Glenn's reason for needing to talk to him. He was sure it wasn't to seek admiration for her efforts in those traumatic years. It was more likely that she was trying to excuse her sister's conduct and, ultimately, Harry's.

The lessons Mrs Glenn had learnt on her way through life would feature strongly in her care of her nephew. She had coped with her feeling of being cheated and had acted to defeat her demons, just as Mrs Boulton had done.

The lesson for him couldn't be more clear, and he felt ashamed.

19

'I've to sit me exams on Monday morning, sir,' came the voice over the telephone. 'The interviews are in the afternoon.'

Norman was clearly so eager to impart this news that he hadn't bothered with any preliminaries.

'Good morning. Do you want a last bit of coaching, Norman?'

'No thanks, Mr Kemp. I think it's up to me now.'

'Would you like me to show you the way to the Merchant Navy Centre on Monday?'

'No thanks, I've already been. I went there last weekend to check where it is.'

Kemp laughed.

'We're being independent, are we?'

'Got to happen sometime, Mr Kemp.'

'Good luck. I'll be thinking about you.'

Kemp put the phone down. He could do nothing now except hope that the boy's ambitions would be realised, but somehow it didn't seem quite so vital. He felt sure that Norman had turned the corner and wouldn't be going backwards, whatever the result.

The phone rang again. He took a deep breath as he recognised Helen's voice. The long wait was over but he felt cautious – very cautious.

'Hello, Peter,' she said. 'Can we arrange a meeting without you asking any questions? I don't want to get side-tracked.'

Kemp gritted his teeth but she spoke again before he could phrase an appropriate reply.

'I'm off to see my family tomorrow and wondered if

you'd like to take me to the station? If we left early we could have breakfast together. I've something to tell you.'

'Are you inviting me tonight?'

'No, not tonight. I've to pack and arrange for things to be done in my flat while I'm away.'

'You've the rest of the day to do those things.' He paused briefly, thinking, 'If it's over Helen, why don't you say so?'

She must have picked up the latent savagery in his reply for she remained silent.

'As it happens,' he said, an acidic note in his voice, 'I can't see you tomorrow morning. I'm duty officer.'

Surprising him, she failed to react to the news that her carefully thought out plans couldn't be carried out.

'Well, can we meet at lunchtime instead? I want to talk with you before I go to my parents. The trains are quite frequent to York, so it doesn't matter if I get a later one.'

Curious about her flexibility, he waited for an explanation for her lengthy absence. It had gone on too long. He also wanted answers about her secrecy. Whenever they had talked on the phone there had been inconsistencies, a lack of congruence or a discordant note in her voice. When they were together and she was being secretive there were always signs – a fluttering of her hands, pink rising at her throat or a defiant look that belied her words.

'Helen,' he said firmly, 'if we're to meet you must be more open with me.'

To his astonishment, her response was compliant.

'You've been very patient. I promise that when we meet I'll tell you everything you want to know.'

Out-manoeuvred, he gave way.

'I could meet you at lunchtime. It would have to be over this side of London, though.'

'I'm leaving from Kings Cross,' she said quickly, 'so I'll be in the Great Northern Hotel from one o'clock. Will that be all right?'

Her contrite tone suggested she knew that they had scouted rather dangerous territory.

'Wait inside the hotel lounge if you're there first,' he replied, adding spontaneously, 'I've missed you.'

He put the phone down immediately, annoyed with himself for not waiting to see if she would respond to his overture. In spite of the mixed feelings that her call had raised, something within him stirred. It seemed that she hadn't quite given up on him and he knew he hadn't given up on her, despite the efforts he had made to get her out of his system.

Later in the day Ben Sears rang. He was brief.

'Do you remember you promised to take one of my boys to Blackheath?'

'Yes, of course,' Kemp replied. 'I've been keeping appointments to a minimum. Only Monday is sacrosanct. I have to be at the other end of the office telephone in case members of a recruitment panel want to talk to me.'

'Good man. Well as luck would have it, they've picked our Open Day. You're planning to come?'

'Yes, Tuesday – but the work has to come first.'

'You'll be all right. Our events don't get underway before about three and you should be back well before that.'

'What about the paperwork?'

'I'll leave a file with the porter at the gate and I've included a rather odd letter you can look at. What time shall I tell the house parents you'll arrive so they can make sure Ronald's ready?'

'What time's his appointment?'

'Ten o'clock.'

'I'll collect him at eight-thirty sharp.'

There was a rustling of paper in the background.

'Right, he'll be waiting for you at the main gates. Thanks, Peter. Bye.'

Kemp rose from his chair and went over to examine the cactus plant. The delicate red shoots breaking out from the prickly green always gave him a sense of wonder. New life.

He gazed out of the window, totally preoccupied with what Helen would say. She had promised to answer all his questions – an incredible promise after her prolonged secrecy. He wondered if he would be able to get away sharply tomorrow. Being duty officer was an unpredictable assignment.

He locked up and went down the stairs, wondering what Mrs Boulton would say if she knew that he was meeting Helen again. He still found it peculiar that having tried so hard in the beginning to get him to find a girlfriend, she was so disapproving of his choice.

She was in reception. He made for the exit, creating as much distance as he could without appearing impolite.

'I'll see you in the morning, Mrs Boulton. Is there anything in the offing for the duty officer?'

'There's no indication of anything turning up,' she replied. 'You should be able to get away on time.'

'Thanks. Goodnight.'

He left quickly in case she speculated on some difference she could see.

In the office the following morning he felt considerable excitement about seeing Helen. In spite of her inexplicable mood swings, it was not in his nature to give up easily on someone who had meant much to him, but this time she had some serious questions to answer. Shortly before twelve Mrs Boulton phoned.

'There don't appear to be any problems, Peter, so if you want to get away that's fine with me.'

'Thanks Mrs B. It'll take me a little time to complete what I'm doing. I'll pop my head in before I go.'

Twenty minutes later he showed no more than his face through her door before swiftly making his way off the premises. There wasn't a problem parking at the hotel and he made his way eagerly to the lounge, surprised to find Helen coming forward to meet him. How good she looked!

'I saw you arrive.'

She smiled, proffering her cheek. It was conventional. He had come to expect more, even in public places. They stood at the entrance to the restaurant and a waiter approached. Conscious of train times, Kemp asked for a table straight away. The manager came over to escort them.

'Such service,' Kemp smiled, aware that he had used those same words the first time that they had dined together. She looked enquiringly at him as they chose from the menu. He waited for the manager to move away.

'It seems I always get superior service when you're with me,' he said. 'I remember the restaurant manager at Beauchamp Place conjuring up a table from nowhere for you.'

She gave a tight smile, obviously not amused, so he changed the subject.

'What time is your train?'

'I'll get the first one after we've finished.'

She breathed deeply and reached for his hand.

'Peter, we had such a wonderful time at the beginning,' she said softly. 'I'll never forget you.'

A waiter approached with a basket of bread rolls.

Kemp said, with a coolness that surprised him, 'That sounds like goodbye.'

She studied him closely.

'Well, it's up to you really. I know it's been difficult for you, so I want to tell you my whole story.'

He tried to keep his voice even.

'Good.'

'I've never lied to you, Peter. I don't have a job. I own my flat and I don't have to work.'

'That's three questions answered on the button.'

Immediately he asked the obvious fourth. Leaning across the table he said, 'How can you afford a lifestyle like yours?'

'I've a small income.'

Considering the clothes she wore he thought it could not be that small, but he said nothing.

'When we met I told you I'd given up my boyfriend. He's an older man and wealthy – the chairman of a big company – and I was his personal assistant for a short while. He took me abroad with him sometimes and took me out for wonderful meals when he was here.'

'And you went with him to Brussels quite recently, didn't you?'

'Yes. So what? It didn't mean anything.'

'Is he married, Helen?'

'Yes.' She looked at him defiantly. 'But it's in name only.'

He looked at her with curiosity, trying to get an up-to-date measure of her. He thought he knew what was coming.

'One thing led to another and he offered to buy a flat for me and to give me a small income. We're like friends now and he's always generous. He likes to see me in expensive clothes because he shows me off to his business contacts. He's a bit of an artist and I pose for him.'

Kemp remembered how Helen had posed for *him* at the beginning of their romance. Imagining it to have been exclusively for his benefit, he had held it as a treasured memory. As if she had read his thoughts she spoke of their first meeting.

'Initially I didn't want to get serious about you. We made love and it was so wonderful that I forgot all that. The reason I didn't want to get involved was because I knew that Gunnaur would be back from time to time. You see, I couldn't afford my allowance to end before I was ready.'

Throughout this one-sided conversation she was stiffly upright but retained hold of his hand, her eyes unwaveringly upon him. It was Kemp who chose to avert his gaze. He knew that he should be more dynamic and walk away.

Sensing his indecision she put her other hand across the table, trapping his between them.

'After you and I had been together for about a month, I told Gunnaur about you. He really does care for me.

He said the flat was legally mine and he wouldn't contest it, but he wanted a last month to show me off, as he put it. At the end of that time, if I still wanted to go, he would accept my decision and not bother me again. Those were his words.'

She stopped talking, waiting for him to react, but he said nothing and gave no eye contact. She introduced a combative tone, her head angled in a defiant mode.

'I thought he wasn't asking a lot of me, having given me the flat.'

Softening her voice again she said, 'Now you know why I asked for a temporary separation from you. I didn't really want it.'

At that moment the waiter appeared with their food and she had to let go his hand, which had laid passively in hers.

'That's only half the story,' she said with a small smile. 'Shall we have lunch and continue afterwards?'

He stirred as if he had been asleep.

'I think I'm off food.'

'I think I am too,' she agreed instantly, and moved her chair back.

Kemp called for the bill. Perplexed, the waiter asked if anything was wrong with the order.

'Nothing at all,' Kemp replied, adding dryly, 'I've already had enough to digest. Please serve us coffee in the lounge.'

He escorted Helen to a remote table in the corner.

He was surprised to find he wasn't feeling angry. Instead he almost felt a sense of relief at having his fears confirmed. Subliminally he had known there had been emotional complications: now at least he was free from the doubts that had plagued him.

The table was smaller, and it meant they were closer together. Her scent was evocative. For a moment he felt himself being drawn into a familiar pattern of behaviour. He looked into her eyes before his travelled down, tracing the curve of her breasts. He watched them rise and fall. She was breathing more quickly than normal and it was obvious that her confession hadn't come easily. She looked beautiful.

What did she want of him?

She took a deep breath.

'Thank you for hearing me out, Peter. It does get better – much better, I promise you.'

She was quiet until the waitress had served their coffee. They drank slowly, using it as a respite. She searched for his hand again, holding it tightly.

'What happened subsequently with Gunnaur was special. He took me to the most wonderful places and I met such interesting people. I do enjoy the luxuries of life and he was so wonderfully kind – but it was no good because I kept thinking of you.'

She paused and took his hand to her mouth, kissing it before continuing.

'Then I knew it was going to get awkward, which made me difficult, I know. But you are trained to understand after all!'

Removing his hand to readjust his position, Kemp made no effort to replace it.

'Don't be hard on me, darling' she said, noticing this. 'Gunnaur didn't take all that much of my time. I was on my own a lot – thinking. Anyway, you'll be pleased to know that I made a decision.'

Waiting for these words to sink in, she became much more intense.

'Despite losing the allowance, and despite your preoccupation with your work, I told him that I was sorry but I was giving him up to be with you.

'That's because I'm in love with you, darling, and I want us to be together.'

Her words came in a rush and her colour deepened.

'Please, darling, love me!'

He had heard those words before. He couldn't reply that he loved her. She had played fast and loose with his affections for too long. He should tell her there was nothing left. Alternatively, out of kindness, he could take her in his arms and hold her until the emotion brimming in her eyes had abated and she was in control again. He was rather shocked to realise that he really didn't want to do that.

But she wasn't waiting for his reply. There was a curiously triumphant expression on her face.

'I've only one more thing to tell you.' She reached for his limp hand. 'You should know that when I told Gunnaur of my decision to give him up he was quite upset – and then he made me the most wonderful offer.'

She paused for effect.

'He said he'd bought me the flat because he cared for me. I inspire him and if I'd continue to pose for him, he'd ignore the fact that you exist and make my allowance permanent.'

She waited for the financial implications to sink in.

Kemp could see the half-truth very clearly: he had become experienced at it. He thought of letting it pass, but there was a spark of residual anger in him.

Twisting his mouth, he said derisively, 'You did say, "Pose for him"? Oh, but it wouldn't end there would it, Helen?'

The words created their own vacuum. Even the restaurant seemed to be holding its breath.

She chose to be bold and confront the implication of his words. Looking him straight in the eye, a flicker of irritation crossed her brow.

'Oh, for goodness sake, Peter! You're talking about five minutes – five minutes of non-experience for me. You don't think I enjoy it, do you?'

He was speechless.

Helen, a strain of exasperation creeping in to her voice, continued, 'Gunnaur said that he'll confirm the allowance by instructing his solicitors to get in touch with me. Please remember, Peter, that I won't see him much because he's always travelling.'

She stopped there, obviously convinced of the excellence of her negotiations. She put her hands in her lap and waited.

Kemp saw himself in a decorative box. She would take him out and play with him when she wanted, then put him back and close the lid. Gunnaur would be in a similar, well-appointed box, the boxes probably laid side by side for convenience. There was no conflict for her: she would endeavour to make it work. All he had to do was refrain from asking questions and enjoy the comfortable lifestyle.

The lovely Helen had bewitched him, but he now saw her much more clearly. She was lovely only on the outside – the side, fortunately, that Gunnaur wanted.

'It wouldn't work for me, Helen,' he said simply.

He wasn't angry with her. She had brought him a kind of beauty and had prodded him out of his insularity but he knew they could never stay together. Their values and beliefs were too different. He was well aware that all he wanted now was to put her safely on the train and never, ever, see her again.

'Let's get you to the station. Your parents will be anxious about you.'

He rose and she waited by the exit as he paid the bill. They crossed the short distance into the station.

'Do you have your ticket?'

'Yes!' She stopped by the barrier and half turned, again striking an appealing pose. 'You're not going to be difficult are you, darling? It's an amazing opportunity and will give us a good start for our future together.'

This time he was less impressed and her pose, attractive as it was, had no effect.

'It won't work, Helen.'

She tossed her head and pouted.

'Peter, one gets used to having nice things and having time to spare to pursue interests. It's an offer in a million and we'd be together and be comfortably off. I've risked so much to negotiate this settlement.'

She seemed determined to prevent him making a hasty judgement, and he could see that she was genuinely disappointed that her careful build-up and absolute honesty hadn't produced the desired result.

'This is your platform, Helen.'

She moved very close to him, straightened his tie and stroked his chin.

'Darling,' she coaxed, 'take a little more time to appreciate how good this offer is.'

She took an envelope from her bag and a train ticket. He noted that it was for first class travel.

'Darling, I'd like to tell my parents about us this weekend. I've written a letter to you.' She offered him the envelope. 'My parents' phone number is in it. I thought it would be a nice way of introducing you if you talked to them over the phone.'

He couldn't resist asking, 'What would they think of your plan, Helen?'

'They know about Gunnaur. They took some time to come to terms with my friendship with him, but they know he's been kind to me. This visit is a reconciliation. I wouldn't tell them about our arrangement of course, but they'd be glad that I'd met you.'

Impulsively she added, 'I've tried to make everything up to you. Please, darling, ring me and tell me that we'll be together.'

'I'm sorry, Helen. It's over.'

'Be practical, Peter. This thing with Gunnaur isn't important. Don't be old-fashioned.' She pushed the letter into his hand. 'Please, darling.'

She turned on her heels and walked away from him; a beautiful girl with corn blonde hair, great poise and an excellent taste in expensive clothes. He was well aware that she was turning heads – all but his.

He stood at the station exit looking for a waste-bin. Standing over it he tore the unopened letter into shreds. Her favourite scent had been sprinkled on the envelope and was now on his hands. He went to the hotel cloakroom to wash and splashed water on his face. He studied himself in the mirror, searching for any change in his demeanour.

Deviating from his usual route home, he reached the point where the doomed romance had begun and spent a little time in St James's Park. It was a liberating ritual. He found the tree under which the beautiful stranger had kissed him. He found the bench on which they had sat, each of them isolated but in very different ways –

she leaving a relationship behind and set on remaining alone, he trying not to be a loner.

This roller-coaster affair had so nearly jettisoned all his confidence. Trust, meaning, a sense of purpose had all begun to appear suspect. The warnings his colleagues had given him about the need to have a personal life had led him into this fantasy. He accepted they hadn't been wrong – rather, his lack of experience had made him blind to Helen's hedonism.

And now? He felt free but at a crossroads in his personal journey.

'What you need is a good woman,' Mrs Boulton had said.

She would be pleased to discover that he and Helen had parted.

20

'When is the Merchant Navy interview board going to ring you?'

Mrs Boulton was clearly anxious.

'I think they will only ring if Norman is a borderline case. I know the morning is taken up with the written examinations and they interview in the afternoon. The board may speak to all the applicants or only to those who've passed the exams.'

Mrs Boulton came to see him several times during the day, in case he had received a phone call while she was dealing with other matters.

At about four o'clock the telephone rang. Picking it up, Kemp recognised Norman's voice, sounding somewhat strangulated. Almost simultaneously Mrs Boulton came into the room without knocking.

'It's Norman, isn't it?' she hissed.

Kemp put a finger to his lips.

'Speak up, Norman. I can hardly hear you.'

'I've been shouting, sir. I'm hoarse. Me voice has gone.'

'What have you been shouting for? What's wrong?'

'I'm so happy, sir and I've been trotting round the park with the runners.' The boy was clearly trying to catch his breath. Sounding in tears he croaked, 'I frightened this old man sleeping on a bench.'

'Stop gabbling Norman. Are you telling me you were accepted?'

Kemp held out the phone out to Mrs Boulton, who was holding her breath. Had the lad really succeeded against all the odds?

Mrs Boulton listened, her face expressive.

'That's absolutely wonderful, you clever, clever, boy Norman . . . Goodbye.'

She handed the silent phone back to Kemp.

'He's gone.'

'Would you have it any other way?' Kemp responded, with enormous satisfaction.

The good news travelled round the office at speed, for everyone had been aware of the young man's ambition and the tension that had existed.

At five-thirty Wilkinson came on the phone. He was uncharacteristically jovial.

'I take it back, Kemp. That young man was impressive but you'll have to advise him of the genteel nature of this locality.'

Kemp was bemused.

'Why's that?'

'My security staff said he went carefully through our dignified portal then launched himself off the top step shouting, "Yes! Yes!" and raced down the street.'

The selection officer was clearly amused.

'Great lad,' he said. 'And yet he was so controlled during the interview. You can send us more like him. Well done.'

Kemp repeated what Wilkinson had said to Mrs Boulton.

'You must be very proud,' she commented.

Reacting immediately Kemp said, 'He did it all himself, Mrs B.'

Arriving at Wellington the next morning, Kemp acknowledged the greetings of the porter.

'I've got a young man waiting for you, sir. I hope

you're coming back in time for the start of the Open Day this afternoon?'

The porter handed him a large envelope.

'I certainly am. I wouldn't miss it,' Kemp replied.

Ronald came out of the porter's lodge, spruced up and eager to leave. He was an athletic looking lad with short curly hair crowning a high forehead. They began their journey to the other side of London.

'I've wanted to join the Army for as long as I can remember, sir,' he told Kemp. His enthusiasm never waned as he chatted non-stop until they reached Blackheath.

Unfortunately, enthusiasm was not enough: Ronald failed his entrance examination. A young officer gave the news to Kemp and suggested he go back to his car. Ronald would be brought to him after they had finished talking to the boy.

While waiting, Kemp re-read the letter the superintendent had left with the other papers. Sears had given little attention to it, but learning of Ronald's disappointment made the letter more important. Before the boy came back to the car Kemp read it once more for something nagged at him.

It was headed 'Strictly Confidential'.

Dear Sir/Madam,

I was to be a godmother to Ronald Stone but before it happened his mother had to give the boy up because she could not cope. I have always remembered him and would have liked to help.

I should not get involved now but as I know he will soon be leaving the residential school because of his age, I would like to know if he is going to be all right. It's not that I can do anything for him, but it would give me peace of mind if I knew he is happy.

Although I was his mother's friend, she disappeared a long time ago. If it is any trouble please forget this letter. I will not write again.

Susan Glover

The letter had poignancy, but also an odd feel – so much so that it caused him to alter his plans.

Ronald didn't notice the change of route on the way back, but Kemp was becoming obsessed with an urgent desire to see the woman who had written that letter. He stopped at a newsagent and invited Ronald to choose something to read, explaining that he wanted to make a short visit. The lad chose a couple of comic papers and sat in the back of the Rover to read them.

Pulling up outside the superior block of private flats that Susan Glover had given as her address, Kemp left Ronald in the car.

'I'll be about half an hour,' he said, closing the car door.

He went through an archway, walked up the steps to Flat 2 and pushed the doorbell. After a short wait a well-dressed woman opened the door to him. She wore a business-like suit of navy blue with a necklace of pearls at her throat, a wedding ring and a fine diamond engagement ring on her left hand. She looked to be about thirty-five, younger than he had imagined.

'Could I speak to Susan Glover?' he asked, doffing his hat.

The colour drained from the woman's face. She looked either side of him and said, 'Who are you?'

Kemp gave her his card. She examined it before

looking past him to see if anyone was watching then stood back to let him in.

'It was I who wrote to you,' she said, taking his hat and putting it on a stand by the door. 'I didn't expect anyone to come in person. I was about to go out.'

'I was in the area and it seemed an opportunity not to be missed, given that you said information about Ronald would give you peace of mind.'

'Did I say that? I suppose I did. I'm not sure I should've sent the letter.'

The v-necked blouse she wore failed to hide the flush rising in her neck. Her hands were like small, fluttering birds.

There was an awkward pause.

'I didn't use my married name in the letter. You weren't expected to come here. I was only watching out for a reply by post. You see, my husband doesn't know that I . . .' The flush had reached her cheeks and after pausing for breath she asked, 'How's Ronnie?'

Asking the question seemed to help her recover her composure. She invited him to sit down but made no attempt to tell him her real name. Almost humbly she said, 'I only wanted to learn how Ronnie was getting on. I couldn't have him here.'

Kemp spoke slowly.

'There's no intention of asking you to have him with you. That's not why I came. Was there any reason why you didn't give your married name in the letter, Miss Glover?'

'Oh, it's just . . . you see . . . '

She looked desperate.

'Is it that you're closer to Ronald than you're saying?'

She was aghast, her eyes wide and her body rigid.

'What do you mean? It's just that I've never told my husband that I . . . had this . . . interest in Ronnie.'

Kemp looked at her in disbelief.

'All right,' she burst out. 'I'm his mother. I knew this would happen. I should never have sent that letter. I made up a name in case my husband should see a reply.'

She looked defiant.

'I've a family of my own now.'

Tears welled in her eyes and ran slowly down her cheeks. She looked down at her hands, touching her fingers together before looking fearfully at him.

'What happens now?'

'What would you want to happen?'

'My husband . . . he's such a good man but I don't think . . . You must think I'm an awful woman. You could never understand how difficult it was for a single mother trying to care for a baby and hold a job down at the same time. My parents disowned me and Ronnie's father deserted me.'

Unwilling to get involved in the rights or wrongs of a young woman abandoning her baby over a decade ago, Kemp tried to be a passive listener. She was clearly trying to convince herself as well as him. He gained an impression that she had been living continuously with the fear of exposure.

Suddenly excusing herself, she rose from her seat and hurried out of the room. Kemp anxiously watched her go. He couldn't begin to imagine the misery of walking away from your own child and waking up to that feeling of emptiness each morning. He walked to the window. He could see below the roof of his parked car. No doubt Ronnie, as she called him, was preoccupied with his comic. It would have done him no good to know whom Kemp was visiting.

She was gone a long time. He went over to the door she had gone through, listening for movement. He guessed she had gone to the bathroom and was worried. He moved quickly away when sounds suggested she was returning.

She came back and went over to the fireplace, bringing back a photograph that she handed to him. It was a snapshot of a happy family in the sunshine. Two children, the eldest looking no more than eight or nine, were picnicking happily with their parents. It was difficult to reconcile the woman who had deserted Ronald with the one displaying such motherly pride in the photograph.

It was quite clear that so-called Susan Glover was in a panic. She couldn't sit still or find words that would settle the excessive tension that was showing in her face and in her jerky movements. The silence continued unabated as she found an album of photographs of the children to show him.

Why had he come, he asked himself? It had been a knee-jerk reaction. Had he been seeking another Harry-type miracle that would make up for Ronald's career disappointment? He settled for the fact that he had merely been pursuing all avenues, but right now he needed to stop her frenetically providing evidence for him of a life that had nothing to do with Ronald. He broke the silence.

'How can I help you?'

She stood rigid.

'Is Ronald all right? Is he in good health?'

'Ronald is strong, capable and very fit.'

'Does he miss his mother?' she asked tremulously.

'I think he learned to live without one and it isn't a top priority anymore.'

She winced.

'You don't think I should come back into his life?'

'It's not for me to express an opinion. It's your decision and your life.'

'Does my husband have to know?'

Her eyes pleaded for help.

'Again, that's your decision.'

She looked at him helplessly, making him feel he had failed her. There was a delay before she spoke again.

'Will you be telling the authorities?'

He took his time answering the question. He supposed that to some extent he was 'the authorities'. Susan's husband would need to be a fine man indeed to accommodate such dramatic news. Assuming the marriage survived, he could foresee a range of outcomes if Ronald re-entered his mother's life. He saw the husband rejecting Ronald and the children resenting the impact of this stranger on their parents; he saw Ronald comparing the children's cosseted up-bringing with his own and becoming jealous; he even saw this mother, despite her evident heartache, finally rejecting Ronald again because he was re-writing the settled family standards of behaviour.

Eventually he said, 'We all make choices which we later think were wrong, but we can cause greater harm if we try to undo them.'

Because she was looking so thoroughly miserable, Kemp tried to take this philosophy a little further.

'Rather than take that risk we can see it as a debt, and give more to the ones we can reach.'

'What do you think I should do, please?'

She twisted her hands in her lap, unable to interpret his words and apparently plagued by distant memories of a fateful decision that had never given her relief. It occurred to him that she wanted someone to share the blame for a final parting.

Dredged from the past, that rash part of Kemp that could never bear to see people in deep distress took over. His current profession had taught him to snuff it out with icy logic, but this time he wouldn't. After all, he thought, he didn't know her real name and had no confirmation of her story. She was just a very vulnerable individual pathetically seeking advice.

'I think you'd do well to devote all your energy to your young family, who need you,' he replied, giving her his card, 'but you're free to contact me at any time.'

She took it gingerly, her relief evident.

'Oh no. Not if you don't think it's necessary.'

He hadn't said that, but he wasn't prepared to argue. Bidding goodbye he walked away but she hurried across the room and reached the door before him. She held the handle, keeping the door closed.

'Before you go . . . Do you think I could have my letter back or torn up, please?'

Every emotion she had felt over the years seemed to be expressed in her eyes.

Kemp considered carefully. He could see what it meant to her, but it was one thing to give advice and quite another to destroy evidence. For her peace of mind he would give her the letter and make a short report in the file. It would contain this address and only the name she had given him.

One day, perhaps, Ronald might come looking and

Kemp had no right to deny this in advance. He hoped for the young man's sake that his life would be too full to want to do that.

He extracted the letter from his attache case and watched her tear it into quarters. She put the pieces carefully back into the envelope, added his card and then offered her hand with some semblance of calm.

'Goodbye, Mr Kemp. Thank you for coming.'

'Goodbye.' He made a small movement in the direction of the photograph album on the table. 'You've a lovely family.'

As he walked to the car he thought it likely that her eyes were on him, wishing he had never come. He tried to draw some benefit from the diversion he had made: for himself if not for her. Both of them had made bad decisions in the past at a time of high drama. She would never be free. He could change, reach out to others and be free to love again, in the best sense of that word.

Of a sudden he was very clear that Helen had been a passionate intrigue and he was lucky to have escaped from his mistake, but Susan couldn't escape from hers.

There was silence in the car as he drove back to the residential school. Ronald didn't want to talk about his disappointment, and when they stopped at a cafe he welcomed the prospect of food. He chose a substantial meal, automatically making his mouth too full to be able to answer questions.

Kemp spent the rest of the journey convincing Ronald that he had many other opportunities open to him. The boy recovered his spirits sufficiently to confide his discomfort at having to tell his friends of his rejection.

'Tell them straightaway,' Kemp advised. 'Admit you're

disappointed. There's no sense in play-acting. They'll probably be on your side and say that the Army's loss is civvy street's gain. Actually, I think that's probably true.'

He was pleased to see Ronald respond and glad he was showing resilience.

Turning into the grounds of the school they were reminded of the Staff Open Day. Marquees had sprouted in the grounds and there were sideshows and competitions for the children.

'In the next two weeks,' he told Ronald before letting him go, 'I'd like you to think about what you're good at, what you'd would like to be doing in five years time or where you'd like to be. Don't fix on any one thing. Think of alternatives, chat with your housemaster and talk with your teacher.

'People haven't been discussing your future with you because you were stuck on one thing. If you broaden your preferences and write them down, we can discuss them all next time I come.'

Ronald gazed with interest at the activities going on in the grounds, confirming Kemp's belief that the lad would bounce back from his disappointment.

'Okay now?' he asked.

'Yes, sir. Can I go?'

'Yes, but I'll be back in about a fortnight to see what ideas you have. In the meantime, have some fun at the sideshows.'

He gave the young man some coins and Ronald sped away.

The house-parents, when Kemp found them, were sympathetic about the boy's failure but not unduly worried. They confirmed that although Ronald was single-minded he was also reasonably positive, and tended to seek other openings when an opportunity closed. He told them of the advice he had given and the arrangement to visit again.

Walking from the car park, he aimed to the right of the dining room building, using it as a short cut to the large staff marquee where fellow guests were milling about. Seeing a sign for the buffet, he headed in that direction. The building had a large kitchen and two dining rooms, and he could see the teachers busy with the catering. Among them he recognised Kathleen Ashley. She had her back to him, but to his surprise he bumped into her as he went past the end of the building.

'Hello,' she said, out of breath. She must have spotted him through the window and hurried to the point where they had, inevitably, to meet. He was flattered, and pleased to see her again. She had on a white overall with the sleeves rolled up in a businesslike manner.

He turned warmly to her.

'You're doing your bit it seems.'

She was wearing a wide, black ribbon that pulled her luxurious dark hair away from her face. It evoked a memory of the last time he saw her, when she agreed to meet Eric O'Reilly's prospective foster parents after the cricket match. With a start he recalled that he had never acknowledged her help. He looked at her thoughtfully, wanting an opportunity to thank her.

Without make-up, her expression was roguish. A generous mouth showed lips that were full and sensual. Mischief lurked in those dark eyes, so different from Helen's blue. Her bubbly personality sparked a desire to flirt with her and he said, 'How much longer before you're free to join the festivities?'

She gave a little smile.

'Not very long now.'

He pointed at the hospitality tent.

'Good. Perhaps you can find time to have a drink with me. I'd like to thank you for looking after Eric.'

'That would be very welcome.' She turned away from him. 'I'll be about fifteen minutes.'

She flung the words over her shoulder. Left on his own in the middle of the path, he went to the marquee where immediately a tray of sandwiches, home-made lemonade and orange cordial were offered to him. He selected a sandwich and, looking around the room, sipped lemonade. Seeing nobody he knew, and growing impatient, he decided to collect Kathleen from the kitchen. He returned to where they had met, just in time to see her walking in the opposite direction. She was still wearing her apron and turned when she heard him behind her.

'I've cut myself,' she said, 'and I'm looking for the nurse.'

Her left hand was wrapped in a tea cloth. She gestured with her other hand to the first aid tent.

'It's not manned.'

'Are you willing to let me try out my first aid on you?' Kemp asked, guiding her into the tent without waiting for her reply.

He wasted no time in examining the cut, gently easing the flesh away until he saw the dark-red depth of the wound. Compliant though she was, it did not prevent her from flinching.

'It looks clean. Shall I bind it for you? Ideally it should have a stitch.'

Kathleen bit her lip.

'Please carry on. I think it'll be okay.'

He gently bathed and dressed the wound at a leisurely pace, enjoying the closeness of her. The faint fragrance of her scent beguiled him and he found himself slowing down further as he bandaged her hand, but he resisted the temptation to build on the intimacy they were sharing and the moment passed. Somehow he was sure that she sensed this, for she drew back from him slightly.

'I need to return the overall and tidy my hair,' she said. 'I won't be long.'

He watched her walk back to the main building then returned to the marquee, deep in thought. It was now much more crowded. Talking to a member of the teaching staff he was introduced to a younger man named Alan, who was also a guest. He was about to ask him what business he was in when the sight of Kathleen entering the tent distracted him.

'I've been practising first aid,' he said to Alan, by way of conversation.

'On the girl with the bandaged hand? I don't blame you.' Kemp raised his eyebrows. 'Her name's Kathleen. She's a teacher – been here for three years. '

'I know. We've met a few times.'

'She doesn't look like a teacher,' said Alan.

Interested in this aside, Kemp looked across at Kathleen again.

'Why not?' he queried. 'What does a teacher look like?'

'Well, then!' Alan said meaningfully.

Kemp looked at Kathleen afresh. Without her overall he could see how her frock emphasised her shapely figure. She had released a little more of her hair from the ribbon. The dark waves, pushed further forward, were framing her face. She was sideways to him but angled enough for him to see the way her dark hair rested on her shoulders, drawing attention to her straight back.

She turned and caught him looking at her. He guessed that she might have read the frank appreciation that was going on in his mind, but it didn't deter her from smiling back at him and coming over to join the three of them.

'Cook says I'm relieved of duty.'

She held up her bandaged hand for the group's benefit.

'The bar's open now, Kathleen,' Kemp said. 'I want to buy you a drink for the help you gave. What would you like?'

He returned from the bar with their drinks. They clinked glasses, standing close together and looking around the tent. He felt good being beside her. For a moment or two their intimacy excluded the other two men.

'I spoke to Eric both before and after the match,' she said, 'and introduced the visitors.'

He wished he had been the first to raise the matter of the help she had given. His visit to O'Reilly had turned out so well, and Eric had responded so positively to his weekend away with his foster parents, that he had become relatively unconcerned about the lad's future. Nevertheless it was a poor response to her willingness to help.

'Can you tell me about it?' he asked, trying to make amends.

'Well, as you know, I introduced the foster-parents after the cricket match. I also met Eric again two days ago. He told me it was the best time he'd ever had, and he waved to me this morning so I'd say he's very happy.'

'I managed to sort out his dad,' said Kemp, 'which was a great relief.'

'Your work must be varied and very rewarding.'

'Yes, both.'

He wanted to tell her more, but he saw that his two male companions, excluded from the conversation, were growing restless. He moved to include them. Kathleen began to talk animatedly to her colleague.

It wasn't fair, thought Kemp, with a sudden switch of mood, to pursue this opportunity with Kathleen. He had barely left Helen's arms. Kathleen didn't deserve to be used to erase a memory.

'I'm going to have to leave now,' he told Alan. 'Enjoy the rest of the day.'

Kathleen was talking at the time, but he somehow knew that his words had registered with her. He gave a small wave.

On his way to the car he was furious with himself. Why had he fled so abjectly? Had he still not overcome the fear of becoming too involved?

A pebble lay on the grass in front of him. He kicked it viciously into the undergrowth.

21

A 'thank you' message from Norman was passed on by Mrs Windsor when she phoned to say that he had left to report to the training ship.

'He said he wishes it was a ship and not a land-based camp.' She laughed. 'In just a few days his language has acquired a nautical flavour. There are seven others in his group and he said they are all good shipmates already.'

'You've been a very good friend to him,' said Kemp. 'Can I invite you to have a celebration lunch for all that you've done for him? Perhaps you would like to go to one of the Lyons Corner Houses?'

'Thank you, Mr Kemp. It's kind of you and I'd be delighted to accept but I'm going on holiday the day after tomorrow. I thought it best to get away for a while to give me the chance to adjust to Norman not being around. I'll be away for two weeks, staying with my cousins in the village where we were born and grew up.'

'That sounds good. What about meeting when you return?'

'I'd like to. I'll be in Town on the twenty-first, if that suits you. I can make my own way to the restaurant. The one in the Strand would be the most convenient for me that day, if it's not too difficult for you to get to?'

They met as arranged a little over two weeks later. Kemp was at the restaurant first and rose to greet Mrs Windsor as she walked towards him

'I do like the waitresses' uniforms here,' she said, looking around. 'They're prettier than most. Oh! I must tell you that a post card from Norman was waiting for me when I arrived back from my holiday. He really is enjoying himself.

'You know, my life's changed so much since Norman came. So many people like him – well, it's impossible not to, isn't it? – and he was friendly towards them all but didn't get close to any of them. Perhaps it was because he wanted to devote his time to his studying. He's so independent, and I love that about him. He's so keen to learn about life. It's as if he's been locked away and is now impatient to learn everything. He shared his discoveries with me.'

'What kind of discoveries?'

'Oh, the smallest things. He recently asked why cutlery was laid out as it is and I said it was convention. Two days later he asked if I knew why we shake hands with the right hand, and when I said I didn't know, he told me it was because in the olden days soldiers would have their swords sheathed on the right, and offering your right hand was a sign that you'd put away your sword. He guessed that also had something to do with the way a table's laid.'

As she talked, Kemp saw that this fifty-year-old woman had found a new purpose in life with Norman in her house. In the short time at her disposal she had become the listener that Norman had needed, and in so doing, had helped him to develop and mature. Her eyes were sad as she recounted stories Norman had told her of his empty life in Hackney.

Their meal was brought to the table and they were quiet for a while.

'You know,' she said when the plates had been cleared, 'he's never spoken an unkind word about his grandmother. Indeed, he said she should never have had to look after him.'

'I've never visited her but I understand she was a bit of a grouch,' Kemp replied.

'Norman told me about the gangs in his district, and how the local children had to pretend some allegiance to them or else they were beaten up.'

'That's very likely.'

'He told me of a small number of his age group who, ignored by their parents, banded together to challenge authority. Norman disliked the fact that they were destructive, but it made them feel powerful. He said that didn't make sense to him because they always ran away afterwards.'

'Yes, there was a lot of questioning churning over in that head of his,' Kemp commented.

'He painted word pictures for me,' she smiled. 'They were his perspective of life in the East End.'

'It would seem that you gave him attention and affection before it was too late – thank goodness.'

'It's never too late, is it?'

'Perhaps not, but there does seem to be a time when they give up listening and start being cynical,' Kemp said, 'believing their own tarnished view of life is all there is.'

She looked distressed.

'Getting them to change after that must be very difficult. What age is it?'

'I don't think it's to do with age – I think it's when they give up hope. But now I think we should stop being so serious and talk of cabbages and kings.'

Mrs Windsor wholeheartedly agreed. She had never been privy to the ugliness, violence and despair of the world Norman had known, and he had opened her eyes to it. In spite of her own tragedies, her heart obviously went out to others less privileged.

When their deserts were brought she said impulsively, 'I think of you as a friend now.'

'I'm pleased that you do. We've Norman to thank for that, so shall we drink a toast to him and his achievements?'

'With the greatest of pleasure,' she replied, raising her glass to his.

When Kemp returned from visiting prospective foster parents the next day, he was told that there had been an urgent phone call. He fleetingly thought that if he had been grieving on the break up of his relationship with Helen, he would have had no time to dwell on it. The triangle of victim, rescuer and persecutor had turned and he was being rescued by the demands of his clients.

To his dismay the message was from Mrs Jacques, the foster mother of Gordon Church, one of the youngsters for whom he thought he had made a successful intervention.

Gordon had been abandoned when he was three years old and had been labelled sly and untrustworthy for most of his childhood, the result of persistent thieving. It was alleged that the politeness and good manners he exhibited were practised to disguise the petty theft. Four attempts at fostering had broken down because of this compulsion.

Gordon was thirteen when Kemp first met him, and he thought him an appealing boy with an engaging manner. He believed that the lad was finally beginning to mature and counselled him in an attempt to break the destructive cycle, convinced that he was worthy of another opportunity.

Wanting to find a foster parent who would match with Gordon on several levels, he believed he had found an ideal person in Mrs Jacques. A widow with a son, Raymond, of Gordon's age, she had answered one of Kemp's advertisements for a foster home. She was open about her motivations for fostering.

'I'm afraid my son is something of a 'Mummy's boy,' she had said. 'I'm hoping he might develop more quickly by having a friend of his own age. I would also welcome the opportunity to make a contribution to a youngster who's had an unfortunate start in life and, of course, the allowance enables me to provide for Ray and me that much better.'

Having the ability to manage her affairs without making a fuss had been a deciding factor in Kemp's decision to ask her to take on Gordon. He had informed her of the boy's background and given her some reassurance.

'My opinion is that the pilfering was the result of acute deprivation, and I think it's a phase that hopefully has ended.'

Promising to contact Kemp immediately if there was any repetition of the unacceptable behaviour, Mrs Jacques took Gordon into her home. The hoped-for friendship between Gordon and Raymond had not yet materialised, but during the ten months Gordon had lived with the family there had been no problems.

The telephone message had priority over the other things Kemp had planned and he went straight out to Mrs Jacques' home. She looked upset when she opened the door to him.

'Thanks for coming so quickly, Mr Kemp. I'd hoped never to have this conversation with you, but I'm sorry to tell you that I've lost money from my purse on four different occasions recently. The first time it happened I thought I'd mislaid some coins or forgotten that I'd made some purchase or other, but it isn't possible that I'd do that repeatedly.'

Kemp was dismayed.

'I'm so very sorry, Mrs Jacques. I find it incredible that, given his history, Gordon could believe the losses would go unnoticed. The compulsion to steal is evidently deeper rooted than I'd imagined. I'll remove him from here as quickly as is possible.'

'I've been marking the notes that are in my purse at the moment,' Mrs Jacques said. 'I'm sure the money will surface soon and we'll have the evidence we need to confront him. I'm dreading doing that as I've become very fond of him and I'm so disappointed, for his sake as well as mine, that it's come to this.'

'It was a good idea to mark the notes. Being faced with hard evidence should prompt Gordon into a confession. If he does that, it'll be an important stage in coming to terms with the problem.'

She was looking depressed, probably because her good intentions had been so misused, and Kemp felt guilty.

'I'll need to see Gordon privately as soon as he returns. Raymond gets in first, doesn't he?'

Miserably, Mrs Jacques nodded.

'In that case an interview in the house would be inappropriate. I'll wait outside in the car and whisk Gordon away to talk to him privately. Hopefully, Raymond won't see me.'

'There's a car park nearby, the first turning on the left,' Mrs Jacques pointed out.

Raymond arrived home without seeing the car. Ten minutes later Kemp waylaid Gordon and drove the short trip to the almost empty car park.

'How are you getting on, Gordon?'

He listened to the boy for some time and had to give credit to him for a seemingly sincere and untroubled account of progress. When Gordon stopped talking there was a long silence before Kemp said, 'So you really think you've settled well?'

The answer came without hesitation. 'Yeah!'

'Is there anything troubling you that it would be better to tell me about?'

'No,' Gordon said, apparently subdued by his counsellor's grim face and the tone of his voice.

'School okay?'

'It's okay, sir.'

'Do you like Mrs Jacques?'

'Yeah! She's nice.' Gordon's face brightened.

'How do you get on with Raymond?'

'Okay.'

'You sound a little less sure of him?'

'No, he's all right. Keeps to himself, that's all.'

'You would tell me if anything was wrong, wouldn't you?'

Gordon responded more animatedly.

'I do like it, sir! I like Mrs Jacques very much. She's good fun.'

He appeared totally devoid of guile and Kemp had to remind himself that the boy had the reputation of being a consummate liar as well as a thief. Confronting the lie could serve to entrench the boy further if he chose to deny it. A voluntary admission of guilt would be a step forward to rehabilitation, but it might never come.

'Unfortunately, Gordon, some money is missing.'

He paused but Gordon didn't speak. He chose words that edged him a little closer.

'It's unfortunate that this has only happened since you joined the family.'

'It ain't nothing to do with me, Mr Kemp. I ain't done nothing, not since we had that talk.'

Kemp gave Gordon full marks for his acting ability, but it meant that they could make no progress in diagnosing what was triggering this compulsion. He would have to doggedly continue until Gordon owned up.

A tapping on the window of the car interrupted the interview and Kemp opened the door. Mrs Jacques stood in front of him, tearful and harassed. She beckoned him out of the car.

'It isn't Gordon,' she said haltingly. 'The marked money has gone and he hasn't entered the house since I laid the trap.' A sob caught at her throat. 'I've confronted Raymond and he's admitted that he's the culprit. He's produced the rest of the money. He didn't really want it.'

She wept openly. Kemp had closed the car door and now put his arms round the sobbing woman, trying to calm her.

'He said he didn't need any of it, but did it to get rid of Gordon. Oh, I'm so upset at accusing Gordon. That's so bad of me! Ray's locked himself in the bedroom, and – I'm so sorry – could you please come back to the house, Mr Kemp?'

'We shouldn't leave Raymond by himself,' Kemp said. 'Sit in the front, Mrs Jacques.'

He led her by the elbow to the passenger door.

'Do you mind if I get in the back with Gordon? Although he's innocent, I think he'll have to leave, poor dear. We were getting on so well . . . I suppose that was the trouble.'

She broke down again.

Gordon had watched Mrs Jacques's distress but couldn't hear what was being said. He moved to get out of the car but Kemp motioned him back in and opened the other door for Mrs Jacques. Distraught, she embraced Gordon, who looked utterly bewildered.

'I'm so sorry, darling, so sorry!'

Within minutes they were back at the house. After checking that Raymond was still locked in his bedroom, Mrs Jacques returned downstairs and asked Gordon to sit down. She then told him everything. The boy wore a haunted look as she reached the terrible conclusion.

'I knew Raymond was immature but I'd no idea of the extent.' She dabbed her eyes. 'I'm afraid I'll have to ask you to leave, Gordon. It seems that my son isn't grown up enough yet and I'll have to give him all my attention.'

Tearfully, she dropped her hands to take hold of Gordon's, only to let go of them and hug him instead.

Gordon was upset. Muffled by her hug he said manfully, 'It's okay, don't cry.'

Sally Jacques untangled herself and made her way into the kitchen. After providing tea she again went up to the bedroom.

'Come down and talk to us,' she pleaded, tapping on the bedroom door.

'Leave me, Mum.'

To the two involuntary listeners at the bottom of the stairs, Raymond sounded choked.

'I can't come down now, Mum.'

Kemp turned to Gordon and saw that the hunted look he remembered had returned. He put his arm around the boy's hunched shoulders.

'We should get out of the way right now, Gordon,' he said. 'Raymond and his mother need to sort things out and we have to talk about finding somewhere else special for you to live.'

Mrs Jacques, returning, caught the end of this and was desperate to right the wrong she had done.

'Oh! Gordon, darling, I shall miss you terribly. I'm so sorry. Will you ever forgive me?'

She held out her arms and Gordon went to her. Holding him, she spoke softly.

'You will come to see me often, won't you, please? I want you to have a going-away party. We'll have it tomorrow. Will you come, Mr Kemp?'

She was still holding Gordon but had pressed his face to her bosom as though she, too, could not stand to see the hunted expression. Kemp misunderstood her.

'I was hoping . . . Will it be convenient for Gordon to stay until the end of the week? I want to give him the chance to choose his new home and that will take a little time.'

Mrs Jacques released Gordon.

'I don't want you to go, dear. You do understand that, don't you?'

Looking woebegone, she turned to Kemp.

'Of course he can stay until you've found somewhere nice, but I'd still like to have Gordon's party tomorrow, if that's all right with you?'

Acknowledging her determination, Kemp inclined his head.

There was an awkward silence while Mrs Jacques busied herself patting some cushions into place.

'Raymond will be sent over to his aunt during the party,' she said quietly.

Gordon looked very unhappy.

'Oh no, please don't do that. I'd like Raymond to be at my party. Please, Mrs Jacques?'

'I'm not sure he'll want to, Gordon. He's too embarrassed. But if he changes his mind then yes, of course he can attend if you want him there. Under the circumstances, it's very generous of you.'

Kemp wanted to bring an end to the embarrassment both Mrs Jacques and Gordon were suffering. He turned to the boy and said, 'We'll go out for a meal to give Mrs Jacques a chance to talk to Raymond.'

Miserably, Mrs Jacques went to the door with them.

'Thank you for coping with this awful business. If it's just the two of us Raymond may come down and talk to me.'

'When we come back it'll be late, Mrs Jacques. If you don't mind, I'd like you to concentrate on Raymond and not talk about it anymore with Gordon. I want him to keep out of the way in the morning too, and go to school as though nothing has happened.'

Kemp looked at Gordon, seeking agreement.

'That would be the kind thing to do.'

When the boy nodded Kemp added, 'We'll sort things out, won't we, Gordon?'

Gordon gave a weak smile.

'I'll be okay, Mrs Jacques,' he assured her.

Before she could say anything, Kemp said briskly, 'Of course you will. I'll have a plan to discuss with you after the party. Come on Gordon, let's get something to eat and forget the whole sorry business for a couple of hours. Goodbye, Mrs Jacques. I'll see you tomorrow.'

The following afternoon, deliberately arriving at Clapton before the boys returned from school, Kemp saw that Mrs Jacques had created a table of appetising food. In the centre was a large and inviting chocolate cake with the word GORDON written in icing sugar across the top.

'I've been rather extravagant with my sugar ration,' Mrs Jacques said, 'but Gordon deserves a treat.'

As usual, Raymond arrived home first and although he could not have failed to notice Kemp's Rover parked outside, he went straight to his bedroom. Gordon came soon afterwards and sat with the adults.

Raymond must have been watching for Gordon to arrive, for he came down looking shamefaced and handed him a letter. He stood by while Gordon read it, then both boys disappeared from the room. Mrs Jacques looked across at Kemp with furrowed brow, clearly having no idea of what was going on.

When they returned Raymond went to his mother and conducted an urgent, whispered conversation. Kemp kept his distance but Raymond came over to him.

'I'm sorry for all the trouble I've caused, Mr Kemp,' he said haltingly, his eyes cast down. 'Will you please let Gordon stay with us? I really want him to.'

His mother looked on, trying to hide her anguish.

'What does Gordon say?' asked Kemp.

'He says he understands what I did and doesn't hold it against me. Please, sir, can he stay? Mum says it's all right if you say yes.'

Mrs Jacques was crying again. Both boys took an arm

each and led her across to the chocolate cake. Gordon cut a slice and handed it to her.

'What's this for?' she said, attempting to stem her emotion. 'Is it to stop me blubbering?'

'Mum of the year!' said Gordon spontaneously, to Raymond's vigorous applause.

They embraced her before she hurriedly left the room. Kemp found her sitting in the kitchen, dabbing her eyes.

'I've had a horrid time but I think it's going to be all right.'

'I'm sure it will,' said Kemp.

She went to the cupboard and took out a bottle of sherry. They went back into the lounge to toast the boys and found them in a corner, swapping anecdotes. Gordon gave Kemp a proud glance.

Turning to Mrs Jacques, Kemp said quietly, 'This whole episode might have been a blessing in disguise. It's the first time Gordon has ever been on the side of the angels and it's done a lot for his confidence. As for your son, with the rapport he and Gordon are now establishing, you may well find Raymond has moved a little away from your apron strings.'

Mrs Jacques was delighted with this conclusion. With all the goodwill evident, the household had found a satisfactory equilibrium again. Once more Kemp knew that it was better that he should go.

He locked the car away and walked to his flat. His colleagues' pressure for him to have a private life was making more sense, but despite Mrs Boulton's favourite 'other fish in the sea' saying, he felt it would be difficult to find a partner who would understand, and be content to share, the pressing demands of his vocation.

Having promised to return to the residential school to help young Ronald sort out his career prospects, he now went to the phone. He left a message for the house parents that he would see the boy on Thursday. His resolve growing, his next action was to write a brief note to Kathleen, addressing it care of the school. In it he spoke of his impending visit to Wellington, and invited her to dinner that same evening. He suggested he could meet her about six. He had already given her his business card but included his home and office numbers for good measure, then rushed out to catch the last post.

He was engrossed in a book when Mrs Boulton rang.

'I don't know what plans you have,' she began in a subdued voice, 'but it would be extremely helpful if you could come into the office on Sunday morning for about an hour. I'm afraid it's got to be when other staff aren't present. It's confidential and I need your help, but I can't say more now.'

Only twice before had she ever asked him to come in on a Sunday morning, on both occasions with the same proviso. He wracked his brains about whom or what it could be.

He thought of Harry. His was the one scenario that had defied logic: it had appeared too magical for him to be convinced that it would last. Because he was so anxious not to have bad news of Harry, he decided to check that source and rang Mrs Glenn. She reassured him straight away, but dropped her voice at the end.

'There's something I want to tell you, Mr Kemp. Don't tell him I told you.' She spoke in a conspiratorial whisper. 'He's got himself a girlfriend. A really nice girl, two doors down. They're walking out for the first time this evening.'

She sounded happy.

'Gosh! How did that come about, Mrs Glenn?'

'How do these things ever come about, Mr Kemp? I wasn't aware he knew she existed, but one of my boys introduced them. He's dressed himself up in a new suit. I think it's the one you got him. Thank you for what you done for him.'

He found the praise extraordinary.

'I've done nothing, Mrs Glenn.'

'Me hubby and me think of you as a friend of the family for what you done for Harry,' she said firmly. 'You didn't have to do as much as you did.'

'It's my job, Mrs Glenn,' he said with satisfaction. 'It's the way you and your husband have always cared and loved Harry, even when he didn't know it, that counted.' He paused. 'You should be very proud of yourselves.'

'You found us, Mr Kemp,' she said simply.

The news of the leavening influence of 'a really nice girl' upon Harry was worth a trip to his drinks cupboard. He poured out a whisky and toasted Mr and Mrs Glenn and their family, which included a lucky young man named Harry Weston.

There were still a couple of hours of daylight left, so he drove to Epping Forest and parked. He strolled through the trees, at peace with himself for the first time in ages. Couples passed him, also enjoying the peace and the fresh air.

He wasn't envious of them – indeed, he was glad to be no longer bewitched – but it didn't take long for him to return to wondering what the emergency was that had required Mrs Boulton to call him.

22

The Montgomery Estate was quiet on Sunday morning and none of the residents were out on the road. Judging by the number of windows with their curtains drawn, a lie-in seemed popular. Kemp locked his car and went to the main door. While he was searching for the key Mrs Boulton released the lock from the inside and let him in.

'I think you'd better go straight to your office,' she said. 'You've a visitor.'

'A visitor?' He frowned. 'Male or female?'

'Male.'

Puzzled by the guessing game he asked sharply, 'Has he got a name?'

'He didn't say,' she replied, and abruptly turned away.

What had got into her? Mrs Boulton was always very strict about security and confidentiality. She had never before left a stranger in his office. He ran up the stairs to find Norman standing by the window. He was admiring the deep red flames of the cactus plant, now fully at its best.

'Lovely, ain't it, sir?' Norman said by way of greeting.

He was wearing a dark navy blue Merchant Navy jacket. They shook hands and then Norman removed his beret, which he had been wearing at a jaunty angle, carefully tucking it into a pocket before removing his jacket. Pointing with his finger he said proudly, 'How about that, sir?'

There was a new, bright yellow V-stripe on his arm with a red MN in the middle.

'I've been chosen to be in charge of me group, sir,' he

said with a wide grin. 'Good, eh? Even me gran's impressed. She wants me to go round to her friends with her to show me off, but first she said I had to visit that nice Mr Kemp. That's you, sir – and she ain't never met you. Good, ain't it?'

'Quite clearly she doesn't know me!'

Norman grinned.

'She's dead keen for her friends to see me, so I thought I'd ask her what had happened to me bad blood.'

He paused dramatically before saying, 'Do you know what, Mr Kemp? She hit me. That's assault, ain't it? Then she said she didn't mean it and I was lovely.

'Funny, but Mrs Boulton said the same thing when I came in on Friday. I'm not lovely, am I?' He gave a covert glance to see if he still had the attention of his audience of one. 'But, handsome perhaps, eh?'

He paraded his arm again.

Although Norman was deliberately play-acting, it gave Kemp a tremendous boost to see such a transformation. They went to join Mrs Boulton, who saw his stripe for the first time and listened proudly as he told how, after the first week, he had been selected to lead his small group. Then the ever-surprising senior clerk produced a carefully wrapped cake, already on a plate, from her shopping basket. Placing it on her desk, she handed Norman a knife.

'This cake, young man,' she explained, 'has been baked in your honour to launch you as a Truly Nomadic Norman.'

'Well done, Mrs B,' Kemp said, touched that she must have planned this celebration after Norman had called in to the office on Friday evening. Norman took hold of her hand. She didn't resist until he kissed the back of it, when she snatched it back, but Kemp could see that she was amused and flattered.

'Go on with you!' she reproved. 'You're growing up far too fast, young man.'

Inviting him to make the first cut, she then took the knife from him and continued slicing the cake. She handed a piece to each of them on a paper napkin. They waited until she had helped herself before tucking in.

Mrs Boulton had manoeuvred Norman centre-stage and, as if on cue, he launched into tales of his recent experiences. They stood close to the excited young man and Kemp was surprised to see that Norman was already slightly taller than the senior clerk.

'The best bit was in the first week,' said Norman. 'It's the tradition to climb this tall mast in the quadrangle. It was a bit scary at first.'

He perched on the edge of Mrs Boulton's desk, something her senior colleagues would never have dared to do. She seemed not to notice.

'So far,' he continued, 'me team's only had guided tours of boats in the dock, with a lot of discipline training in the camp. Boat drills are done every day. Me squad's a good one and we get on well together.

'Next week though, we'll be practising on the water. That'll be good.'

During a lull in the questions he declared, 'I mustn't be late for the Gran parade.'

Mrs Boulton looked puzzled, then understood as he volunteered information about his grandmother. Evidently the relationship was repaired.

'She says she's very proud of me and don't want me to stay nowhere else, but I told her I've got me own place now with Mrs Windsor.

'By the way, Mr Kemp, Mrs Windsor sends her regards and hopes you'll call in some time, if only to hear how I'm getting on.'

He stood up and put a hand in his back pocket, producing a carefully folded ten-pound note.

'If you don't mind sir, I thought you'd find a good cause for this since I've given up me charitable status.'

He had obviously prepared the last few words for this occasion. Aware that this marked the boundary between his old life and the new, Kemp responded seriously and handed the note to Mrs Boulton.

'This lady can be relied upon to find a deserving cause. Thank you, Norman.'

The young man nodded gravely.

'Can I give you a lift back?'

'No, I don't need a lift, Mr Kemp. I got me own transport. I came on me new bike. Well, it's really second-hand, but it keeps me fit. You have to be fit when you're at sea. I bought it with the money they collected for me at the laundry. I'm keeping it at Mrs Windsor's.

'I've named her as me dependent,' he confided. 'The Merchant Navy now makes Mrs Windsor a small allowance from me pay.'

Mrs Boulton beamed.

'Funny!' he said, 'I didn't have a home and now I've got two!'

The mischievous twinkle was back in his eyes. Kemp guessed that this was probably the last time he would see Norman – in a roundabout way he was saying goodbye. The look in his eyes bore eloquent testimony to the fact that he had learnt the meaning of respect, and with it had come responsibility.

The irrepressible youngster offered his hand to Kemp

in a grown-up way. It was a brief handshake, perhaps just a little longer and a bit firmer than for a normal parting, but not overtly so. Kemp smiled back, offering his friendship in return, but neither of them said a word.

Mrs Boulton, standing to one side, seemed to have a problem with her eyes and left for the ladies room.

Watching her go Norman said, 'You did care sir, didn't you?'

'I did and I do, Norman. Good luck.'

The young man smiled.

'You can make your own luck, can't you?'

Recalling that Norman had discarded his blue jacket in the office upstairs, Kemp went to fetch it. Entering his room he was again struck by the sight of the spectacular cactus plant. It was indeed lovely, as Norman had said, but the young man would never know the symbolism he attached to it.

Picking up the jacket, Kemp turned towards the door. As he did so he saw the familiar green of a charge sheet lying on top of the in-tray. He stopped to read the attached note from Andrew McGovern.

Tony Mills, convicted of theft from high street shops. Age 14yrs. No known home address, but is obviously from Tyneside. Clearly had a tough home-life, experiencing violence and abuse. There's evidence of old scarring on his body, arms and legs.

He would be more appealing if he were less combative. (It takes some effort to repeat to yourself: 'Every insult is a cry for help'). He's been placed in the Stockwell hostel.

Good luck – Andrew

Kemp felt the adrenalin rise at the challenge of one more youngster needing, but not wanting, help – living only for the moment and indifferent to the future. Tony would need to be a priority and go to the top of the list, and Norman would now come off it. Hurrying downstairs he was in time to see Norman holding Mrs Boulton at arm's length as they completed an old-fashioned dance step.

Pausing on the stairs Kemp called out, 'It's all right Mrs Boulton, I won't tell anyone.'

'I should think not,' she snapped.

He smiled, interpreting her rebuke as a confession that she needed to preserve her battle-axe persona to hide her feelings. She wasn't so different from him, after all.

Grinning rather sheepishly, Norman let go of Mrs Boulton but to the astonishment of both watchers the lady executed a quite passable pirouette, ending with a curtsy. Norman immediately forgot his embarrassment and attempted a responsive bow.

Helping him to put on his jacket, Kemp and Mrs Boulton walked outside with the confident young man. The estate was still deserted. They watched Norman undo the heavy chain that secured his bicycle and waved him off.

Kemp drove Mrs Boulton home and walked with her to her gate. She reached in to her shopping basket and handed Kemp a parcel which contained the rest of the cake.

'If you listened to me,' she said, 'you wouldn't keep needing these handouts.'

He froze, about to deliver the mother and father of all broadsides, when he saw her laughing at him. To pay her back he embraced her, in full view of any of her neighbours who might be watching.

Two hours later he was back in Woodford, changing into his gym kit for a session in the loft when the phone rang. A pleasant voice, one that he was beginning to know better, declared a little breathlessly that she would be delighted to have dinner with him next Thursday and would remain at school until he came for her.

'That's next week, Kathleen,' he said impulsively. 'Are you free this evening by any chance? We could have dinner – that's if you know a restaurant that'll be open near you? It's only a little over an hour's drive for me.'

She hesitated for the briefest of moments.

'What a lovely surprise! The King's Arms Hotel has a restaurant that caters for non-residents too. If you can hold on for a moment I'll look the number up for you.'

He heard the sound of pages rustling then took the number down.

'I'll book it for seven o'clock because it probably won't stay open late on a Sunday night. Where shall I call for you?'

Kathleen gave him her address then added mischievously, 'Are you sure that you can spare the time from your rescuing?'

'I don't rescue,' he said, sure of himself. 'I do what you do.'

'What's that?'

'Open windows.'

'I like that. By the way, my friends call me Kathy.'

Putting the phone down, Kemp went across the room to look out on a clear sky. The trees along the edge of the pavement were casting shadows and a couple passed by with a little girl, who was holding the man's hand. As they came out of the shade into the sunshine she skipped forward happily, not letting go of his grasp.

It made him think of so many of his young clients without a hand to hold on to; unloved, insecure, knowing more of ridicule and rejection than of encouragement and challenge, and wearing their belligerence as a shield; and he was aware that his determination to help was as strong as ever.

He took time dressing, wondering if he was truly free of the oath he had made after his parents' death. He wandered into his study. Looking at the photograph of a happy boy standing beside his parents he said, 'I think I might have arrived, Mother, Father. Sorry I took so long.'

Kathy was waiting at her front gate.

'Have we time for you to meet my parents, Peter?'

He followed her along the path to the front door where a couple stood, arm-in-arm. After a short conversation about their garden, he and Kathleen left.

'This is a lovely way to spend a summer's evening,' she said, as he opened the car door for her.

During the ten-minute drive she answered his questions about her family and her home. As they walked into the hotel she slipped her hand through his arm and kept it there until they were shown to their table.

Inevitably, she asked about his parents and he was able to tell her, easily and without halting, that he was orphaned while still at school. Her eyes grew large and he saw them well up.

'I'm sorry,' she said.

He hastily reached out and managed to catch her fingers.

'It's all right. I was one of the fortunate ones, I was well loved while they were here.'

They were soon talking freely, sharing experiences about the young people each of them looked after. Kathy fastened on to the Department's newspaper game. She was able to identify the flying saucers headlines because Eric had told her the story of his father's behaviour. But she cringed at the reason for the headline relating to Kemp's visit to Hackney slipper baths, and the importance of the precious bar of soap.

Asked to repeat the story about the 'inept council official', he did so, but when, later in the evening, she asked to hear it for a third time he caught the sly smile on her face and flatly refused. They ended the evening as friends.

One morning, three months later, Kemp met Mrs Boulton in Reception and asked her to come to his room. Once inside, in a serious tone he said, 'I suggest you sit down, Mrs Boulton.'

'Has something happened?'

'I'm afraid so. It's going to come as something of a shock to you.'

She sat down abruptly.

'Who is it?' she said sharply.

'It's me,' Kemp said. 'I got engaged last night.'

'To Kathy?'

'None other.'

The severe expression faded, replaced by a dawning smile that reminded him of the lovely woman he had seen in a photograph with a handsome soldier beside her.

'About time, too,' was all that the T.O.B. had to say.